A Box of Texas Chocolates

The Final Twist

L & L Dreamspell
Spring, Texas

Cover and Interior Design by L & L Dreamspell

Copyright © 2009 L&L Dreamspell. All rights reserved. No part of this publication may be reproduced, stored in a retrieval system or transmitted in any form or by any means, electronic, mechanical, photocopying, recording or otherwise without the prior written permission of the copyright holder, except for brief quotations used in a review.

This is a work of fiction, and is produced from the authors' imaginations. People, places and things mentioned in this anthology are used in a fictional manner.

ISBN: 978-1-60318-140-2

Visit us on the web at www.lldreamspell.com

Published by L & L Dreamspell
Printed in the United States of America

Contents

A Box of Texas Chocolates   5
Copyright© by Linda Houle

Getting a Clue   21
Copyright© by Pauline Baird Jones

Dying for Chocolate   37
Copyright© by Laura Elvebak

The Invisible Hand Will Smear Chocolate   47
on the Face of Tyranny
Copyright© by Mark H. Phillips

A Recipe To Die For   57
Copyright© by Sally Love

The Bavarian Drop Killer   71
Copyright© by Cherri Galbiati

Bitter Sweet   89
Copyright© by CeCe Smith

The Cowboy's Rose   109
Copyright© by Betty Gordon

Books and Bon Bons   127
Copyright© by Charlotte Phillips

Valentine's Day   143
Copyright© by Diana L. Driver

Jadead   153
Copyright© by Iona McAvoy

Deep in the Heart of Texas   169
Copyright© by Autumn Storm

Truffles of Doom   185
Copyright© by Mark H. Phillips

A Bona Fide Quirk in the Law   201
Copyright© by Cash Anthony

A Box of Texas Chocolates
by Linda Houle

Pouring rain. Another Houston deluge, and no sign of an end any time soon. Megan held her breath and made a run for it—a mad dash to her mailbox and back through a waterfall of water. Hopping inside, she slammed her heavy wooden front door then promptly slid on the wet ceramic tile entryway, plopping down on her ample rear with a loud smack.

"Oh...crap. I hate rain!"

She paused before rising, looking at her splayed out legs surrounding the pile of scattered ads, bills, and magazines. Nothing felt broken, except her ego. At least nobody saw. Nobody taunted her with *'Megan the Moose, Megan the Moose, you're so fat you have a mile wide Caboose!'*

Shaking her mousy brown shoulder-length hair like a wet dog she tried to make sense of her crazy thoughts—why did she dredge up that horrible chant from her Collins Junior High School years? She'd worn clunky hard-soled shoes and often slipped on the sidewalk whenever it rained. A slightly overweight thirteen-year-old klutz for sure, but she didn't deserve to be bullied.

Ten long years ago. Her tenure of Junior High torment that added another twenty pounds to an already chubby physique—she'd resorted to stress-eating to block the emotional pain. Not only teased but also shut out of the fun she used to have with her best friend Debbie. Miss Smarty Pants of the world Catherine Farrantino moved to Texas, and took away her only friend.

Catherine developed a crush on Debbie's brother and

discovered the best way to spend time with him—by becoming his sister's new BF—plying her with expensive gifts and even family vacations to Italy with the Farrantino family. The gullible girl went along with anything Cathy wanted, even coerced into joining in the teasing. Unbelievable. And cruel.

I know why I'm remembering that horrible time in my life—because she's back. 'Catherine the Great'—my Junior High arch nemesis—is my new boss at Variety Plastics...

Two weeks prior, the tall, skinny, overly made up bleached blonde walked through the office door, shook Megan's hand, and winked when she recognized the girl. "Remember me?" she'd drawled. "Gee, your…weight hasn't changed a bit, in ten years." Then her lips puckered like she'd just eaten a dill pickle as she fought the urge to laugh and taunt her again with the same sing-song nasal chant.

I should have slapped her right then and there—once a bully always a bully. But I'm better than that, I'm older and wiser.

Megan struggled to her feet, scooped up the mail, then slammed it down on the little wooden stand by the door. *I won't let her make me quit—I need that job, I have car payments and…* Her hand knocked one letter back onto the tile. A sideways glance revealed a Texas flag decorating a large return address label on what looked like a greeting card.

My birthday isn't for months. Snatching it up, she slipped a chipped fingernail under the edge of the flap and tore it open. An invitation—to a party? *I haven't been to a party in ages.* A slight smile formed on her lips. Brenda Garrison, her buddy at the plastics factory, had invited her over for a party Friday night.

Not just any party—a theme party called 'A Box of Texas Chocolates'—the unusual card announced she'd play one of the characters. It instructed her to prepare the enclosed recipe to bring for the chocolate dessert table.

"Chocolate Death Kisses?" she wondered aloud. What type of cookie has a name like that? *Must be part of the 'theme'—a murder mystery/chocolate party. And I'm supposed to role-play, as*

'Kandy-Kiss Klein'—*a broken-hearted alcoholic bimbo, hell bent on getting revenge on the gal who stole my boyfriend...*

Megan laughed out loud. The invitation suggested she dress the part too. *Wear your tightest little black dress with too many gaudy accessories and jewelry—overdo and smear your eye make-up, ala Tammy Faye Baker.*

"What a hoot—me, in the role of a dressed-up and made-up bimbo?" She spoke to her sweat suit clad reflection in the entry-way mirror, hair still dripping and bedraggled, the polar opposite of sexy.

Oh why not? What the hell, it'll be fun. I'd better call Brenda to RSVP.

"So Megan, are you game for Friday night?" Like fingernails on a chalkboard Catherine's voice, and the question sent a shiver down Megan's spine, and she dropped her recipe card. She'd been making a shopping list—ingredients for her cookie contribution, 'Chocolate Death Kisses.'

She pivoted her swivel chair around to see Miss Smarty peering into her tiny gray cubicle. "Wha...*you're* invited to the party too?" How could Brenda do this to her? As soon as Catherine appeared at Variety Plastics Megan told her, in confidence, all about the Junior High torture queen.

"You know, it's too bad this party's for women only," Catherine drawled "or else Bradley would be there." As she spoke she twisted her fingers through at least six gold chains draped around her bony neck.

Oh I get it now. She's already getting thick with Brenda to spend time with her husband Bradley Garrison, the tall, dark and handsome stockbroker. Some things never change. Megan took time to think before she spoke again. "Brenda is my dear friend and I plan to be there *and* have fun." Her eyes narrowed and she wanted to say something more but stopped. She'd have to warn Brenda to watch out for that no good vamp. "So, who're you going to be? And what are you bringing for the dessert table?"

Catherine smoothed her short skirt and turned her back on the girl as if she hadn't heard the questions. Then as she sashayed away her head shot to the side and she answered "I'm 'Leilani Lovechild' and my dessert is 'Pele's Chocolate Revenge'—something with coconut in it, I think."

Megan felt a volcano of bile rising from her stomach into her tightened throat. *Yeah, I'd like to give you 'Pele's Revenge' myself.* She pictured the unpleasant woman falling headfirst into a flaming volcano.

"Who else did you invite?" Megan munched on a sour cream flavored potato chip as she and Brenda sat at a table for two in the break room, sharing their usual foot-long ham and cheese subway sandwich lunch.

"Maria in accounting. Delma and Sylvia from packaging. Vivianne and Julie in shipping—then you, me, and Catherine. It's a mystery party for eight women, and we all get to play a role. One of us is a killer…" A giggle turned into a cough as Brenda tried to talk and eat at the same time. She gulped from her sweaty soda can, patted her mouth with a yellow napkin, then laughed even harder.

"Even I don't know 'who done it' because that's part of the game. I'll hand out booklets at the beginning of the party and we'll follow the instructions. The invitations were all pre-printed and I just had to decide who got to play which character."

"And you got to pick your own character first, of course." Megan yawned.

"Of course." Brenda started shoving trash into the takeout bag, almost ready for the second half of their workday. "I'm 'Tootsie-Pie Porter' and I'll make the 'Chocolate Pie to Die For'—probably the night before since I won't have time after work on Friday."

"I'm going to the store today to get my ingredients. I brought the recipe card with me—I left it on my desk. What other goofy characters are there?" Megan stood up from her chair without scooting it far enough back and almost fell. Her eyes scanned the room to make sure Catherine wasn't around to see and sighed with relief at no sign of the unpleasant woman.

"Well, let's see if I can remember. There's Cherry Dee Light, and Stormy Deeds. Carlotta Cheesecake, and Muffy Mini Chips. One more…" Her eyes shifted from left to right, searching her memory. "Oh—Toffee Truffles."

"Of course." Megan wondered who made up such silliness. Then she started thinking about all the chocolate they'd be devouring. "I hope everyone is a good cook and can follow the game's recipes. Especially Catherine. She doesn't look like she's ever seen the inside of a kitchen."

Megan's closet nearly exploded with t-shirts and sweats, but no little black dresses. Buying a sexy dress to wear one night to a party didn't make sense so Brenda loaned her an outfit. Now Megan stood in her steamy bathroom, arms contorted, as she attempted to zip herself into a two-sizes-too-small spandex dress.

"Now I know how Brenda landed such a hottie husband—she must have been wearing this dress…ouch!" Her skin felt the pinch of the zipper's teeth. A little more twisting and turning and she had the dress fastened. Good thing Brenda also loaned her a full body shaper to go under the dress. Though now Megan couldn't take in a full breath of air no matter how hard she tried.

She applied her makeup four layers thick, added every bead and bangle in her jewelry drawer, then grabbed her box of chocolate cookies on the way out the door.

It took so long to stuff herself into that dress she was the last to arrive—*drat the luck*. Megan made quite an entrance into Brenda's large ranch style home. Someone wolf-whistled. She vowed to find out who and get back at them later.

"Oh, Megan *dahling* you look *mahvelous*." Delma drew out the words in her half-serious half-sarcastic greeting.

"I'm not Megan, remember? I'm Kandy-Kiss Klein. We're supposed to be in character from the start aren't we?" Megan thought she'd overdone the costume part of the game but blushed when she saw some of the other outfits. "Don't we have name tags or something?" She mumbled to Brenda, dressed as Tootsie-Pie Porter—outfitted in a cute flower print sleeveless dress and sixties era headscarf.

"You're right—I forgot! Here they are." She fumbled around in a box sitting on her elegant sideboard, surrounded by chocolate, chocolate and more chocolate. "Set your dessert over here. Everyone, come get your name tags."

"I'm not sure if I can wear a name tag." Catherine's commanding nasal tone blasted them as she approached wearing a Hawaiian print string bikini covered by a skimpy plastic hula skirt. Bright colored plastic flower bands surrounded her wrists and ankles and a matching lei adorned her neck.

"I guess we could stick it on your…flowers." Brenda/Tootsie-Pie coughed to suppress a laugh.

Megan tried not to stare at Catherine's…flowers. She took her first good look at all the other women in their creative costumes. Vivianne as Cherry Dee Light had a semi see-through French maid's outfit that Megan suspected was lingerie. Again, she tried not to stare.

Maria as Muffy looked suited up for a tennis lesson, in a white mini skirt and midriff-baring tank. At least *she* got to wear comfortable tennis shoes. Then Julie as Toffee Truffles looked like a fifties era coffee shop waitress, in a pink ruffled apron and cute little cap.

Delma as Carlotta dressed as a Vegas lounge singer, in a floor-length silk strapless dress, shimmering with huge silver sequins. Megan wondered when Delma would have ever worn such a dress or if she created it just for tonight…she'd have to ask later.

Sylvia as Stormy Deeds sat by herself on the couch, sipping wine, hiding behind dark sunglasses. She'd donned a leather bustier, studded jeans, and embossed boots. The tattoos on her arms looked real.

"Come on everyone, get another drink and your booklet and let's get started." Brenda/Tootsie-Pie clapped her hands to interrupt the loud chatter.

"Wait—where's your powder room?" Catherine ordered that the game not begin until she'd freshened up.

Brenda's mouth formed a scowl. "Around that corner, first door on the left." She pointed. "Hey, those are for later." She saw Catherine/Leilani pause at the buffet then snatch a chocolate cookie. Brenda snorted and put her hands on her hips, watching their new boss-lady sashay and shimmy her hula skirt as she headed down the hall.

The women picked up their booklets and found places to settle down on the comfy overstuffed couches and matching loveseats. Sylvia was already seated and showed no signs of getting up so Megan picked up the Stormy Deeds booklet and handed it to the tattooed lady, then sat down beside her.

"Thanks." She tipped her sunglasses down and winked. No doubt the woman who'd whistled earlier. Definitely the least enthused about the game, yet costumed for the part—or was that her normal weekend attire? Megan realized she didn't really know that much about her co-workers. She'd worked at Variety Plastics only six months, and spent most of her free time with Brenda.

Vivianne/Cherry tapped her long fingernails on her wineglass, impatient at Catherine's long absence. "Can't we just get started already?"

"Maybe I'd better go check on her." Brenda/Tootsie-Pie got up to investigate.

Everyone could hear the knocking on the powder room door and "Are you all right in there Catherine?" Silence. You could have heard the proverbial pin drop as all the women craned their necks to listen.

Brenda rapped again, followed by the creak of the hinge as she opened the door a tiny bit to peek inside. A piercing shriek echoed from the hall—Brenda, or an embarrassed Catherine?

"Oh my GOD—someone help, please!" Brenda shouted and the women leapt to their feet all at once and bumped into each other in their haste.

Megan reached the door first. Catherine lay sprawled across the terrazzo tile floor, hula skirt tossed aside. Looking away from her unclothed bottom half Megan focused on her face and checked for breathing. Nothing. She gulped when she saw part of a 'Chocolate Death Kiss' cookie on the floor.

The women all tried to press together to get a look inside the small powder room, some could see, others could only hear as Megan announced "Catherine Farrantino is *dead*."

"This is just part of the game, isn't it?" Julie/Toffee squeaked.

"Ah…no…and could someone please call 911?" The murder party had turned into a *real* murder scene—one of the women standing in the hallway was a *real* killer.

"NOBODY TOUCH THE CHOCOLATE!" Megan warned the women, not knowing if someone laced all the desserts with poison. But it was one of *her* half-eaten cookies on the floor and *she* didn't add poison to her recipe. Maybe Catherine swiped a couple desserts off the table?

"Look at whatever you brought, ladies, and tell me if some of it is missing. I want to know what else Catherine ate right before she…died." The women moved en mass to the buffet table to scrutinize everything.

"Brenda took our desserts from us and re-arranged them on her own platters. All but yours, Megan, since you arrived late." Maria cast an accusing glance at Megan/Kandy-Kiss.

"No way! I'm not a killer." The sound of police sirens interrupted them and Brenda hurried to open the front door.

If it hadn't been such a horrible moment for the Variety Plastic employees the expression on the officers' faces would have made them laugh. Four men charged in with guns in hand only to stop in their tracks and stare open-mouthed at the oddly dressed ladies.

"What's going on in here? A slumber party?"

Noticing they all seemed fixated on Vivianne as sexy French Maid Cherry Dee Light, Sylvia/Stormy the biker chick stepped forward to defend the group. "Hi Dave."

"Sylvia? What in blazes are you doing in the middle of a crime scene with all these bimbos…" The officer startled at a *very* familiar face.

"These are my co-workers at the factory, Dave. We're, um, at a murder party." She turned around. "Ladies—this is my husband, Officer David Drake."

"And someone called about a murder." Another officer pushed further into the room, looking for a victim.

"I did." Julie/Toffee squeaked. "She's in the bathroom, over there." Her arm raised up, pointing.

"Everyone stay put."

"Don't worry, officers…" At that moment the women collectively collapsed onto the nearest sofa, loveseat or chair, the group adrenaline rush had subsided.

"What kind of a joke are y'all playing on us tonight?" Officer Drake returned from the powder room and scowled at Sylvia.

"Huh?"

"There's no dead body in the bathroom." He holstered his gun while the other men searched the rest of the house and yard.

"But…" Megan felt faint.

Four officers searched but Catherine Farrantino's body had vanished, along with the half-eaten cookie.

"She wasn't breathing, I swear! We came out here to look at the dessert buffet to see what all had been eaten, in case something else was poisoned. She didn't just get up and walk away—did she? Is her car still here?" Megan looked to Brenda for help. She also felt like a fool—how could she have been mistaken about Catherine—she swore the woman was *not* breathing.

Brenda ran to the front window and stared out at the street. Catherine's silver Lexus had also vanished. While they were busy looking at the buffet she'd probably slipped out the back door.

Embarrassed, Brenda turned. "I guess our new boss wanted to play a sick joke on us. She's an odd woman. I'm…sorry officers."

Sylvia approached her husband and chatted quietly, trying to avoid any trouble for her co-workers. The unhappy look on the officers' faces spoke volumes, but they left without further questioning, assured that this was just a sick practical joke by a very mean woman.

"Well…" Brenda shut the door behind the men. "Thanks Sylvia, without your help we might have all been in a bit of trouble tonight."

"Hey, since Catherine didn't really die, I guess that means we can eat the chocolate?" Delma side-stepped toward the buffet.

"Yes, let's eat." Maria zeroed in on the pie, ready to have a big slice.

"WAIT!" Megan held her arms out to block the hungry women. "What dessert did Catherine bring?"

"Pele's Chocolate Revenge—those coconut macadamia brownies." Brenda pointed.

"Nobody touch them. No telling what she may have put in or on those things. If she's warped enough to pull a fake death stunt then she's nutty enough to give us all a case of food poisoning."

"You're probably right." Sylvia agreed. "Maybe I should have them checked too—I've got a few connections downtown, through Dave."

"Wow, that'd be great. Thanks." Megan helped Sylvia bag up Catherine's dessert.

"How about your 'Killer' cookies Megan? Wasn't there a piece of one in the bathroom?" Maria shot Megan a suspicious stare.

"Well, yes. But she didn't really die, did she? She's gone, her car's gone, and besides, I did NOT put poison in my cookies!"

"At least we don't *think* she died. It's still pretty weird how she vanished." Delma frowned, not ready to believe Megan—who couldn't tell dead from alive and got them and the police worked into a frenzy.

"OK, suit yourselves, don't eat my cookies. But they're delicious—I ate a few earlier, while they were cooling." Megan confessed.

"I'll have one, I'm not afraid." Julie picked up one of the Chocolate Death Kisses and popped it into her mouth. She sat down on the couch, savoring the morsel. After a few minutes she made a funny face, gagged and coughed then tumbled over onto the floor.

"Call 911 again—HURRY!" Brenda screeched.

Megan bent down over the woman but she'd already stopped breathing and all efforts to revive her failed. This time they checked her pulse. Too late, again. But…if those cookies were poisoned and Catherine really did die, where did her body go and what about her car?

Thanks to Sylvia, Megan was taken in for questioning but not held for the night—though not home free by a long shot. One woman died after eating a cookie she'd baked. Another woman was still missing. The police promised they'd search for Catherine.

Advised to stay home, Megan waited for the phone to ring with the report on her cookies and all the other desserts. The police had also checked her kitchen and pantry and found no traces of poison. She didn't even use mouse traps let alone rat poison—yet when they finally called they'd found rat poison in Julie, but none in any food from the dessert buffet.

Somehow only one of the cookies held the poison. Or maybe two if Catherine really died from another Deadly Kiss. Somebody could have hidden in Brenda's house and dragged off the body, stealing the woman's car in the process. But who, and why? Or Catherine did the dirty deed and sneaked off into the night. What a confusing mess. And fate dealt Julie the poisoned cookie. Any one of them might have eaten it.

Deep in thought, Megan jumped when the phone rang—the

police again? "Hello?" Brenda.

"Hey Bren, what's happening at your place?" Brenda also stayed at home for the day.

"Uh, Bradley is missing. He agreed to stay out with his buddies last night until after our party but he should have been home by midnight. I've tried his cell but he's not picking up or returning calls. He didn't show up at his office today either." Her voice grew quieter as she spoke.

Megan's first thought—did Catherine and Bradley run off together? She didn't want to say it but her silence said it for her.

"I know what you're thinking and I'm thinking the same thing. It's making me sick—I thought Bradley loved me."

"Oh, honey, I don't think…"

"Yes, you do. Should I call the police?"

"You mean you haven't reported this to the police?" She sucked in her breath. "Didn't they ask where your husband was last night?"

"Yes of course, but he wasn't a person of interest in Julie's death so they didn't go looking for him. I wasn't sure where he'd gone anyway. Probably bar-hopping."

"Call the police, *now*." Megan didn't want to sound too stern but after all, *she* was prime suspect in a murder and if Bradley was involved the police should be after him.

"OK, bye."

Megan crossed her fingers, hoping Brenda would make the call, but just in case, she also contacted Officer Drake.

"Your suspicions were correct." Officer Drake's call woke Megan early the following morning with some important news. "We've already called Brenda Garrison to let her know—we located Bradley. With Catherine Farrantino, traveling in her silver Lexus—they almost made it into Mexico."

"Oh dear. What about the poison and Julie and the possible charges against me…"

"Slow down. Let me fill you in." Dave cleared his throat.

The Final Twist

"It turns out Bradley had a relationship with Catherine, in California, before he married Brenda. When she returned to Houston she sought him out and they started scheming about ways to get rid of Brenda. He's the one who bought the murder game and suggested she have a party, agreeing to help Catherine fake her death and disappear—the poisoned cookie she baked, to match your recipe, was slipped into the dish and meant for Brenda. Though I don't know how she expected Brenda to eat that particular cookie. Maybe her plans changed since you arrived late? In any case, they tried to frame you since Catherine bullied you in school. They knew you hated her." He paused at her sharp intake of breath.

"So I'm off the hook?" She already knew the answer.

"We have Bradley's confession. He and Catherine are being hauled back to Houston as we speak."

The women from Variety Plastics stood in a solemn line in front of the gravesite. Poor innocent Julie. Megan sidled over to Brenda and whispered "I'm sorry about Bradley."

Brenda's response surprised Megan. "Thanks, but you know what? We were never 'right' together. I should have seen the signs, then maybe this wouldn't have happened…" she stopped as the gravesite service began.

"You know what I want to do?" Brenda and Megan sat in their same familiar chairs in Variety Plastic's break room, sharing their favorite lunch, a huge ham and cheese subway sandwich.

"What?" Megan sipped her root beer.

"I want to finish what we started—the murder game, I mean."

Megan's jaw dropped and her eyes widened. "How can you possibly want to, after…after…"

"As a tribute to Julie—we'll stuff our faces with chocolate and drink wine." She sounded so excited, how could Megan refuse?

"And who…"

Before she could even finish her question about who would play the missing characters they both heard a clatter of high-heels and saw their new boss, Marla Jackson, enter the break room. A nice woman—not at all like Catherine.

"Hi Marla—come here a minute." Brenda waved and her eyes sparkled. "How would you like to get better acquainted with your employees?"

"What did you have in mind?" She placed her hands on her hips.

"She's a natural to play Leilani Lovechild."

"Yes, I can see that." Megan winked.

"What in the world…who's…" Marla smiled and pulled up a chair.

"Leilani—a character at a party, at my house, this Friday night. Featuring chocolate and…"

"Don't say it!" Megan put one finger upright in front of her lips.

"M. U. R. D. E. R. There, I spelled it but I didn't say it."

"Are you talking about one of those murder mystery parties? I've always wanted to try that!" Marla grinned.

"Yep. It's called 'A Box of Texas Chocolates'—you get to dress up and play a character, drink wine and eat a lot of yummy chocolate."

"Sounds great. Count me in. Just give me the details."

Megan knew *this* time everyone would enjoy her 'Chocolate Death Kisses'—and everyone else's delectable creations. She couldn't wait to start baking.

Enjoy your own taste of Texas chocolate with the recipe book *A Box of Texas Chocolates—Recipes to Die For* available from L&L Dreamspell. Visit this web page for more information: http://www.lldreamspell.com/ABoxofTexasChocolatesRecipes.htm

Did you know that you can play the *real* murder game mentioned in this story? *A Box of Texas Chocolates—Murder Mystery Party* is available from L&L Dreamspell. Visit this web page for more information: http://www.lldreamspell.com/ABoxofTexas-ChocolatesParty.htm

A Box of Texas Chocolates

Getting a Clue
by Pauline Baird Jones

"Miss Trapini."

Most people said her last name like it was a curse, but Conall didn't, even though his family had been on the side of the law since they arrived on U.S. soil. Her family couldn't find the legal side with a map and a magnifying glass—not that they'd tried.

"Lieutenant Molony."

They both paused on their separate ends of the phone line. She wasn't sure why. They just did. It was part of this thing they had going. If she could figure out what the "thing" was they had going, she could cut back on her chocolate therapy. Or not. It was such a freaking cliché to drown her sorrows in chocolate, but nothing else she'd tried worked like a good dose of chocolate.

She closed her eyes, her hands clenched on the phone as she braced for what came next.

"I was wondering if you'd be free to come in for a chat this afternoon."

When the "chats" started a couple of years back, Conall had offered to come to her apartment, but she'd said no. It was hard enough having him in her head, without having him actually in her apartment. And, even if she wasn't in the family business, she *was* a Trapini. It didn't look good to have a cop car parked outside the place for too long. Chats at a police station were, oddly enough, not a problem for her family. It was expected that she be familiar with the inside of a police station.

"What time?" Even if she wasn't free, it was better to agree.

Conall had no problem sending a squad car for her. His little brother had a shiny, new badge. Who better to practice on than a Trapini?

When the call ended—abruptly of course—she turned to her assistant, Carol.

"Can you cover for me this afternoon?"

Carol looked worried, possibly because Anna went from the phone straight to the éclairs.

Anna's "I'm fine," was understandably muffled. When she'd swallowed, she gave Carol a weak smile, explained the request, and added, "I told you about my family."

What she hadn't told Carol was that she was in love with the enemy. Anna had been in love with Conall since the first grade, but a Hatfield and a McCoy had a better chance of getting together than a Trapini and a Molony.

"You didn't tell me about this Molony." Carol crossed her arms over her chest. It was her "truth time" pose.

Anna looked down at the éclair. It was preferable to Carol's all too perceptible gaze. "There's nothing to tell."

"Except you're totally into him."

Anna licked the chocolate off her finger. "Not totally."

"I thought you said Trapinis are good liars?"

"I'm an aberration."

"You ever been out with him?"

A Trapini out with a Molony? Stars would collide first.

"I've been under with him." Carol's eyes widened in shock. "Well, under the slide with him. I was nine. He was ten." He'd kissed her. She liked it so much she kicked him. He'd laughed, like he knew.

"That's it?"

"Well, there was a New Year's dance in high school. We bumped into each other." He'd kissed her again, a much better one this time, and then he asked her if she was going to kick him. For the space of two heart beats, she'd stared at him and thought, *he likes me.* Then his date grabbed him and her date grabbed her and the evening went flat as a pancake. That was when she started serious chocolate therapy. She'd been a dabbler in it until then.

Chocolate wasn't a perfect substitute for Conall's kisses, but it was more fun than an eating disorder. Of course, most things would be. And she'd been able to turn her obsession into a positive when she started her own business: *Anna's Delights*. Chocolates and pastries, Italian-style. Recipes stolen by a long dead Trapini, though she didn't put that in the advertising.

Her dad claimed the only good business was one that laundered money, but it turned out a lot of people needed chocolate therapy, too.

The location in Old Town Spring was almost as therapeutic as her delights. It had a folksy, family charm that helped her forget how many holidays she'd spent visiting family in prison. Outside spring was trying to get its game on and shoppers were trying to help with shorts and tees. Her tree out front looked very zen: no leaves, but some buds scattered on bare limbs.

"What's he look like?"

"Conall?" Carol nodded. Anna sighed. She shouldn't be thinking about how Conall looked. It was almost as dangerous to her well-being as actually seeing him. "He's…a better version of Pierce Brosnan. Black Irish. Blue eyes. Long and lean." Anna leaned her elbows on the glass counter top and let her brain off the leash. "He's going to age well. His dad is still hot—with touches of gray." Was it okay to think a guy's dad was hot? Etiquette wasn't high on the list of Trapini family lessons. "Enzo broke his nose in a fight once, so it's not perfectly straight, but you have to get really close to tell. He has great bones." And a perfect ten butt. She faltered to a stop. And ate another éclair. Words didn't do Conall justice. How did you describe the kiss factor of his mouth or the way his hair begged to be brushed back when it fell against his forehead, without descending into lame?

"Sounds like you had a lot of interaction—between the families, I mean."

"The Molony's lived across the street from us. Still do." Anna smiled a bit weakly. "Saved on gas having the cops so close." Now there was a tag line: The Trapini's, the "green" wise guys.

She'd stayed put until Conall moved out. And she'd had the strength of character to get a place that *wasn't* across the street from Conall. One might be obsessed with a man, and still be able to resist turning into stalker girl. It did take an impressive amount of chocolate and pastries, however.

"I'm pathetic," she admitted with a deep sigh. There'd never been anyone else and heaven knows she'd tried to find someone who could make her forget him. But her heart had refused to pat, let alone pit-a-pat, for anyone but Conall. "I'm beyond pathetic."

"You should tell him," Carol said, patting her shoulder. "What have you got to lose?"

"My pride?" She thought a minute. "Oh, wait. My family stole that."

"My point exactly. Tell him."

"And what if he laughs at me?" Or worse, what if he quit hauling her butt in for questioning?

Carol handed her another éclair.

It was a good thing her metabolism was still winning against her chocolate consumption.

They did the interrogation room version of their usual greeting, then Conall indicated her usual chair. Anna turned and straddled it, resting her arms on the back while she pretended to look at something besides Conall. It was the same room, they always used, the one without the two way mirror. Better not to have an audience for their exercise in futility. The smell was the same: a mix of disinfectant, sweat, coffee, burgers and Conall. He smelled really good, but then he always did.

He looked good, too. She'd manage to convince herself he wasn't all that and then she'd see him again and find he was more. Today he was wearing jeans and a tee shirt. Neither was particularly new, but they loved his body almost as much as she did. His dark hair was unruly, like he'd shoved his hands through it a few times. If he were on the trail of a Trapini, then he probably had done it more than a few times.

He stared at her for a whole minute before he took his usual seat across from her. Long ago she'd decided it was a cop power play. Of course he was a good cop. He was good at everything he did. So was his family.

Her family was good at getting it wrong. True to that family tradition, she'd gotten it wrong by falling in love with a Molony. Her family kept wondering when she'd find a "good" Italian boy and settle down. Of course, their idea of "good" was a good second story man.

She should have gotten over it, briefly thought she had when Conall followed the family footsteps into law enforcement. His first collar was her brother, Paolo, for pity's sake. But he'd looked so hot in his uniform when he testified at Paolo's trial, Anna had had to put on her sunglasses on so no one would see her staring at him. She'd contained the drooling by pretending to be upset by the trial. When she dabbed her eyes with a tissue, she'd sopped up the drool on the way to her eyes. She'd gotten some major sympathy points from Grandma Trapini, but it wasn't enough to save five pounds of chocolate from going down.

She became very familiar with his shiny, new cop car and had ample opportunity to examine the fit of his uniform in her rear view mirror—both coming and going. He stopped her on a regular basis during his time on routine patrol. She might have asked for it by going a few miles over the speed limit and letting her safety inspection tag expire. It was worth a ticket and made her dad feel better about her Trapini creds. Any court date was better than no court date.

When Conall got promoted, he and his new partner stopped in the shop now and again. Hatch was a fan of her dark chocolate Rum Victoria's. Conall was all about the éclairs. It was the one thing they had in common. Could one build a relationship on a pastry?

He'd started bringing her in for "questioning" about two years ago, when Enzo upped the criminal ante with some B&E. There was no question her family provided him with plenty of fodder for questioning. It was the only bright side of being a Trapini. A pity it was also the downside. Her family put the hopeless in her hopeless passion.

"You cut your hair."

She fingered the shortened strands around her face. Did he like it? His tone told her nothing, but then it never did. Conall could teach a sphinx how to be a better stone face.

"Yes." She shrugged indifferently, but the air in the small room felt thick with her longing. It amazed her he couldn't feel it. Clueless had to be a guy thing, because it wasn't a Molony thing. They *always* had a clue.

She studied him. He'd been in the shop recently, but he hadn't dragged her in for questioning for four, long months—a period that had been oddly devoid of family trials, now that she thought about it. That had to be some kind of record—and a reason to be *very* afraid.

"How's the family?" Irony weighted his tone.

"Fine?" Did he know something she didn't? Since they were all free on their own recognizance fine was probably a bit optimistic, nor was it likely to last. "And yours?"

"Doing great."

Of course they were.

"That's good." She almost sounded sincere. You'd think she'd know how to lie better. She'd had every opportunity to learn from the best. The only thing she'd ever lied about was her unrequited passion for Molony, and that was really a lie of omission, rather than commission.

"So, what did they do this time? And which one did it?"

Conall threw a folder on the table, the contents spilling part way across the scarred surface.

With a wary glance his direction, Anna drew it closer and

began to sort through the contents. It took her a few minutes to realize what she was seeing.

"Someone is sending your sister *my* chocolates?" They weren't having her ship direct. She'd have noticed an order to a Molony.

"Enzo. His prints are all over them."

He hadn't bought them from her. She'd have noticed that, too. No wonder Enzo had been so eager to help her set up her website. She should have looked that gift horse in little more closely in the mouth. By stalking a cop's sister, while ripping off his own, Enzo had achieved a new level of stupid. She was also aware of the other irony.

"Enzo has a crush on your sister?"

Conall looked almost offended. "Why wouldn't he?"

"I didn't know he had that good of taste." It was, she hoped, a good save. It was true. Erin was great. She came into the shop regularly. It was sort of funny. Two Trapini's mooning over two Molony's. At least she hadn't resorted to stalking, at least not technically. Speeding and the odd expired inspection tag were attention getting devices, and totally different in their level of pathetic.

"So you know nothing about this?"

"He didn't buy them from me." If asked, he'd tell her he picked them up when "they fell off the truck." She had a suspicion he'd fallen off the truck and hit his head at crucial stage of his mental development. "Is Erin okay?'

"Now that she knows it's Enzo she thinks it's funny."

Of course she does. Anna felt color creep into her face. Her family was a laugh riot. Her smile was a bit stiff. "I'm glad."

"How did he know her favorites?"

She probably knew, but she didn't *know*. She tried not to know what her family did and they tried to help her not know stuff. They knew she was a lousy liar, even if Conall didn't.

Why did he drag her in here anyway? It was a question she should have asked herself before. She frowned. Conall had a reason for everything he did, a good reason. He'd never even gotten a hint of a lead from her that she knew of. So what did he get out of these meetings?

"I don't know." She did know she wanted to crawl across the table and taste his sternly compressed mouth. Carol said she should go for it. For the first time, she was almost ready to try. She had the awful feeling there wasn't enough chocolate in the world to make her feel better if she walked away from him again.

Of course she didn't know anything, but if he didn't ask her about the case, then she'd want to know why she was here and then what would he say? What could he say?

I pretend to interrogate you because I need to see you. I eat your éclairs to see you. I keep tabs on your family, trying to find ways to see you.

Today her pink tee shirt said, "You know you want to." Truth by tee shirt. It was tucked into jeans that fit her lean hips so perfectly, they should have been a crime. She always wore pink. He thought pink was a cute, little girl color until she started using it as her "signature color," whatever the hell that meant. All he knew was that on her, pink wasn't for little girls.

In some ways she looked just like the first time he'd seen her. He'd been in second grade, she had just started first. His heart had tried to pound his way out of his chest then, too. He'd thought, *I'm going to marry her.* Of course he had to notice the one girl in the world he couldn't have. Molony's like to do the impossible as regularly as possible, getting Anna Trapini—or forgetting her—was the only thing he'd failed at.

Stay away from those Trapinis, both parents had said. They're nothing but trouble. How did you avoid temptation when it lived across a narrow street and looked like Anna Trapini?

He'd disobeyed them twice. The first time when he kissed her under the slide and she kicked him in the shins. The second time he kissed her, she hadn't kicked him. The memory still made him smile. And he still wondered what the look in her eyes had meant. Now that's a question he wanted to ask her.

Would she laugh? Would she care?

He pretended to look at the file, but he couldn't keep his eyes off her. The shorter hair suited her face. Even at six, her face had been nice to look at, strong and determined, but soft, too, like girl. Her hair looked like dark sable. It moved when she did, releasing her scent into the air around her. It was a mix of chocolate, vanilla and essence of Anna.

He'd only been real close to her those two times, but he remembered everything about both of them. Her skin was silky soft to the touch. Her mouth had trembled under his and he thought she leaned in and responded, but someone bumped them apart and he wasn't sure.

Her eyes were dark and cool. They watched him watching her, hiding her thoughts as effectively as Fort Knox hid gold.

If he took her hands, if he pulled her close and kissed her Trapini mouth, so lush and pink, would she kick him or kiss him back? Would she realize that they belonged together?

A Molony and a Trapini belonged together. *Right.* Both their ancestors must be rolling their eyes—not to mention over their in their graves. The living family would probably do an intervention. The thought of her family and his in the same room outside of a police station made his eye want to twitch.

He'd planned some questions to ask her. They'd sounded good at the time. If he could just remember them, he could ask them. Only he couldn't. He should say something about Enzo and the chocolates. He should say something about anything.

He cleared his throat. His mind stayed blank, no not blank. It was full of Anna fantasies. He'd seen her at Gianni's with Marco Gianni last week, and the only thing that had stopped him from going over there and punching some lights out was her obvious boredom. Come to think of it, his date had looked bored, too. He'd have introduced her to Marco, but he was a second story man and would probably be back in jail before the seasons—or his underwear—changed.

He rubbed his face, trying to rub away the thought of her long, soft body against his.

Okay, just because her family was a nightmare and everyone they both knew would think them being together was a bad idea, didn't make it a bad idea. When he was within sight, sound and smell of Anna, the only bad idea was letting her walk away from him again. He'd been doing it for since they were both six years old and it wasn't working for him anymore.

"Was there something else you wanted to ask me?" She pushed her hands into her hair the way he wanted to, releasing a wave of her scent into the stale air.

It almost stopped his heart.

He wanted to ask her if she liked him. He wanted to tell her how proud he was of what she'd done with her life. She'd started her store herself, worked damn hard to make it a success. She'd kept it honest, against the odds and family pressure and her lame ass brothers kept trying to mess it up for her.

"Why do you let them do it, Anna?" He didn't realize he'd used her first name until he saw her eyes widen. Her mouth parted, too, becoming perfect for kissing.

She stared at him.

He stared at her.

And then a miracle happened.

Anna Trapini *smiled* at him. She'd always been great, but that smile was beyond great.

"There isn't any *letting* where my family is concerned," a pause, "*Conall*. You know that."

She'd said his name. The cautious warmth in her voice seeped into his heart, erasing the cold chill that had lived there for all the years he'd loved Anna Trapini from a safe distance. It wasn't, he finally realized, possible for any distance from her to be safe. Nothing was safe or right when they weren't together.

"You know I'm going to have take Enzo down."

She didn't look away, didn't even blink. "You always do."

"If you get in my way—"

She stood up, pushing away from the chair. Her movements were deliberate. She turned the chair around and eased it back in place under the battered table top. She left her hands resting on the top, as if she needed the support.

"When have I *ever* gotten in your way, Conall?"

She said his name again. He stood, too, because it was good manners and urgent necessity. He stepped to the side, removing the table as an obstacle.

"You're always in my way. You've been in my way my whole damn life."

Her eyes widened again and pulse started to pound against her neck. He spent a whole minute watching it, imaging his mouth just there, against her skin soft—

"Conall?"

She sounded uncertain. Anna Trapini never sounded uncertain. She took a step that might have been toward him—or toward the door.

"No."

"What?" A tiny shake of the head sent her scent toward him again.

"You're not leaving until I have my say."

"Okay." She propped a hip against the chair, crossed her arms, and fixed her brown eyes on him with an intensity that twisted his insides into a knot, while igniting a tiny threat of hope. "I'm listening."

"You're in my mind when I'm awake, in my dreams when I sleep, and you've between me and every other woman I wanted to love instead of you."

Her lashes swept down, lingered for what seemed a long time, then lifted with agonizing slowness.

"You put a lot of effort into it?"

Conall felt a tingle of unease head down his back. "Into what?"

"Getting me out of your way so you could love someone else?"

His tie suddenly felt very tight. He tugged at it. It didn't help.

"You're so good at everything, I'm sure you were *very* thorough."

He swallowed, his throat dry as the Sahara. "My heart wasn't it in."

Her lips pursed. "What about the rest of you? How much of that was in the effort of forgetting me?"

Anna Trapini was jealous. His tie loosened at this realization.

"Distant was a word I heard a lot. Too into my job. Too somewhere else. My last date dumped water on my head because I was looking at you. You were with Marco Gianni." Just in case she had forgotten the guys *she'd* dated the last few years.

She rubbed a finger along the top of the battered chair and Conall envied it. He was jealous of everyone and everything she'd touched that wasn't him.

"I remember that night. I didn't see you looking."

She'd been looking at him, too.

"Well, I was. If he'd touched you—"

"He tried, but I stopped him." The look she gave him through the thick fan of her lashes lit a brush fire inside him. A tiny, pleased smile tipped up the edges of her mouth. "Is that all you wanted to say to me?"

He felt like he'd made it the other side of a minefield and wasn't eager to go back in.

"There is something I need to *do*. " He closed the gap that separated them before he finished the sentence. It was the closest he'd ever been to Anna Trapini since high school, but it wasn't close enough.

His hands settled at her waist and then they slid around to her back. His arms had to follow and her slight, supple body finally came into contact with his. She didn't resist, which was both good and legally wise. Resisting an officer was against the law.

He withdrew one hand, so he could tilt her chin up. His thumb brushed across her mouth and it parted, as if she'd been waiting for him, too. Her chocolate-vanilla-Anna scent was even better this close to her. Her lashes lay against her pale cheeks. He wanted to see her eyes, needed her to look at him. A pulse at her neck beat at light speed. He touched that spot, her skin as warm and smooth as he remembered. He bent there first, pressing his mouth to that spot and felt her shiver the length of her body.

"Conall." His name was both a sigh and a demand.

"*Anna.*" He gently mocked her tone. That lifted her lashes. What he saw there was encouraging, but he wanted more. He bent, put his mouth on hers, felt it tremble and then soften in welcome. She tasted like her chocolate éclairs. He'd always loved her éclairs. He deepened the kiss. This was good. *This* was safe. This was finally *right*.

Outside of their embrace, the world might have rocked. Molony and Trapini ancestors might have rolled over in their graves. He didn't know. He didn't care.

He was kissing Anna Trapini like his life depended on it, because it did.

Conall finally put a millimeter of space between them. She looked as dazed as he felt. He wanted to say something. Maybe to ask her when, how long, how much, but the words clogged his thickened throat. So he kissed her again. That worked, too. She was with him. He could feel it. When he had to pull back to breathe, she murmured a protest, her hands both insistent and exploratory at the back of his neck.

He hugged her close, but the need to look at her was almost as great as the need to hold her and kiss and never let her walk away from him again. He managed a smile, but his hand shook as he smoothed her hair back from her flushed face.

The door opened and his partner, Hatch poked his head in the opening. His eyes widened and then he grinned. "It's about damn time."

Conall looked at him with a frown. "What?"

"You're the only two who didn't know. It was getting embarrassing."

He looked at Anna, worried how she'd feel about this frank outing. She grinned and shrugged.

"I'm a Trapini. I'm used to being embarrassed."

Conall felt how big and stupid his grin was, but he didn't care. "I can live with the humiliation, if I have you."

Anna leaned back just enough to look up, then down. "You appear to have me, Molony."

"So when's the wedding?" Hatch asked.

Anna jerked in his arms. "Wedding?"

"There's been a pool about you two for like, forever."

A cold ball of fear formed in his gut at the look on her face. "Only way you can have a Molony, Trapini, is legal."

"We haven't even had a date." The protest lacked serious heat and she was still leaning against him and almost purring. Had he thought her eyes hid things? They weren't right now.

"You've been dating since, like grade school, Anna," Hatch pointed out. "You just didn't know it."

Conall felt his tie tighten around his neck as she considered this. Slowly a smile tugged the edges of her mouth up again.

"No wonder you love me, Molony. I'm a cheap date."

Hatch laughed. So did Conall, but not for the same reason. It was going to be all right. He didn't even care if her family came to the wedding as long as there was one eventually. He stroked her back and saw little flames in her eyes.

Her head tipped to the side. "Way I heard it, you have serious commitment issues."

"Heard from who?"

"Where do you think your dates came for their post date carbohydrate therapy?"

Hatch straightened and crossed his arms over his chest. Conall felt a tinge of unease at the look on his face.

"Do you know what he said to me the first time he saw you, Anna?"

She shook her head. Her hair stroked his face and he had to

dig his fingers into the mass and hold on to keep from kissing her again.

"He told me, I'm going to marry her."

Conall had forgotten that part. So much for his secret heart's desire.

Anna looked at him. "You were seven."

"A very smart seven," he said, a bit smugly. He liked being right almost as much as he liked hugging Anna.

"You're a Molony."

"Always will be."

"I'm a Trapini."

"Not if you change your name to Molony," he felt compelled to point out. "You've always been more Molony than Trapini anyway."

She hadn't pulled away, but he could feel her thinking. He could also feel her wanting it. What held her back?

"Your family won't like it. They don't, they won't like me."

The light bulb went off.

"They'll love you, Anna, but not as much as I do." No one could love her that much. "Do you love me?"

"I think I'm going to barf." Hatch's words and tone didn't match, so they ignored him.

"Of course I do, but the shock will kill your dad."

Conall frowned. His dad was taking blood pressure medicine.

"Did you forget the part where I said everyone knew but you two?"

This time they both looked at Hatch. Conall considered this, shining a new light on some things his mom had said recently.

"I think you might be right," he admitted.

"Your family always has a clue," Anna conceded, "but not mine. They never have a clue."

But it turned out they did.

36 A Box of Texas Chocolates

Dying for Chocolate
by Laura Elvebak

Three toddlers, two girls and one boy, sat in a circle on the bare attic floor. Three sets of rosy cheeks and fine, fly-away hair. Claire watched them lean forward, pudgy hands reaching, but not touching. They giggled as they slapped at the colorful rattles.

Claire edged toward the door. The toddlers grew more aggressive with their toys, egging one another on. Soon they would be grabbing one another's playthings, and there would follow yells and cries. "Just like your mothers," she thought. She gave the room a second glance. Nothing could hurt them in there. The attic was perfect for her purpose.

She turned the doorknob and let herself out. She waited a moment and listened by the door. No sound. Satisfied, she locked up and pocketed the key. The steel insert her husband had built to fortify the room was indeed soundproof, just like the one he built for the room downstairs, the one he called the "panic" room. His excuse for the attic had been to provide him with a quiet refuge. The panic room was supposed to protect them from intruders. But the real reason for both, she discovered, was to keep anyone from hearing her cries.

She softened the furrows on her brow and exhaled as she descended to the main living area. A glance at the clock told her she had timed everything right. In five minutes the first mother would arrive. That gave her enough time to bring out the chocolates. They lay in five beautiful rows of six on the deep red silk that lined the bottom of the box. Each mouth-watering morsel nestled in its own cup of crinkled black paper that curled around the edges of the candy. Only one paper holder sat empty. The largest one in the middle that had held the fanciest piece.

The kitchen looked spotless. Tonight her husband would not be served dinner just the way he demanded—a salad with no wilted leaves, his steak rare on the inside, burnt on the outside. Tonight the kitchen smelled of live things, plants and flowers, with the rarest of ingredients to sweeten the chocolates.

The doorbell rang. Lacey Richards could wait a few extra seconds. Claire carried the box of chocolates into the living room and placed it on the coffee table. She made sure the box was exactly centered. Jerry would have insisted. But, on second thought, he wasn't there to watch her. She pushed one corner down a fraction of an inch. A tiny thrill shivered her spine. She smiled and went to open the front door.

Lacey Richards stood on the porch, irritation showing on her sharp features. Taller than Claire, Lacey didn't have the awkward movements one would expect of someone with her proportions. No baby fat that Claire could see. How did these women bounce back so fast after having babies?

Claire moved aside to avoid being run over. Lacey steamrolled in. Claire supposed this aggression was built into attorneys from birth.

"Where's the kid?" Lacey demanded. "I have a dinner party to get ready for. The caterers should be at my house."

"Come in, Lacey." Claire knew it was a little late for an invitation, but said it anyway to hear her own voice. "The children didn't get to nap until late. They're still sleeping, and I hate to disturb them. Anyway, I wanted to visit with you and the others. They should be along shortly."

Lacey sighed as if she were being terribly inconvenienced. "I don't have time, Claire. I'll wake up Darius. Where is he?"

"I made a treat for us," Claire said, ignoring Lacey's question.

To her relief, the doorbell rang before Lacey could protest further.

Sharona Milton burst in, emitting a stream of chatter that rose to a crescendo of endearments, exclamations and announcements. Claire wondered if she had been forced to remain mute all day in her cubicle at the newspaper office and that's why she released words like a bubble machine. Maybe she was trying to make up for her petite frame which might have disappeared into the cracks of the sidewalk if it weren't for the soft rolls of fat that, on her, somehow looked cuddly and cute.

Sharona spotted Lacey and paused for a nanosecond before she caught her breath. "Oh, Mrs. Richards, I was hoping I'd catch you here. You're usually out of the door and gone who knows where before I get here, and I've been dying to meet you. I've wanted to talk to you about a legal issue I'd like you to look at and that I know you will jump at as soon as I tell you all about—"

"Stow it," Lacey interrupted. Her piercing eyes could have rendered almost anyone speechless. For a moment Claire thought it worked on Sharona. Lacey pointed at her. "I don't make appointments. That's what my secretary is for. She answers my phone between eight and five. Is that clear enough?" While she spoke, she pulled out a business card and thrust it into Sharona's hand.

Sharona held up the card and broke out in a huge smile. She acted as if she'd been given the keys to the judge's chamber and a free pass to Disneyland. "Why, honey, I can't thank you enough. I'll surely call her first thing in the morning. I will do that, don't you worry your head about nothing. You got yourself a client, and no ordinary client. Just wait until you hear my case—"

"Fine, fine," Lacey said, her eyes sparking. She whirled on Claire, but before she could repeat her demand, someone pounded on the front door.

Claire rushed past the two women to open the door to Rita Caldonas, dressed in the wildest colors Claire had seen north of the Mexican border. Once a top Vogue model, Rita designed clothes and jewelry and appeared daily on the Home Marketing show. Her bracelets clanged as she reached to touch Claire's arm.

"Darling, you look so tired. What is wrong with my favorite

little babysitter? You need some jewelry to perk you up. We must make time for a jewelry party, dear. But as usual, I'm in a rush. Contracts to go over tonight. You know, the usual." She waved her hand to encompass "the usual," taking for granted that Claire would understand.

Rita spied the two other women, put dainty fingers to her lips and glanced at her watch. "Oh dear, it is late, isn't it? I'm always the last one here. Well, I won't interrupt. Where's my little bambina?"

Claire turned her back on Rita. "Lock the door," said the voice in her head. "And don't forget their purses."

Claire nodded as if in a trance. She felt her blood race as she turned the deadbolt on the door and used her key on the second lock. She felt certain at least one of the women would have heard the lock turn, but then she realized no one had paid attention to her movements. Why be surprised? They never did. They didn't even notice when she snapped up their purses and tossed them in the hall closet. She was little more than a maid to them, paid to watch their children while they led their busy lives, and she stayed imprisoned in this house.

She minced her steps until she cleared her way among the women. "The babies are sleeping. Before we wake them, I'd like to discuss something that's been bothering me."

Her tone sounded whiney. She hated that. She always acted awkward around these mothers. Next to them, she felt plain, unsophisticated, dumpy. Her wispy brown hair never did what she wanted, but hung limp and dull. Her skin always turned blotchy this time of day, and she felt driblets of sweat run down her back.

"Claire," Lacey's voice cut through the quiet. "What's the matter? Is it your husband again?"

Claire blanched, but recovered quickly. Was she that transparent?

She took a deep breath and sat in the upright chair her husband always used, the one that faced all the others. "Why would you say that, Lacey?"

Lacey waved her hand as if the question were irrelevant. "Aren't husbands always the root of all trouble?" She laughed and looked for the other women to join her. "I've told her how to handle him, and that she needed to sock money away without him noticing. Never hurts to have a cash reserve for emergencies."

Claire noted that Sharona had turned her attention to the chocolates.

"Did you make these, Claire? They look delicious." Sharona selected one and popped it in her mouth. The other two mothers followed her example.

"They are," Claire agreed, not able to suppress a smile. "I call them my Truth or Dare chocolates."

Rita's fingers hovered over the box a second time, but withdrew her hand at Claire's words. "You're acting very funny, Claire."

"It's a dream I had. Only I'm beginning to think it wasn't a dream after all."

"You're not making sense, honey," Rita said. "Where is Jerry?" She looked around the room as if expecting him to magically appear. "He's usually home by this time, isn't he?"

"Oh, you noticed," Claire said. *Of course you would.* "Don't you want to hear about my dream?"

Lacey made a show of looking at her watch. "Really, Claire, I'm sorry you're having problems, but that isn't any of our concern now, is it? It's getting late and we have things to do."

Claire folded her arms and hugged herself. "Yes, I know. But this is important to me."

Sharona sat and motioned to the others. "Let's listen to her. After all, she's been watching our children for a year now. I think we owe her a few minutes."

Claire's head buzzed. The women paid attention to Sharona, but never to her. Anger washed over her, taking away the fear that usually paralyzed her. Calm settled over her like a foggy night. She lifted her chin, and the women settled in front of her. Lacey chose an armchair, while Rita perched on the sofa.

"This sounds serious." Rita said, frowning.

"Well, get to it," Lacey said. "We don't have all night."

Claire sucked in a deep breath. "I dreamed one of you is having an affair with my husband."

Sudden silence met her, but that didn't last long. Protests burst from their lips that looked to her like colored bubbles growing and popping. She barely heard the sounds they made as she watched the bubbles bounce and float and splatter against the ceiling.

She raised her voice. "Then I dreamed I made chocolates. Special chocolates that would tell me which one of you deserved to die."

For a second they all stared at the coffee table. Then Lacey's hand flew to her mouth and she coughed twice. Sharona gagged. Rita drew back and opened her mouth, but nothing came out.

"What—what are you saying, Claire?" Sharona stammered. "Did you put something in the chocolates?"

"You wouldn't, you're our babysitter," Rita said, looking worried.

"So you had a dream." Lacey swayed as she stood. "Big deal. You don't really believe one of us would have an affair with your husband."

Claire looked up at her. "Why not? Isn't he good enough for you?"

Sharona hurried to her side. "Honey, we've seen how he treats you. No wonder you've let your imagination run wild." She turned to the others. "I was leaving one day when I heard him yell at her over a salad. I guess he thought I'd left. He dumped the whole salad bowl over her head. I heard her crying, but he made her clean it up and fix him a new dinner."

Rita shook her head. "You need a break, honey. Have you ever worn any of the clothes I've given you? New clothes always give me a lift. I know that you don't drive, but you need to get out once in a while. You poor girl. He won't let you, will he?"

"No wonder you're acting Looney-Tunes," Lacey said. "I never realized. But really, dear, that's no reason to go off on us."

Furious, Claire stormed to her feet. "I'm not a little girl." She stopped and made herself take several calming breaths. She couldn't lose it now. When she felt more in control, she said, "I know one of you has been sleeping with Jerry. You trust your children with me, but when it comes to my husband, you treat me like I'm an imbecile."

"That's not true," Sharona argued.

Claire looked at each of the women. "Jerry said you would never tell me the truth. That's why I decided on the chocolate test. Only they will expose the liar." She pointed to the box of chocolates. "Are you feeling any after effects? If you're innocent, they won't hurt you. They only kill liars and adulterers."

Rita backed away. "You didn't poison us! I feel fine."

"That could mean you're innocent," Claire said. "Or it could mean I've injected a slow acting poison for which only I have the antidote."

"I don't believe you," Lacey said, but her expression told a different story.

Sharona clutched her stomach. "I'm feeling sick. Someone call 9-1-1."

Claire didn't move.

Rita moaned. "We need to get to the hospital."

Lacey gave up her calm exterior and went into action. She searched the room frantically. "Where's my purse? I want my cell phone. Damn you, Claire."

Claire shrugged. "I'll get your belongings when I'm ready."

"Bitch." Lacey glared at her. "Get them now."

"Please," Sharona pleaded.

"As soon as the guilty party confesses." Claire tried to sound reasonable. "I suggest you don't delay. The side effects of a poisoned chocolate could be fatal."

"You won't get away with this." Lacey snarled. Then she stopped as if struck. "Where's Jerry? What have you done to him?"

Claire smiled. "He's unavailable." She looked at the empty

paper cup in the center of the box. Jerry always said he deserved the best and she expected him to pick the largest and fanciest chocolate. He didn't disappoint. "What do you care?"

Lacey took a threatening step toward Claire. "This is getting out of hand. Nobody wants your stupid husband. You need a doctor. Your head is screwed on wrong."

"Yeah," Rita said. "He's nothing but a lying SOB anyway."

"Rita's right," Sharona said. "He's not worth this."

Claire lifted her eyebrows. "I thought none of you knew him, but that's not what I'm hearing."

Sharona paled. "Oh, my God, you're serious. You've really poisoned these chocolates." She sank into the chair cushion.

"Not all of them," Claire said. "Truth or Dare, remember?"

Rita grabbed Lacey's hand and pulled her down on the sofa. Lacey yanked her hand away and looked away.

Claire looked pointedly at her watch. "Time's a ticking."

"Okay, okay!" Sharona wailed. "It was me. Jerry knew my marriage was in trouble. He wanted to comfort me, but it got out of hand."

Lacey's eyes widened. "You slept with him, too?"

Rita bolted upright. "That bastard. He told me I was the most beautiful girl he'd ever seen. He almost talked me into leaving my husband."

Claire felt the room spin. She hadn't expected all of them to confess. "He slept with all of you?"

"Why wouldn't he?" Sharona blurted. Then, as if realizing how that sounded, she covered her mouth and avoided Claire's steady gaze. She peered down at the chocolates. "Claire, tell us the truth. Are they really poisoned?"

Claire didn't answer right away. She didn't owe these women anything. She took care of their children five days a week for a year while they had a life, and they underpaid her miserably for the privilege. Moreover, they thought they could get away with sleeping with her husband. Take, take, take.

But she took something from each of them, too. She listened

to Lacey's legal advice, accepted Rita's fancy hand-me-downs she could never wear in front of Jerry, and learned how to plant a legal notice in the newspaper. But these tidbits were offered without thought, crumbs to a beggar.

They never considered her as a person or even as a long suffering wife. She only existed to babysit their children, be the invisible wife of their lover. They were having second thoughts now, weren't they? Oh, yes. Claire felt a sudden urge to laugh.

The women, on the other hand, were growing more distraught.

"Tell us," Lacey demanded. "Should we go to the hospital?"

Claire turned her gaze slowly upon them. "I don't know. I only chose a few pieces, but they got all mixed up. I don't know which ones were special."

"I can't believe you'd do this," Rita moaned.

"Where are our children?" Lacey said. "Tell us you haven't harmed them, too."

Did they just now remember them? "They're in the attic," Claire said. "You can take them home now."

"I knew you wouldn't hurt them," Sharona said, relief showing in her face. "You've always been good to the children."

"That's right," Rita murmured in agreement. "God, I hate the thought of finding another babysitter."

"But, of course, we couldn't…" Sharona started, but let the rest of the sentence drop.

Lacey shook her head. "The chocolates weren't poisoned." She turned to the others and tried to sound convincing. "She was lying. Can't you tell? I feel fine. I'm taking Darius and going home to my dinner party."

They followed Claire upstairs. She unlocked the door and let it swing open. For a moment no one spoke. The room was dead silent.

The babies hadn't moved far from where Claire had left them. They were still on the floor surrounded by plump cushions. But instead of sitting up, they were curled up on their sides forming a circle, eyes closed and fingers reaching out but not touching.

The three women sucked in a collective breath. Rita made a soft whistling sound through her teeth.

"Are they sleeping?" Sharona whispered. Her tone implied that she really wanted to ask, "Are they dead?"

The children stirred at the sound and the mothers ran to them with cries of relief. One by one, they carried their babies from the room. Claire followed them to the first floor. Wordlessly, she retrieved their purses from the closet and unlocked the front door.

"You are certifiable," Lacey said to her before leaving. "I better not get sick or die. I'll sue the hell out of you."

Rita paused at the door. "Honey, get help before it's too late."

Sharona refused to look at her as she rushed down the porch stairs to the street.

Claire locked the door after them and took a deep breath. After several moments, she reached into the closet for the suitcases, filled with clothes Rita had donated over the last year, and placed them by the door. She strode to the living room, snapped up the box of chocolates and took them into the kitchen. She chose a dark chocolate for herself and dumped the rest in the sink and turned on the disposal.

With all evidence gone, she stopped in front of the panic room. "This is goodbye, Jerry. Too bad you can't hear me. You're the one who insisted on the soundproofing. Like everything else you owned, it's the very best money can buy. I'm going away for a while, Jerry. Call it a well deserved vacation. They say Brazil is beautiful this time of year, but there are so many choices."

She slipped the chocolate into her mouth and savored its dark sweetness. "Like you always told me, it's all in how you pick them."

The Invisible Hand Will Smear Chocolate on the Face of Tyranny
by Mark H. Phillips

"You are playing a dangerous game, Mr. Kinkaid." Latarra stirred her hot chocolate and then breathed in its scent. Her face took on a brief image of ecstasy. I wondered what would happen to her when she tasted it for the first time. What would happen to her handler?

I sipped my own chocolate and said nothing. The harvest of cocoa beans had been superb. SGT 474 was just a shade hotter than Sol and this planet was ten percent more massive and its orbit just a shade closer to its sun. Even in the highlands of the extreme southern hemisphere it was hotter and more humid than any equatorial rain forest on Earth. We were both sweating profusely with only a few rattan fans to stir the heavy air. I watched a trickle of sweat roll into the deep valley between her breasts. Perspiration soaked through her light cotton blouse and turned it transparent. Khaki shorts showed off her long legs which stretched out as she sprawled farther down in the chair. She kicked off muddy boots and socks to cool her feet. She had blisters. Touring the plantation had taken its toll. A beautifully iridescent flutterwing landed on her big toe and absorbed the precious salt from the surface of her skin.

Latarra spoke in a deep, lazy purr. "Our agents have given us the U.N.'s master schedule. The release of chocolate is another century away. Your masters have determined that releasing it now would undercut their coffee profits. Theater of the Absurd, the Swahili language, something called a corndog, the history of the Dutch, 19th century comic books, and a selection of jazz classics are all on the trade schedule before chocolate."

Latarra finally sipped the chocolate. Her eyes went wide and she visibly shuddered. Could someone actually orgasm from drinking hot chocolate? She gave me a genuine grin. All her previous movements had been so deliberate that it was refreshing to see a spontaneous, unguarded reaction. Her grin emphasized her youth, no more than twenty.

The Rell almost always acquire their human proxies as infants. My eyes went to the tiara-like band surgically implanted into Latarra's forehead. It sparkled with tiny diodes as the signals reached out to her Rell handler who would feel what she was feeling, hear her thoughts, or at least some version of her thoughts that would make sense to it. By convention everyone considered a Rell and its proxy as one entity, with a single name between them. Only with significant alteration could her brain physically form and grasp Rell concepts as well as provide the biological circuitry for the entangled tachyon transmitter. Of course, no faster-than-light communication was necessary with her handler on the huge Rell ship orbiting high above.

I sighed and leaned back in my chair. I was older than I currently looked, and trudging over the entire plantation in the heavy gravity and oppressive heat had taken a toll. For some reason I had to show off all my hard work; the vast orchards of cacao trees, the fermenting shacks, the leveled rocky outcropping where we sun dried the fermented beans, and the new brick and iron roasting ovens. How many humans could feel the pride of accomplishment anymore?

The Rell thought as collectively as the kleptocrats of Earth. I knew that I would have trouble making them understand my motivations. How could I make Latarra understand concepts so alien to her race? It would have been so much better to deal with the former trade liaison, but of course that was impossible. "I have no masters. The coffee profits support the kleptocrats of Earth who let the dregs filter down to their pet citizens. I may undercut their profits, but my own profits will be extraordinary, as will yours."

Latarra's eyes glazed over for a few moments. Perhaps the layered meanings and puns of my response threw her and her handler momentarily out of synch. I wondered what it would be like to make love to Latarra. I've heard from others that Rell proxies make exotic and disturbing lovers. They cannot switch off their contact. Sex with Latarra would mean sex with her handler, involving behaviors and reactions not at all predictable. I remembered my only direct encounter with a Rell, a hippo-sized, green polyp with multiple antennae and wasp-like compound eyes. Noxious slime had covered the Rell and the odor was unimaginably strange and nauseating. My idle speculations ceased to arouse and I shut my mind to them. At least Rell taste buds were similar to ours. I sipped some more hot chocolate.

Latarra set aside her empty cup. "I cannot understand your willingness to act against your own species. How can we trust a being that would betray the interests of his own kind?"

"Surely a diplomat understands that humans have multiple ethical systems, not all of them similar to the specieism of the Rell. Aren't the Rell currently addicted to this decade's release of the plays of Shakespeare?"

"I am not so familiar with you humans as my predecessor. But I have read Shakespeare's works. I see you as an amoral Macbeth, consumed by ambition to assume, illegitimately, the status of your betters. You exemplify not an alternate moral system so much as evil, do you not? You have fallen into a sort of madness, your greed outweighing your duties to your fellow humans. You are a rogue, unpredictable. Indeed, I now believe that it was your madness that infected my predecessor. Did you give forbidden tracts to the former Rell trade liaison? Forbidden texts fascinated him. Is that why he lost his mind and disappeared into self-imposed exile?"

"You are being overly harsh with me. I am not such a bad person. And you certainly have a moral duty to advance the interests of your people. Whatever my moral status, the deals I'm offering are to your advantage." I put down my drink and offered her a plate heaped with squares of the richest fudge brownies I could bake.

She squealed with pleasure after taking a bite. "It makes my tongue tickle, and causes momentary loss of equilibrium."

"It's full of easily metabolized sugars. Look, Latarra. It's important that you and your masters understand my motivations. I intend to offer you other commodities well ahead of the official U.N. schedule, and well below the negotiated barters. I'm willing to offer you items from Earth's legacy the existence of which the Rell are unaware. The U.N. has withheld access to these items from their own citizens for so long that most people have forgotten they even exist. Acquiring these would obviously be in the Rell collective interest. Your masters need to understand that I will be a reliable source." I handed her a hard-copy list of tantalizing items for sale and suggested payments.

She stared at the list. I watched as her left eye oscillated left and right. She was unconsciously mimicking her Rell handler's gesture of frustration and dismay. "This is not acceptable. Some of the items you offer are, of course, most tempting, but others are forbidden. The reason they are not on the official schedule is that they would pollute Rell society. Releasing these items would be tantamount to an act of war. As for the payments, many of them would entail the release of proprietary technical advances too quickly into Earth society. We will not release the cure for leukemia for three decades, or the secret of the manufacture of chromatic quantum circuitry for another century. Your masters have meticulously planned the release of technologies in a way determined to maximize long-term stability. Releasing tech too fast would make social planning impossible."

"The stability my so-called masters want to maintain is the stability of their power and privilege. Their social planning is transparently self-serving. Somehow I don't think the people dying of leukemia would sympathize with their rulers' amazing patience. Perhaps that patience is more explicable when you factor in the persistent rumors that upper level U.N. officials have access to medical technology not scheduled for release to the general population. Perhaps my supposed masters would not suppress new medical research if they needed the results themselves."

"Your masters should suppress such rumors. Your culture is still far too lenient with its dissident elements." Latarra looked up from the list and stared directly at me. Her eyes narrowed. "Some of these proposed prices are ridiculous. Entangled Tachyon Transmitter human/Rell interface wetware is completely off the table. The Rell monopoly of faster-than-light technology must remain secure. Indeed, you and your workers should not even be on this planet. How did you establish your operation here? Using current Earth technology you would have had to leave Earth sometime in the 4th century BCE."

The tiny audio implant behind my right ear was whispering panicky warnings. Jinaru scared easily. I scratched behind my ear to lower the volume. "How my team arrived here is not germane to our negotiations. You have your secrets and I have mine. Have you ever read the Earth fable about the goose that laid golden eggs?"

Latarra smiled and nodded. She was good at her job, but her handler was not. Her left ear was turning a bright red in a loose correlation with the Rell antennae color change indicating rage.

I shrugged and smiled. "The proposed trades are mere suggestions. If you think a particular price too high, we can negotiate."

"But, even if we made these trades, you in turn would disseminate unscheduled technologies into Earth society ahead of the master schedule. We must not endanger our relationship with the legal owners of Earth's heritage. They would be furious not just at you, but with us. We may enjoy a temporary bargain dealing with you, only to pay for that temporary advantage many times over to compensate your masters for their unplanned losses. They have the whole heritage of Earth locked away in their vaults. Why should we endanger our eventual access to all of that intellectual property in exchange for the early introduction of a sweet luxury item?"

Jinaru was now yelling into my audio link. I had to turn down the volume again. "You have the gall of all exploiters. Since the Rell discovered Earth, you've turned my culture into a damned cargo cult. Earth's masters appropriated the entire culture, locked it away from Earth's own people, and trade it out to aliens in meager dollops. Why trade it out in precious dollops? Because when that's all gone there won't be anything left. Humans no longer create new culture. There is no innovation, no creative drive. Earth's citizens are useless, pampered, uncreative dependents. They were wolves and now they're lapdogs. They have peace, plenty to eat, mindless entertainments, but they couldn't read Shakespeare until after you bought his plays, let alone write something new that Shakespeare would be jealous of. My people won't be able to taste chocolate again for a century—the kleptocrats froze the seeds for the plants and locked them away, at least the seeds left unliberated by my organization.

I stood and glared down at her. "You accused me of not caring for my species. Well, I do care. I want to throw my society into chaos. I want to destabilize the power of our rulers. I want the current generation to have black-market access to everything they should own as their common legacy. And out of that chaos will come new creativity, new product, more than your masters have ever dreamed of. And if, in the bargain, I bring my society closer to your level technologically, we may eventually become equal trading partners instead of selling our cultural treasures for the equivalent in your culture of a few trinkets and beads."

Latarra sat stunned at my outburst. Jinaru stomped into the silence, slammed a holo unit onto the table, and brought up the image of the Rell ship in orbit. She pointed at her ear and glared at me in fury. Jinaru was even more beautiful than Latarra, even though her left eye was wagging and her right ear was as red as a thrust exhaust. Was she pointing at her ear to remind me that I had ignored her audio messages or that "she" as an entire unit was furious? With so many indicators of her dual nature, what was the point of wearing that ridiculous turban?

The Rell heavy cruiser had opened its belly to disgorge a U.N. military craft bristling with rail guns, particle beam cannons, and rocket launchers. From its belly in turn, fighters were emerging, dozens of tiny specks in tight echelons of brilliant atomic fire. Several immature flutterwings entered the hologram to play with and hunt the tiny specks.

The holographic projection faded to static as they hijacked our com signal. The florid, scowling face of Admiral Leland replaced the Rell ship. He had aged considerably since I had last seen him. His handlebar mustache was pure white. It was impossible that he would recognize me—even my genetic structure and brain waves were different. I liked Leland; tough as nails, scrupulously fair, and a patriot albeit with far too little philosophical perspective.

Leland addressed himself to me. The com unit was projecting a holo image of me onto the table in front of the Admiral. "Kinkaid. In the name of the United Nations of Earth, I demand your immediate and unconditional surrender. If you care at all for the men under your command, order them to power down all weapons and defensive screens. I guarantee fair treatment. I will bring you all back safely to Earth to stand trial."

"I'm sorry, Admiral Leland. You're fighting on the wrong side. I do care for my men and for my cause. I wish I could convince you that we too are patriots, but I'm positive I don't have the skill to convince you to go against your orders, at least not in the time we have. Perhaps the examples of men more eloquent than I may eventually do the job. I give you a gift." I looked over at Jinaru and nodded. Leland jumped back as the book appeared on the desk in front of him.

Recovering from his involuntary defensive reaction, he picked it up. "*A History of the American Revolution* by Richard Kincaid. You wrote this?"

"I did indeed. There are few human writers or readers of history left. I think you will enjoy it, Admiral, though you may find that it challenges your notions of a soldier's duty."

Latarra was in a fury. "You will not read it, Admiral. Destroy it immediately. Your masters have placed all of Kincaid's writings on the banned list as well as all books on that particular subject." Latarra turned her fury on me. "You just used a Rell matter transfer device. No human should even know of its existence, let alone be able to use one."

I shrugged. "What can I say? I have friends in high places."

Jinaru's eyes glazed slightly as her handler spoke through her. "Mr. Kinkaid's unit is a loaner. Don't worry. Not even someone as insane as I would allow a savage human to control such technology. His unit is firmly under my control."

Jinaru removed her turban to reveal her sparkling implanted tiara. She turned to face Leland's image. "Please keep and read the book, Admiral. It changed my life. I've always been a collector of banned Earth writings—an inexplicable perversion of mine. But Kinkaid's writings were the ones that finally converted me. The concept of going against my superiors had never occurred to me, let alone the possibility of direct violent confrontation. Richard tempers his views with a strong pacifist streak. He insisted you get a book. I wanted to send you a sizable antimatter bomb. Richard says that you are a misguided, but otherwise admirable patriot. My favorite quote in the book you are holding is, 'The tree of liberty must be refreshed from time to time with the blood of patriots and tyrants.'"

I ignored their further discussion and stepped out onto the veranda. I looked around for a last time. The last of my men disappeared, transmitted to safety along with the last of the precious beans. The sun was setting behind the distant mountains. A dense night fog was already filling the valley below and the cries of howler spiders began their haunting banshee wail. I breathed in the scent of a night-blooming flower not dissimilar to jasmine. I would miss this planet. I regretted never naming it. I could see the contrails as Leland's fighters entered the atmosphere.

Jinaru's handler flipped a switch and we transmitted to some cold, gloomy stone room. Even I had no idea what planet we were now on. The gravity was much less. The air had a rusty metal and sulfur smell. Latarra was livid. No distance could disturb the link to her handler. I didn't fully understand the tachyon entanglement mechanism, but I knew it worked so well that there was no way for her handler to even know where in the universe his proxy was.

Latarra looked as if she might have a cerebral hemorrhage. "Jinaru, once again you demonstrate your extreme antisocial madness. How dare you kidnap my proxy? How dare you act contrary to the will of your betters?" Latarra stamped her bare foot in rage. Was her handler simultaneously stamping one of its viscous pseudopods on the deck of the Rell ship?

Jinaru sighed. "Your daughters and sons will feel differently someday, crèche-brother. You've tasted chocolate. It will spread across the Rell Empire. You could have saved us all a lot of trouble, danger, and overhead by making its spread semi-official. But white, gray, or black, there will be a market. The market's Invisible Hand will smash the evils of monopoly, mercantilism, privilege, and exploitation. It will revive the creative spirit of a stupefied race and alter the destiny of the Rell in exciting, unpredictable ways. The Invisible Hand will bring us products still undreamed of and in our lifespans. You've tasted chocolate. The Invisible Hand will smear chocolate on the face of tyranny. Soon you will taste corndogs and root beer and even the sweetest most intoxicating brew of all—liberty. Warn your masters and Kinkaid's former masters: Freedom is coming. Adapt or die." Before Latarra could respond, she disappeared, transmitted instantaneously to the Rell ship where her handler dwelled.

When I spoke my voice sounded odd in the thin atmosphere. "Do you really believe all that, Jinaru? The line between greedy entrepreneur and revolutionary is fraught with opportunities for self-deception."

"The Invisible Hand allows you to be both with no conflict. The Invisible Hand cares not for your motivations. Act for your own profit and the universe will rejoice. Trust The Invisible Hand to smash what must be smashed and to sculpt what must be sculpted."

"You speak like a religious zealot, Jinaru. The invisible hand is not a god. As there are no masters, there are no gods."

"It now seems to me that sometimes gods and masters require convincing. We shall see. Your doubts distress you. Don't they get in the way of your goals?"

"Well-read humans are always subject to second thoughts, counterarguments, and skeptical doubts. It should make it harder for us to blow up our enemies, though my historical researches make me doubt even that. Someday, you may regret helping us humans emerge from under the Rell collective thumb."

"Perhaps, friend Kinkaid. Perhaps someday you will rebel against the order you and I will now sculpt. Perhaps it is your nature to rebel against any structure that constrains you. If that is an old pre-Rell human trait waking from its long slumber, then I salute it. But enough theory. We have beans to roast. We have chocolate to make. We have some liberty to brew."

A Recipe To Die For
by Sally Love

Gretchen Schultz inhaled the glorious aroma of her chocolate cakes. She slipped her hands into padded red-and-white gingham mitts and lifted a pan from the oversized oven. Every year just as she geared up for the Thanksgiving and Christmas season, the seige by the town's women began. While she spent long hours baking Gretchen's Chocolate Fantasy Cakes, and filling order after order from the most exclusive gourmet outlets in Texas, her so-called friends mounted an assault to steal her recipe.

Only a few positions of honor existed in the Texas Hill Country town of New Pilsen—Mayor, Sheriff, Banker, Lawyer, Preacher, Chocolate Queen. Gretchen had owned the Chocolate Queen title for decades. She began selling the cakes forty-seven years earlier, after her husband of four years died—crushed between two rail cars. The Chocolate Fantasy Cakes supplemented her meager widow's pension.

She stored her prized ingredients in the pantry, in alphabetical order. Well, most of them. The ultra-secret one she hid in a Quaker Oats box.

The baker had turned off her telephone a week earlier to avoid call after predictable call. "I'll scoot over and help you, Gretchen," they'd say, the sing-song voices barely masking their true mission. Gretchen knew they would pry, wander through her small house chasing every clue for the secret to the moist, melt-in-your-mouth, orgasmic chocolate confections.

She updated the standing orders in the computer database—

password protected—with the help of her constant companion purring in her lap.

Gretchen always had more orders than she could fill—even baking through the nights. She could pick and choose at whim who received her exclusive cakes. The small town snoops would have to buy theirs like the rest.

"Wake up, Flour. We're in serious baking mode."

Flour answered with her customary "ee-ee-ee." Even as a kitten, Flour had never meowed like other cats. The vocalization could mean, "Hello," "The mail is here," "I'm hungry," "I'm bored" or "Please scratch my chin."

Gretchen nudged the cat out of her lap and hurried to the kitchen, brushing off pale hairs. She heard a knock at the back. The baker had ignored an earlier front doorbell. The women of her own generation had given up, but their spoiled daughters, the thirty-somethings, were rabid. "You need to leave a legacy," they'd say. "With no children, publishing your recipe will make you immortal in the baking world."

She had huffed at the clumsy ruses designed to filch her recipe, jerked her hands to generous hips and looked down her nose. "*My* cakes have *already* elevated me to that status."

Gretchen pulled back the eyelet curtain with a finger, then let it fall. Opening the door a crack, she frowned at Josie—one of the irritating second generations, complete with fake smile.

"I'm driving to the grocery, may I pick up anything for you?"

"Don't need a thing." She pushed the door closed, nearly nipping Josie's nose. How could she meet shipping deadlines with the constant interruptions? Did the woman really think she'd rattle off an ingredient list?

After supper and an hour of watching *Criminal Minds*, Gretchen glanced at the clock. As her customer list had grown, she switched to wholesale bulk ingredient suppliers. She ordered online and received shipments via UPS. But many of the town snoops assumed she bought everything at the local grocery. Only a few of her extra touches—flavorings such as the tablespoon of buttermilk she had added through the years— were ordinary grocery purchases. She delayed shopping at New Pilsen's HEB until she knew most of the second-generation busybodies were home serving supper. Even then, she had to be careful.

List safely secured in her purse, the baker cased the HEB entrance for her two tormenters. All clear. Gretchen aimed for aisle nine—Baking Needs. She selected Baker's semi-sweet chocolate squares, and the eight-ounce box of Carnation powdered milk, then hurried to the back corner of the store.

"May I help you?" Marian interrupted the restocking of housebrand yogurt cups to corner the baker at the refrigerated milk section. She homed in on Gretchen's half-filled mini-basket like a human Geiger counter.

Gretchen sensed the stocker logging each item in memory. "No, thanks." She forced a half-smile, then reached inside the refrigerator section for a pint of whipping cream and the half-gallon of buttermilk. All except the buttermilk were diversionary purchases she would donate to New Pilsen's food pantry.

At checkout, even though Gretchen chose the staffed express register, Rose, tormenter number two, pushed the teenaged employee away, logged in her store password and swept each item over the scanner. Marian and Rose would compare notes later, each consumed with divining her recipe by compiling lists of possible ingredients.

For years her garden club had coaxed, "Everyone is participating in the bake sale and recipe swap." Shamed, "It's for the church cookbook." Even threatened, "The garden club can rescind your membership." She responded by resigning from the garden club and donating her cakes to select fundraisers. Who needed faux friends?

Each year the pressure intensified. Why couldn't they just leave her alone? How could she halt the incessant hounding?

The next morning, Gretchen fed Flour her favorite breakfast—

two tablespoons of Kozy Kitten, tuna flavored. After a final lick of the lips, the cat settled on a sunny windowsill. The baker slid another batch in the oven. She would have just enough time for the daily constitutional her internist prescribed. She slipped on walking shoes, then dropped the house keys into a pocket.

Two houses south, a neighbor stopped her. "Did you hear?" Mrs. Svboda said. "The most horrible accident! We activated the phone tree. I just left you a message."

Gretchen gave her a questioning look. "What happened?"

"Marian! Marian fell!"

The baker grabbed Mrs. Svboda's hand. "Is she in the hospital?"

"No," the neighbor fished a tissue from the front of her blouse. "She...she's dead."

Gretchen gasped, hand to mouth. "Oh my stars! How?"

Mrs. Svboda blew her nose, stuffed the tissue in her overflowing cleavage. "She fell off a ladder in the HEB."

Gretchen frowned. "The shelves aren't *that* high."

The neighbor shook her head. "Marian was building the Thanksgiving display, stacking twelve-packs of Coke. She leaned out too far and lost her balance. A twelve-pack landed on her head."

The baker personally delivered one of her Chocolate Fantasy Cakes to the grieving family. She hoped she appeared appropriately bereaved for the persecutor who had, with her meddlesome partner, contaminated the last decade in New Pilsen. Gretchen wished she could've figured out a way to permanently deter Rose as well on her endless recipe quest.

Early the following Friday, Gretchen slid the second batch of the day out of the oven. She heard Flour's "ee-ee" as the furball trotted into the kitchen. "Good morning, Flour kitty, did you sleep well?"

Flour peered over her shoulder, then set off. Gretchen followed to the front window.

At the end of the driveway Beth Ann Tomasek from the Lutheran Church stood on tiptoes, head and arms inside the wheeled garbage container. The baker threw open the door and yelled, "Just what do you think you're doing?"

Beth Ann jerked up and grabbed at the bin in an effort to steady herself. The rollers met the pavement and she toppled, leaving a patch of forearm skin on the crumbling asphalt. "You scared me!" Beth Ann sputtered, sprawled on the street.

"Good!" Gretchen didn't offer Beth Ann a hand. "Answer me. What are you doing?"

Beth Ann's face turned fiery. "My Pilates class decided to decipher your recipe by sifting through your trash. I drew the short straw."

"You stupid girl! I'll have you arrested."

Beth Ann struggled to her feet. "You can't arrest me." She winced as she dabbed her shirttail at the oozing scrape. "Once you put out your trash, it's anybody's for the taking." She held her arm close to her waist. "I researched the law."

Gretchen drew her brows into a frown. "The law on *my* property says that you pick up every scrap. If you people want a Chocolate Fantasy Cake, it'll cost fifty-seven dollars and fifty cents—tax included."

Beth Ann recovered several pieces of trash, tossed them in the bin. "Your brochures say thirty-two-fifty."

Gretchen motioned at two tin cans Beth Ann had missed. "The extra twenty-five is what I charge *thieves*."

The baker rolled the bin two feet backward onto her property. She stood watch as Beth Ann limped down the street and around the corner.

Gus rattled his UPS truck into her driveway midweek for the latest shipment of cakes. After he loaded the dolly, they walked to the truck together. As he rumbled off, Gretchen gave him a parting wave. She reached to pick up the weekly newspaper, then slid the paper from its plastic sleeve as she made her way back to the warmth of the house.

Flour waited inside while the baker spread the classified-ad pages on the carpet. The cat padded across the papers, selecting a prime spot to settle.

"My stars, Flour, look here." Gretchen held up the headline toward the cat: "Preacher's Wife Found Dead."

Flour walked over to investigate.

Gretchen grabbed her Walgreens reading glasses. "Beth Ann Tomasek, who disappeared after Bible Study at the Lutheran Church last Thursday, was found early Tuesday at the Westside Landfill. Sheriff Janos Wodnicki reported that Mrs. Tomasek likely had been struck in the head several times with the bloodied galvanized steel trashcan lid found next to her body."

"What do you think, Flour?" As Gretchen scratched around the cat's ears, Flour sank into the want-ads in a limp, purring heap. "Think the Pilates class will concentrate on exercise instead of my cakes?"

Flour half-opened an eye and answered, "Ee-ee."

"I think so, too."

Gretchen tossed her oven mitts at the table and hurried to meet the regular UPS delivery. Flour trailed her mistress. As Gus edged the brown truck to the precise spot opposite her sidewalk, she stepped onto the porch. The driver loaded four boxes on his dolly. He carefully spread a lightweight tarp over the cartons, hiding the logos. Ever since he caught a neighbor sneaking photos of the baker's shipments, Gus made sure the vendor names were covered.

"Just in the nick of time." Gretchen smiled. If she had ever had a grandson, she would've wished him to be like Gus.

As he rolled the dolly inside, Flour beat a quick retreat.

"It's okay, kitty," Gretchen cooed. "She hates those big wheels on your handcart."

Gus placed the boxes of bulk ingredients on two kitchen chairs. "Flour, it's only me."

The cat peeked around the corner.

"Hey, kitty, I have a new mouse for you." Gus pulled a fabric toy from his shirt pocket, bent and shook the mouse at Flour. She immediately switched into stalk mode. Ears flat, the cat eased toward Gus and the mouse, step by slow step. Flour stopped, eyed the mouse. Gus wiggled it. Flour pounced, pinning the mouse with her paws. She transferred it to her mouth and took off.

"Hot cider, Gus?"

"Thanks, Miz G, this Christmas rush doesn't give me time for catch my breath. And I love your cider almost as much as your cakes."

Gretchen poured the steaming brew into a Styrofoam cup, pressed the lid down and handed it to Gus.

The driver accepted with a thank-you nod. He hesitated before propping his foot on the dolly. "Miz G, you're not gonna like what I have to tell you."

Gretchen pulled out two chairs, sat in one and offered the other with a wave of her hand.

After taking a seat, he pried off the cider lid and took a swallow. "One of your neighbors offered one of my co-workers money for a list of the wholesale companies who ship you raw ingredients." He paused, taking another drink of the fragrant cider. "My co-worker is honest. She processes invoices for the Freight Street Distribution Center in Austin. Your neighbor threatened that if my friend didn't cooperate, she'd find a way to get her fired."

"What is the world coming to? Can't these people find a better use of their time than stealing from me? Who is it?"

Gus shook his head, obviously upset.

She leaned toward him, patted his hand. "I have to know, Gus."

He said the name. "It's crazy. Even if Jannah Babka learns that you order sugar from Imperial or cocoa powder pails from Dutch Bakery or almond liqueur from Passion Liqueurs, she could never duplicate the precise amount of each ingredient."

Gretchen gazed past Gus into the backyard. "Why don't they

just leave me alone and let me bake my cakes?"

"Beats me, Miz G. Made me furious." Gus snapped the lid on his cider-to-go and aimed the dolly toward the street. Flour burst through, slapping the mouse along the wood floor. "We thought you ought to know what's going on behind your back."

Gretchen held the front screen open for him to roll through. Gus secured the two-wheeled cart to the truck. He waved as he pulled away.

Inside, Flour trotted to her mistress and laid the mouse at her feet.

She scooped it up and examined the toy. "Wasn't it nice of Gus to bring you a new mouse?"

Flour lifted her head. "Ee-ee," she agreed.

Gretchen washed her hands, fished out her box cutter and opened the boxes. She flipped on the radio. A half-hour later she'd replenished her supply pantry and positioned eight cakes inside the hot ovens.

A week later, Gretchen and Flour stretched out on the bedroom chaise between batches. She turned the radio volume up.

"An update on this afternoon's explosion," the announcer said, "by telephone from New Pilsen's Fire Chief. Chief, tell us what happened."

"Janna Babka prepared her Thanksgiving turkey and filled the propane cooker with peanut oil," said the Chief. "Her sister explained that Mrs. Babka routinely sneaked a cigarette in her backyard. The cooker hose had developed a hissing gas leak. When Mrs. Babka leaned over to find the source of the hissing, the cigarette ignited the propane tank. Mercy Ambulance transported the critically injured woman to County Hospital."

Gretchen walked into the kitchen, lifted the box cutter from the drawer. She shook Ajax powder along the blade, then scrubbed it with steel wool. After rinsing and drying the cutter, she replaced it in the drawer.

Two weeks before Christmas, Gretchen switched into overdrive, omitting her usual breaks between batches. This year she'd accepted even more last-minute orders to counter the ever-rising cost of living. As much as she loved baking, the increasing espionage and her efforts to protect the recipe drained her limited energy. She felt older every week.

The phone rang. Gretchen checked the caller ID: Analytical Food Lab. She'd ignored their earlier call, but picked up the receiver.

"Mrs. Schultz?"

"Who's calling?" Gretchen snapped.

"Reginald Johnson…with Analytical Food Laboratory in Grand Prairie."

"Texas?" The baker frowned. Was this another trick to wheedle the recipe from her?

"Yes. Grand Prairie, Texas." Johnson laughed. "I don't know of another city by that name anywhere else." His voice sounded friendly, not intrusive.

"I'm busy with my cakes, but I'll talk to a fellow Texan."

"This is rather awkward," Johnson began, "but I received one of your cakes with instructions to analyze its ingredients."

"What? Who sent it? I'll wring their necks!" Gretchen threw her oven mitts across the kitchen.

"The woman sent me a check double our usual fee," Johnson said. "Quite tempting."

Gretchen gasped. Fear gripped her. "You wouldn't dare!" If the recipe were discovered, she'd be ruined—financially, of course, but more important, the reputation she'd built would be destroyed.

"I'm calling, Mrs. Schultz, because you registered your recipe as 'confidential' with the National Food Products Association," Johnson said. "And I don't allow this lab to be used for industrial espionage. Especially, since your Chocolate Fantasy is my favorite cake, the one I wait for every Christmas. I count the days until it arrives. I carefully cut tiny pieces to make it last longer, then scrape the plate with a spoon."

"You can purchase more than one at a time, you know." Gretchen smiled at his words, relishing the compliments.

"My belt is already tight," he chuckled.

"So tell me who the spy is." She slid into a kitchen chair.

He told her.

Gretchen sat still a long while, working her way through emotions—first shock, then disappointment, then fury. She knew why Mila Raab tried to extract the recipe with an expensive analysis.

The banker's wife thought of herself as a gourmet cook, but her desserts were ghastly. Mila constantly experimented, but had zero common sense: jalapeno peanut butter cookies, raspberry potato chip mousse.

Mila had, for years, tried to persuade Gretchen to enter the Chocolate Fantasy Cake in the annual Pillsbury Bake-off. These days the prize was a million dollars, but Pillsbury's entry rules prohibited professionals. Mila dismissed the rules and urged Gretchen to lie. The woman wasted her efforts. Gretchen couldn't tolerate liars and she would never enter a contest that published the recipes.

But the thief turned relentless. Every time Gretchen drove out of town, she saw Mila's Cadillac in the rearview mirror. The baker deliberately drove to odd places to throw off Mila's obvious scrutiny. Often Gretchen stopped at Cousin Viktor's Pak-It-N Bar & Grill outside of Willow Springs. Cousin Viktor's job was to delay Mila long enough for Gretchen to slip out the back and drive his F-150 to the source of her special honey. Mila hadn't caught on...so far.

Each cake contained only a single teaspoon of the nectar. Any more could prove toxic. But the tiny amount produced from the surrounding rhododendron and mountain laurel pollen triggered a mild disorienting euphoria.

After this blatant assault, Gretchen must arrange something appropriate for Mila.

On the cold, crisp morning of December 23, Gus loaded the final shipment. Gretchen tied a red bow on an extra cake box. She attached a card, "Merry Christmas to my favorite driver."

Gus accepted the box from Gretchen with a nod of thanks. "Miz G, the other guys are jealous. I'd drive your route for free."

She hurried inside and returned with another box. "For your colleagues." She handed the second cake to Gus.

That evening Gretchen relaxed with her feet perched on an ottoman. Flour lay across her ankles. The TV's talking head appeared, interrupting the lead-in to a rerun of *The Unit*. "Mila Raab was found along Highway 16, twenty miles west of Hye. Tracks at the scene indicated her car swerved from side to side before plunging into a twenty-foot ravine. The sheriff's office is trying to make sense of a broken jar of honey and a spoon found in the floorboards."

She shook her head slowly. "What a shame, Flour." The cat blinked, then jumped from the ottoman to the waiting lap. "More than a teaspoon of that honey addles the brain." She scratched under the cat's chin, prompting a muffled purr.

The afternoon of Christmas Eve, Gretchen leaned her head back against the living room chair and closed her eyes, inhaling the lingering aroma of chocolate. Flour raised up, jumped off the ottoman and hurried away.

The doorbell rang.

Sheriff Wodnicki tipped his hat when Gretchen appeared, apologizing for disturbing her on Christmas Eve. "I wanted to get this visit in before tonight's church service."

Gretchen dismissed the flicker of apprehension. She'd known generations of Wodnickis since they were babies. "Come in, Janos." They were some of her favorite New Pilsen citizens. "I just started a fresh pot of coffee."

He'd always been a big kid. Now he filled her entry as he

walked inside and followed Gretchen through the house. "I wanted your side of the argument with Beth Ann Tomasek. Something about her picking through your trash?"

Gretchen offered Janos a seat. "Hard to believe, isn't it?"

He placed his Stetson on the corner of the walnut dining table and lowered into the old railback chair.

"I just hope her poor family can find peace after such a tragedy," Gretchen said.

"She really dug in your trash?"

"She would've strewn it along my street if I hadn't put a stop to it." Gretchen took a few steps into her cramped kitchen, poured coffee into a mug. She'd poured many a cup of straight black coffee for the sheriff at New Pilsen's community get-togethers.

She set the steaming mug in front of Janos.

"Word is she was consumed with discovering your chocolate cake recipe." The Sheriff sipped.

"The gall of the woman!" Gretchen flinched. "God rest her soul," she added quickly.

"One of the neighbors said you looked pretty angry." The sheriff repositioned his hat a few inches father from his coffee cup.

The baker shrugged. "Just wanted her to think so. I make my living baking those cakes. What if I came poking around the Sheriff's Office, sneaking through your trash? Wouldn't you tell me to stop?"

Sheriff Wodnicki smiled. "I might even threaten arrest for theft of documents. But Gretchen, somebody got mad enough to kill her."

"From what I observed, Beth Ann's hobby was sticking her nose into other people's business. You'll have a long list of residents who argued with her."

"That's what I'm finding out," he chuckled. "That woman rubbed a lot of feathers the wrong way." The Sheriff relaxed into the friend he'd always been.

"I want your opinion of a new sauce I've been testing." Gretchen strolled back into the kitchen.

"Always eager to be your guinea pig." Wodnicki said.

Gretchen poked her head into the dining area and winked. "Coming right up. How are you and the missus spending the holidays?"

While Sheriff Wodnicki filled her in on his family's upcoming trip, Gretchen uncovered a fresh Chocolate Fantasy Cake, then opened the pantry. She lifted the lid off the Quaker Oats box and slipped out her precious honey jar. Flour joined her mistress, rubbing along one leg, then the other. "What do you think, Flour? One? Two?"

Flour peered up. "Ee."

"I think so, too." Gretchen stirred milk, butter, sugar and several tablespoons of powdered cocoa over a low heat. Then she carefully added a half-teaspoon of rhododendron honey—just enough to make Sheriff Wodnicki a tad dizzy and, she hoped, forgetful. She poured the sauce over a generous wedge of cake, filling the house with the sweet scent.

She slid a fork from the silverware drawer, then walked back into the dining room. Gretchen placed the dessert on the table under the Sheriff's nose.

He inhaled as though it might be his last breath. The sheriff drew in the addictive aroma. He smiled as he picked up the fork, cut off a liberal bite and lifted it to his mouth. Janos Wodnicki allowed his lids to lower as he let the flavors melt and mix on his tongue. He opened his eyes. "Gretchen, I declare, with your new chocolate sauce, this cake is to die for."

The Bavarian Drop Killer
by Cherri Galbiati

"Is anyone going to eat that? It's Bavarian chocolate, you know." Rina, pointed at the wrapped candy laying on the pillow, her saliva glands working overtime. "Janelle's not going to eat it. She's dead." Rina slapped her hand over her own mouth. "That came out cold and I didn't mean for it to. It's just...well, you know." Her eyes never left the chocolate.

"You're not supposed to be in here." Danny leveled his gaze on Rina and then kissed her. "The guys will be here in a minute, and I don't think eating the evidence is a good idea."

"Ah ha. So it's true about the chocolate candy being connected to those other murders? Besides, Hannah and I found her, so we do too have the right to be in here." Kissing him back, she pulled on her dog's leash to keep her away from the body crumpled on the floor next to the bed. "Why didn't you tell me about the chocolate connection?"

"Because you gossip." Stating it as a fact, Danny escorted her to the bedroom doorway. "Take Hannah and go wait in the living room. Do not leave," he ordered. "I have to take an official statement from you as soon as Stoddard arrives." He reached down and stroked Hannah's fur, "You did good, girl."

"Speaking of the devil." Rina grinned, pacing up the narrow hallway in the trailer home. Gravel crunched under tires as a car pulled up to the mobile home.

Officer Robert Stoddard marched up the steps entering the trailer with his hand resting on his holstered weapon. "Rina? What are you doing here?" His cobalt eyes absorbed his surroundings, taking her in as well. He smiled, his gaze finally resting on Rina's German shepherd. "Where's Sergeant Gammon?"

Rina blurted out, "Hannah found her and I called Danny..."

"In here, Stoddard." Danny yelled from the back bedroom, cutting Rina off.

She shrugged her shoulders, smiling, as Officer Bob Stoddard slipped into the hallway. Her eyes followed his backside till he disappeared. Eye candy, that man is, pure and simple. She fingered her engagement ring on her left hand. It was fun to look, but for Rina, her soul belonged to Danny.

Rina picked up Danny's voice fussing at Bob about his uniform as soon as Stoddard walked in there. Something about it looking incomplete. The phone rang in the tiny living room. "I got it." Rina called out to the officers down the hall, picking up the receiver. "Hello."

"Rina, dammit. Don't answer that phone." Danny yelled, stomping up the hallway.

She twisted her body so her back faced him, continuing with the caller.

"I need to speak with Janelle. Put her on the phone." Female. Her voice spoke anger in volumes.

"Who's calling, please?" Rina matched the caller's tone, recognizing the voice; but before she could hear the answer, Danny reached over Rina's shoulder and jerked the phone out of her hand.

"This is Sergeant Gammon with the Sandy Creek Police Department. Who am I speaking with?" Danny's expression stayed a mask of stone. Rina listened intently to his side of the conversation.

"No ma'am, Ms. Easton, Janelle's not being arrested, again." He shifted his weight to one leg. "She won't be coming into work and at this time I can't discuss it with you." He held the phone away from his ear as Gloria Easton cussed him out a blue streak.

Rina heard every blaring word and knew her employer's temperament-challenged social skills wavered on so many levels. Watching her fiancé's face turn from blank to animated crimson, she held out her hand. "Let me talk to her before you blow a gasket and get written up for shooting a telephone."

He started to hand over the phone and pointed a finger at Rina's nose. "Not one word about the chocolate." He said through clenched teeth, retreating to the bedroom.

Nodding, she took the receiver. "Gloria, this is Rina Blakely." Glancing behind her, she made sure Danny had cleared the room. "Listen, Janelle's body was found a little bit ago. She's dead. If you know how to get in touch with her next of kin, I'm sure the police would be grateful."

"Uh, Rina?" Gloria's voice came out almost a whisper.

"Yes?"

"What are you doing at Janelle's house? I didn't think you socialized with the trash from the office." Gloria, hawking up an evil cough, lived up to her name—Bitter Bitch Easton. Rina, being Gloria's employee, knew only too well how mean-spirited she could be, noticing she never even asked how Janelle died.

"Having tea." Rina said in her sweetest voice and hung up, not bothering to say goodbye. True, Rina did not socialize with the girls from The Call Box, but she would never consider one of them trash. A diesel truck rumbled by the house, vibrating the windows, as it left the trailer park. She looked out the door in time to see Jimmy Baird driving his tow truck, speeding fast enough to kick up gravel in his quake. Hannah raised her hackles, giving a low guttural growl.

Doing a quick mental run-through of her co-workers, Rina tried to fill in some of the blanks scattered around her brain. Janelle had a loose reputation and rumor had it that her on again-off again affair with Jimmy Baird was currently on again. As well as with the new artist that moved into town six months ago. Even Rina's closest friend, Libby, went crazy about the artist. Tessie Richmond, who claimed to be Janelle's best friend, lived one street over and according to the work schedule was off today. Amy, Tessie's sister, with whom she shares a trailer, would be at work. Which meant Jimmy most likely had just left Tessie's place. Tessie, the hussy with the morals of a housefly strikes again. Janelle should have been at work today, too. She wondered how Tessie was going to feel once she found out that while she had been entertaining the mattress with her best friend's boyfriend, her so-called best friend had had someone's hands around her throat, being strangled to death.

A soft jab to Rina's shoulder spun her around. "Babe, how did you end up here this morning? And how well did you know Janelle?" Danny's questions brought her back to focus.

"We've never hung out together, if that's what you mean. As a matter of fact, I don't know any of the girls from work all that well, other than what I overhear in conversation and to say hi." She tilted her head, feeling a bit guilty. "Working from home, I run all the tallies, reports, payroll and ledgers from my home computer. I only go into the office once a week to drop off the paychecks and unload the stacks of reports on Gloria's desk, or pick up supplies. If Gloria needs anything special done with the accounting, she usually sends me an email. But you know all that already."

"And what brought you here?" He held his hand up, giving a curt nod. "A compressed version would be nice." Danny knew how long-winded Rina could be at times.

"Taking Hannah out for a walk." She grinned, telling a half-truth, wanting to kick Libby's teeth down her throat for getting her involved in a murder. "How's that?"

"Good." He returned her smile, reading her like a book. "Now, want to tell me the real reason you were walking through the Tarver Trailer Park at eight o'clock this morning?"

Rina swallowed hard. "I was checking on something for Libby." She stalled, looking down at her feet, kicking the toe of her shoe with the other heel, waiting for Danny to ask his usual fifty questions. When none came, her gaze swept back up to meet his eyes. "Libby has been seeing Conrad and she heard through the grapevine that he was sleeping with Janelle, too. Since I take Hannah out for a walk every morning, Libby asked me if I could jog through the trailer park to see if Conrad's car was here. It's only a couple miles from the house."

"Why would Libby, and yes, I know who is like a sister to you with an over-active imagination, think this Conrad person would be here this morning?" His eyebrows furrowed in confusion as to who Conrad could be.

"Because they had a date last night, and Conrad broke it at the last minute telling her he had divine inspiration and had to stay with his canvas."

"Are you talking about Conrad Cramer, that hippy artist that drives a beat-up old blue Taurus?" His face beamed as the light came on. Rina nodded.

"I don't believe this." Danny rubbed his eyes. "That idiot's inspiration could be called divine all right. And Jodi Covington can vouch for his whereabouts most of the night. Stoddard caught him leaving her residence at four o'clock this morning."

"But isn't Mayor Covington out of town?" Realization dawned on her as the words left her mouth. "Serves the old fart right, him marrying a woman twenty-five years his junior. Why didn't you tell me?"

"I didn't know Libby was seeing that bum." Taking a deep breath, he blew hot air through his lips. "Look, you don't need to repeat any of that to Libby. If Mrs. Covington wants everyone to know she sleeps around when her husband is out of town, she should be the one to spread the news, not you. Understand?"

"Of course I do." Rina's cell phone vibrated in her pocket. Taking it out she saw the caller ID and grimaced. "It's Libby. She's waiting to hear from me."

"Let it go to voice mail. I need your attention directed here for a bit longer, and then I'm going to drive you home."

Slipping the cell phone back in her pocket, it felt like a hot lava rock. "I hate doing that."

He waved his hand in the air dismissing her. "How exactly did you end up inside this house?"

Pursing her lips, she said, "We walked down the street and as we started getting close, Hannah took off ahead of me, running up to the front door. It was cracked open a bit and she jumped inside. I panicked and charged inside after her hoping she wouldn't get shot, because she blitzed through the house like a crazy dog," Rina paused, feeling her heart race thinking back. "Hannah started barking and returned to me, turning circles likes she does when she alerts that she's found a body. I followed her back to Janelle's bedroom and found Janelle…with her eyes wide open and that cord around her neck. Then I called you excited that Hannah's search training paid off." Then adding the obvious, "And to tell you the body happened to be Janelle Osbourne."

"Did you touch anything other than the phone?" He arched an eyebrow.

"No, I did not." More gravel crunched under car tires pulling up out front. Rina turned around seeing another police car arrive.

"That's Carlson. You and Hannah go ahead and wait in my car and I'll be out in a minute." Danny knew he would need to have the trailer secured before all the neighbors decided they wanted to take a little *look-see*. He motioned Officer Carlson to him as he stepped inside.

"Hi Rina." Carlson spoke as they passed each other. "What are you doing here?"

"Hi John." Hooking a thumb in Danny's direction, "He'll tell you." She tugged Hannah's leash, guiding her outside towards the police car. Passing Stoddard's police unit, Rina caught a glimpse of a small cooler sitting in the front passenger seat and thought, not only did the man have looks to kill, he was also practical. Working the night shift, he brought his own cokes and water, since nothing remained open after 10pm. When Stoddard joined the department a little over a year ago, he volunteered to work nights. Danny never told Rina why, but he did not care much for

Stoddard. Rina chalked it up to male rivalry.

Getting one leg in, after depositing Hannah in the back seat of Danny's car, Tessie came charging up to Rina wearing a pair of boxer shorts and a thin white t-shirt. No bra and barefooted.

"I heard Janelle was strangled. Is it true?" Tessie Richmond's eyes were red and swollen as if she had been crying.

Hannah growled from the backseat of the police car making Tessie jump. "Crap! What's wrong with that dog? She's never liked me. Rina, you should have that animal put down." She ran her hands up and down her arms smoothing over the goose bumps.

Rina coughed in her hand to cover up the snicker escaping her lips. "You must have just talked with Gloria. I only hung up with her a few minutes ago." Rina ignored Tessie's statement about putting her dog down, wanting to instead turn around and praise her. Hannah was a good judge of character. Tessie was correct that Hannah never did like her, and growled at her every time Rina brought the dog to the office.

"Yeah, she called telling me I had to come into work today to cover Janelle's shift." Her voice came out flat. She kept looking around to avoid making eye contact, rocking from one foot to the other like she could crawl right out of her own skin. "Did they find any chocolate candy? Was it the Chocolate Killer?" Her tone held excitement in the last question. "Is Bobby here?" She cocked her head towards the trailer home, referring to Officer Stoddard.

Rina picked up on her interest in Stoddard, but wondered when she felt she could be on a first name basis with him. Something about her demeanor carried an underlying tone. Everyone had been on edge since the two previous murders. Including herself. Except for Tessie's eyes, on this bright sunny morning, they remained dilated. It made Rina wonder if her state of jitters were chemically induced. Rumor had it that Tessie and her sister, Amy, both kept the local dealers in business.

Several neighbors gathered in the driveway. "I don't know,

Tess." She lied, "Danny hasn't told me anything. They just arrived." Rina wished Danny would hurry. "I saw Jimmy drive by earlier, what time did Amy have to go in this morning?"

The question caught her off guard. "Uh, what? Jimmy? You saw Jimmy this morning?" Her body stopped rocking as she tensed and she spoke an octave lower. "He stopped by late last night, but left around midnight." Tessie looked down at her feet, wiggling her toes. "He wanted to talk. He said he knew Janelle was seeing another guy and he was pretty upset." She raised her head and tears spilled over her cheeks. "He said he was probably going to leave town. Permanently."

Okay, the real reason for the red, swollen eyes. Rina's sympathy turned to anger as she realized that Tessie's displaced passion this morning had little to do with Janelle's death.

Danny trotted out with Carlson following, to push the gathering crowd at bay. "Rina, let's go."

Tessie poured on the water works sliding up to Danny. "I sure could use two strong arms to hold me right about now." Her words caught between sobs. "She was my closest friend, you know." She tried laying her head on Danny's shoulder.

"What you need to do is to go home and lock your doors. Don't answer it for anyone. One of our officers should be by shortly to ask you some questions." He said, stepping out of her reach, patting her forearm. To Rina, he said, "You ready?"

Slamming the car door harder than normal, Rina wanted to throttle Tessie. Danny climbed in the police car and started the engine. "You look like you ate something nasty. What's wrong?" He turned the car around dodging a couple of folks who were mesmerized staring at Janelle's trailer, not bothering to get out of the way.

"Tessie and her pseudo drama. It wouldn't surprise me in the least if Tessie didn't murder her *closest friend*, herself." Snapping the seatbelt with a pop, she pushed her head against the headrest.

"Rina, in all fairness, Tessie and Janelle worked together

for several years and they live close by each other. I'm sure she's pretty torn up over this. Those tears were real."

"Oh *puleese*. She's torn up all right but it has little to do with Janelle. She's all broken hearted over the possibility that Jimmy might be moving out of town."

Hitting the steering wheel with the palm of his hand, he exhaled loud enough to show his impatience. "Jimmy who?" He shook his head wondering how many people they knew by the name of Jimmy.

"Don't get testy," Rina scolded. "Jimmy Baird. I saw him, or more like heard him, as he sped by in his tow truck, right after you got there. Janelle and Jimmy have been seeing each other for several months now, from what I hear. And I'm guessing Tessie lied to me about what time Jimmy really left. I bet he just left her bed."

Giving her a sideways glance, "What makes you say that?" Speaking softer now that he knew which Jimmy she referred to. "And I'm sorry for lashing out at you." He reached over and squeezed her hand.

"Because Tess said he dropped by to 'talk' last night, but left at midnight." She made rabbit ears with her fingers. Then slapping her forehead, she exploded. "She knew! You have to turn around and interrogate her right now. Oh, my God, Danny, she knew Janelle had been strangled and I didn't tell her. And Gloria never asked how Janelle died when she called, so Tess couldn't have heard it from her when she called Tess to come in to work. We have to turn around."

He pulled over on the side of the road and thought for a moment. "This is the third murder in the last six months and all three have been strangled. Rina, did you see or smell or hear anything unusual when you barged into Janelle's house? Did Hannah react to anything odd other than finding her body?"

"I saw one of those little clip backings on the floor, next to her nightstand. You know, like the ones you use to hold your SCPD pins on your collar and name tag? I figured Janelle probably uses those for some of her body piercings. It's probably no big deal. Other than that, I didn't see, smell or hear anything. And we certainly weren't doing cadaver training this morning, either." She chewed on the inside of her lip. "The only thing odd I noticed was the Bavarian chocolate on the pillow next to her head. And by the way, everyone knows about the chocolate thing."

"Yeah, we purposely leaked that little tidbit out. What wasn't told is that the candy is an expensive Bavarian chunk chocolate made exclusively from a candy shop up in Maine. It's not sold in local stores. You have to keep that to yourself, understand?"

"I will." She nodded, bringing his hand to her lips, kissing each finger. "I don't tell everything, you know." She gave him a wicked grin, and he rolled his eyes, chuckling as he took his hand back. "Tell me all of it."

"There's never anything out of place or stolen and we're pretty sure this creep knows his victims. He doesn't break in to get to them. These women let him in and so far there hasn't been any sign of rape or a struggle."

"The other two women were found in the Uptown Motel. Right?" Rina knew the first victim, Lauren Vickers. They had gone to high school together. Lauren married Glenn Vickers right out of high school and became the church secretary. Glenn still claims Lauren would never have cheated on him. The Uptown Motel manager swears Lauren had been renting a room there once a week for about a month, before they found her dead body, but had never seen who she came with. And Glenn was cleared as a suspect with an airtight alibi.

Danny nodded, jerking the police car back onto the highway. "I'm taking you home, where you and Hannah are going to stay put."

"But I wanted to watch you give that little *hussy* the third degree." She pouted, puffing out her lower lip.

"Rina!" Danny chastised. "You know you can't come along. But listen, if my hunch is right about all this, Tessie will be the one to verify it for me without her even knowing, then our little town is going to be turned upside-down on its head. The M.E. is on his way and I need to call Chief McAllen." He wiped his brow as a droplet of sweat pilled over his eyebrow.

"What hunch?" Rina's enthusiasm climbed with a hint of skepticism. "And please tell me how on God's green earth Tessie Richmond could turn this town on its head. She's stoned all the time for Pete's sake!" Quieting down, Rina saw the panic in Danny's profile as he drove like a bat out of hell, slowing just enough to slide into the driveway at home.

"Where exactly in the bedroom was the pin backing that you found, and did you pick it up?" The seriousness in his tone meant business.

"On the floor between a pile of dirty clothes and the night stand." She opened the car door. "Why? Is that important? And no, I did not pick it up."

"Yes, Babe, it is. I have to hurry. Y'all go inside and don't open that door for anyone, but me. I mean that Rina, not for anyone but me."

"Not even another police officer?" She teased, standing outside the car, letting Hannah out of the backseat.

"Not anyone, Rina." Danny's face had become as pale as chalk, drained completely of color.

"I can't stand it. You have got to tell…"

"Get inside." He halted her questions. Reaching over, he closed the car door and sped off, squealing his tires.

Rina had her cell phone pulled out of her pocket and to her ear as she unlocked the front door, waiting for Libby to answer her ring.

"Why aren't you answering my calls?" Libby blasted Rina, not a breath of civility in her tone. "I've left a half dozen voice messages on your phone."

"Because I've been at a murder scene and couldn't talk." Rina felt sure that would change Libby's mood. It did.

"Where?" Libby asked, her words coming through hushed.

"Janelle Osbourne." Taking a deep breath, Rina filled her in leaving out the parts she had promised Danny she would not repeat. Except for the part about Mayor Covington's wife sleeping with Conrad Cramer. Libby needed to know what a jerk Conrad turned out to be, in Rina's opinion.

"Oh, my God, Rina. What's happening to our little town? And as far as Conrad, he's history in my book."

"You know who I think you should hook up with?" Rina babbled, "Bob Stoddard. He's gorgeous. And you two would make pretty babies."

"Hey, wait a minute." Libby chuckled. "I'm not sure I want kids, and they certainly wouldn't be with Bob."

"Why not?" Surprise caught in Rina's throat. She thought Stoddard could be a male model and why he chose law enforcement boggled the mind.

"I don't know. It's sort of hard to put my finger on it, but I don't think so. We went out one time last year and well, it didn't turn out all that…you know. He sort of came on too strong."

"You never told me. That's too bad, because you know I think he's one of the most handsome men I've ever seen." In the background, Rina could hear a metal cart clanking on squealing wheels over the hospital floor.

"Looks aren't everything, girlfriend. I have to go, it's time to dispense some meds around here, and my first patient is feisty Ms. Tilly Bentley."

"Your nursing skills are the finest, so give crazy ol' Tilly my best."

After ending their conversation, Rina headed to the shower to wash off the smell of death, the dirt, and to try to fit in the missing pieces. The part that stumped her most had to do with Danny's idea that Tessie could help in any way, shape, or capacity.

Slipping on clean clothes after her shower, she noticed Hannah wasn't in her usual spot on the bed waiting for her. Something didn't feel right, the air didn't feel right in the house. Padding barefoot up the hallway, she called, "Hannah? Come here, girl."

No answer. Nowhere in sight and not even a chuff, as she entered the living room, calling out for her. Rina gulped hard as she rounded the corner, her eyes landing on his shirt. Recalling a conversation she heard earlier in the trailer, she saw he'd brought his mini-cooler with him. The front door stood ajar, and Rina wanted to kick herself for not locking the door behind her. Holding onto the side of the wall to help steady her shaking knees, she stared at her unwelcome visitor. Water droplets dripped from her wet hair, pooling on the floor. Shock and confusion took all the moisture out of her mouth. And fear—fear for herself and for her little German shepherd—as the final puzzle piece fell into place.

"I'll be right back. I need to put on some shoes." It came out squelched, like tuning in a radio station. Her brain flew in six different directions at once trying to decide on playing coy or confronting him head-on. She needed to find a way to get to the phone. "Why don't you have a seat, it won't take but a minute." She knew it was lame and could read his eyes. Eyes so blue they could melt a glacier, now held something so sinister, her heart stopped beating for a second.

"Mmm, the bedroom? That would be a could place to start." Stoddard smacked his lips, picking up his cooler. "I'll go with you." The malevolent look that came over his face made her confront him.

"Bob, how did you slip through the system?" Rina felt her eyes fill with tears. Hard scratching came from the back door, followed by harsh growling. Hannah. Hannah, so trusting with Bob, let him lead her outside to the back yard. A flood of relief surged through her, knowing she was okay.

"What do you mean?" The question threw him off as he blinked rapidly several times. "What you really want to ask me, is *why*, isn't it?" His leer told her he had regained his composure and stood ready to play his own sordid game.

"Okay," Rina started, "*why* do you leave a piece of Bavarian chocolate on the pillows afterwards?" Something told her to not use the words 'murder' or 'kill,' as it might set him off.

Again, the rapid blinking, pausing to collect his thoughts. "My mother preferred Bavarian over all other chocolates. She taught me, when I was twelve, how to leave a piece on her pillow." His voice dropped off, his eyes glazed over with memories.

Rina could not begin to understand what Robert Stoddard went through as a child, nor could she accept his actions as an adult. But for a soft moment in time, Rina wanted to reach out to him. His answer opened a floodgate of questions.

Several cars pulled up in the driveway and Rina did not dare take her eyes off Stoddard. As they listened to car doors slam shut outside, in that fleeting second, Rina knew how this would all end. Her heart shattered from the vision running through her mind.

Chief McAllen barged in through the front door, his six foot frame filling the entryway. "Stoddard, I've been calling you on the radio, why didn't you answer?" The chief's hand gripped the butt of his service weapon, holstered to his belt. Danny stepped up and stood next to his chief. Same stance, hand on weapon.

Stoddard turned to set the cooler on the coffee table. When he looked down, Chief McAllen motioned at Rina, with his chin, to leave the room. Stoddard faced his chief, bringing his hand to his weapon. They looked like an old western getting ready to face off.

Rina tried to move, but her feet felt as if they were cast in cement. From the corner of her eye she watched Danny, gesturing her to walk backwards. A single teardrop fell from her eye as mixed emotions tugged at her heart.

"I tell ya, Chief, I had more pressing matters that needed attending to than to talk to you on the radio. No disrespect, sir." Stoddard seemed to have changed his focus.

"None taken, Stoddard. Why don't you hand me your weapon and we can sit down and talk. Face to face, instead of over the radio." Chief McAllen started forward and before anyone could take another breath of air, Rina saw the clench in Stoddard's jaw, the flex of his arm muscle as he jerked his Sig Sauer .45 out, not meaning to hand it over. The chief discharged his weapon as Stoddard aimed at Chief McAllen's face. Stoddard never got off his shot. Rina knew why. The common term is: Suicide by Cop.

Before Stoddard died, his eyes met Rina's. His final words on earth, were to her.

"I am what I am. It is what it is."

Rina's knees buckled and before she hit the floor, Danny had her in his arms. "How did y'all get here so fast? How did you know?" Tears flowed free as she squeezed her eyes, pressing her face into the crook of Danny's neck.

"Shush for now, we'll talk later." His breath came out hurried as he wrapped his arms tight around Rina, wishing he could erase the horror he had seen in her eyes.

The next day, many questions were answered, but the main ones would never be…nor would they be understood. The mind of a murderer lives in the most unsuspecting.

"I overheard you chewing him out about his uniform at the trailer. I didn't notice until I saw him standing uninvited in our house yesterday, and realized his name tag was missing from his shirt." Rina stroked Hannah's fur with long even strokes over her shoulders. "I forgot to lock the front door, and when I came out after showering, Hannah wasn't in the house and Bob stood in our living room. The pin backing belonged to him, didn't it?"

Danny nodded.

"When did you know it was Stoddard?" Rina swiped at her eyes, wondering how she could have thought him so handsome.

"I suspected when Lauren was murdered. Things didn't add up, and there was no way to prove it. Chief McAllen and I started watching him real close. And then you mentioned the pin backing, and…both Tessie and Jimmy Baird."

Rina's forehead creased. "Jimmy Baird?" Not believing her ears.

"Yep. He had gone to see Janelle night before last and saw Stoddard's police car in her driveway, got pissed off and drove on by to smoke a joint with Tessie and Amy. He said it wasn't the first time he had seen Stoddard over at Janelle's, but didn't say who he had seen there when he dropped in to visit with the Richmond sisters." Danny raised his arms over his head to stretch the kinks out of his shoulders. "Jimmy told me that he had forgotten his stash and drove back over early yesterday morning to retrieve it. He saw Stoddard's car at Tessie's. Said he thought Tessie was probably being popped for the drugs, so he left." Danny coughed and laughed, "Jimmy waited for an hour and then went back to the Richmond's house, saw no cars, and hoped to catch Amy to let him in so he could get his weed, because he thought Tessie had been hauled off. When he left there, he rounded the next street, saw the police cars in front of Janelle's. Poor idiot thought the whole trailer park was being busted."

Rina arched her eyebrow. "What exactly was Bob doing at Tessie's?"

Danny lowered his eyes, "What do you think they were doing? That's why Stoddard showed up so fast at Janelle's when I called him to get there. He was one street over and we never even knew it. He was the one who told Tess that Janelle had been strangled."

"And all this time I thought it was Jimmy who had been in bed with Tessie. Boy, did I have that scenario all wrong." Rina looked up and grinned. "Did Jimmy ever get his stash?"

"Yeah, he did. He broke in through their back door, thinking no one was home. He saw his baggie on the kitchen table, grabbed it and hauled ass out of there. That's when you saw him speeding by. He had no idea Tessie was still at home."

"What was in the cooler?" Rina changed subjects.

"Two plastic baggies. One had some clothesline cord in it and the other had two wrapped pieces of Bavarian chunk chocolate. He kept the cooler filled with ice so the chocolate wouldn't melt."

Snuggling close to Danny's side, Rina felt her eyelids grow heavy. "How Danny? How did he slip through? I asked him the same question."

"Did you get an answer?"

Not speaking the words out loud, Rina shivered as Robert Stoddard's final words haunted her.

A Box of Texas Chocolates

Bitter Sweet
by CeCe Smith

Lorie struggled out of her dream, swimming in a pool of honey. The garage door rumbled as Luke pulled his car out. A glance at the clock showed 5:30 a.m. No goodbye, she didn't expect one after their bitter fight last night. The sound of pelting rain on the window signaled the start of a gloomy day. She peeled herself out of her cocoon as she heard snoring and grunting coming from under the covers.

"Don't worry, Tank, I know it's early," she said, as her bulldog lifted its head. *You got that right* he seemed to say as he snorted and burrowed deeper. Lorie shuffled down the stairs heading to the kitchen for her caffeine fix. She paused on the stairs thinking of Luke and the work and love they had put into this old house. She gripped the hand rail remembering the jokes about the children they would have sliding down the staircase. She wanted that happiness again.

She lit the logs in the kitchen fireplace to take the chill off and started the coffee. Next to the copper sink lay a small, beautifully wrapped box. She smiled. Maybe Luke wasn't as angry as she thought.

A muffled thud on the front door announced the arrival of the newspaper. After retrieving the paper she filled her mug, and carried it with the box to a chair by the fire. As she enjoyed her coffee, she heard the thump, thump of Tank coming down the steps.

"Look Tank, Luke bought us a box of candy." He wagged his

body, as all bulldogs do, and smelled the box. He gave a disgusted snort before he sprawled at her feet.

"Not interested are you? Good thing, I don't intend to share." She took a sip of coffee and opened the box. The sweet aroma of cocoa mingled with the fresh scent of coffee made her groan. The box held four lovely gold wrapped confections. Lorie opened one, put it in her mouth and closed her eyes, savoring the morsel.

"Ah, Tank, this is how a day should start, a breakfast of coffee and chocolate." She had another, then stuffed the box in her purse, and headed upstairs to shower.

On the way to work, she relived the argument with Luke. The first three years of marriage had been storybook wonderful, but this last year turned grim. Luke's job demanded more travel, which put their plans for children on hold. Since they married in their thirties, they had agreed on having children as soon as possible, but lately his enthusiasm had waned. Every time she brought up the subject of having a baby, they ended up having a major fight, and last night was no exception. They were finishing dinner when she mentioned their neighbor, Abbie, was pregnant. Luke lost it and pushed himself away from the table with such force that he spilled his glass of wine. He said he wanted their lives to stay as is, just the two of them. She couldn't believe her ears. What was he talking about, just the two of them?

The ringing of her cell phone brought her back to reality—maybe it was Luke. "Hello, Lorie Madison."

"Lorie, it's Sam. Your nine o'clock is early." He chuckled. "And he seems to be in a big hurry to get that daughter of his married."

"Oh, Sam, you."

"Sorry to disappoint."

"No, I'm sorry; I thought you might be Luke."

"I could if you'd let me."

She laughed, "Tell Mr. Abbot I'm on my way."

"Will do."

Sam lightened Lorie's spirits. They had dated, and been best friends in high school, but went their separate ways in college, and lost touch. She became a graphic designer, and Sam worked with the National Science Foundation doing Postdoctoral research in Montana. They bumped into each other at the Atlanta airport. They sat in the airport bar for hours catching up with each others' lives. Sam decided research was boring, and Lorie wanted something different. They both agreed they wanted roots, and wanted those roots to grow in the small town where they grew up. They still couldn't figure out how it happened, Kismet, or too many vodka martinis, but four years later they were in business together.

Sam's mom left him five prime acres in the heart of Seabrook, just the spot for the "Garden of Eden." With Luke's help they designed and built a unique florist shop with carved wood flowers and vines, straight out of a fairytale. Lorie loved working with flowers and Sam was in his element growing unique plants on the acres behind the shop. Life was sweet. She was in business with her best friend, and married to the man of her dreams…at least he had been.

Lorie hurried into the shop to greet Mr. Abbot.

As Sam watched her approach, his heart quickened. God, she was beautiful. She still looked like she was sixteen, golden brown hair bobbing in a pony tail, and her usual denim shirt and jeans. No one looked as good as her in denim. She reminded him of one of the graceful willow trees he grew out back.

"Mr. Abbot, so good to see you." He gave Lorie a big hug and bent down to give her shadow, Tank, a belly rub.

"Okay, Tank, go play with Sam, I have business to attend to."

The bulldog grunted and went over to sit next to Sam.

"Come on Tank, we have some plants that need watering."

Tank followed him out the back door. Sam filled a large

ceramic bowl with water. He walked over to the shade of a large tree and lay down.

"Here you go, boy."

Tank glanced at the water and plopped over one of Sam's arm with a sigh.

"Yeah, I feel the same way. "

He scratched Tank's head and closed his eyes.

Sam's mind drifted back four years to his chance meeting with Lorie at the airport. God, he hadn't thought of her in such a long time, and then there she was. He felt the same goofy way he did in school, all tongue tied and shaky. She was his first love, and in that moment he knew she was the reason he had never settled down. Lorie was the missing ingredient for a happy life.

Little did he know that Lorie was in love with someone else and a wedding was around the corner.

The Bulldog yawned.

"Hey, buddy, at least I get to spend my days with her. After seeing her again, I was prepared to follow her to the ends of the earth, Luke or no Luke."

Tank opened one eye and snorted.

"Now, don't give me attitude. When she came up with the nursery idea, I jumped at it. You know, you're not very grateful. If it wasn't for me, you wouldn't even be here."

"Do you mind if I interrupt this conversation? It seems very intense. "

Sam jumped up, brushing himself off.

"Lorie, I was just reminding Tank that I'm the one that saved him from that pet shop."

"That's right, Tank, you were the best gift ever. You might have rescued him from the shop, but I had to talk Luke into letting me keep him."

"Right. I genuinely had no clue your husband didn't like animals."

"So you said at least a hundred times. No matter, Tank's here to stay!"

Lorie looked at her watch. "No more daydreaming boys, we have seedlings to unpack."

They had finished sorting the plants when Lorie's cell phone rang. She grabbed for her purse but it spilled on the floor. Lorie quickly picked up her phone, but it was too late.

"Gee, expecting an important call?"

"Oh, Luke's out of town again on business and I thought it might be him."

"Well?"

She looked at the cell, "No, Mr. Abbot."

Sam bent down and picked up the candy box that had fallen out of her purse.

"Well, what do we have here? You've been holding out on me."

Lorie reached for the candy, but Sam was faster.

"No, no you must share." He opened the box. "Just two left." Sam unwrapped the chocolate. "Okay, open up."

Lorie smiled as he put the candy in her mouth.

"Hey watch it, you almost bit my finger."

She laughed and opened the other. Your turn.

"Ah, ambrosia."

He took a step forward, put his hand behind her head, pulled her close and kissed her.

⁓

Just then a bell rang, signaling a customer.

"Hello, anyone here?"

The voice sounded far away. Lorie opened her eyes and looked at Sam. It took a minute to sink in. Dear God, they were kissing!

She pushed Sam away and rushed to greet the customer.

"Hi, Hank, I was in the back…working. I'll bet you're here for some flowers for that lovely wife of yours."

"You got it. It's our anniversary." He looked up as Sam came out of the stock room.

"Hey, Sam."

Sam nodded and moved behind the counter.

Hank looked at the box in Sam's hand.

"What do you have there? Candy?"

"Yeah, but sorry it's gone."

"Yes, I can see that and I know who ate it all. You two have some left on you faces."

Lorie's hand shot up to her mouth and rubbed off the chocolate.

Sam licked his off with a smile.

One of the wrappers fell and Hank picked it up. "Maybe I should order some of these sexy candies."

"Sexy candies?" Lorie asked.

"Well, look here at this wrapper, it says 'Passion'."

Lorie snatched it out of Hank's hand, "Let me see."

"Go on, read it." Hank held it up to the light, "See, right there, it says 'Passion'."

Lorie looked at another wrapper, 'Desire'."

"Oh, my!" Lorie's face turned apple red.

"My God, girl, since that candy got such a rise out of you, I think flowers and that candy would make a great anniversary gift. You know what they say, just because there's snow on the roof doesn't mean there's no fire in the furnace."

Lorie was speechless.

Sam bumped her on the arm. "Lorie, where did you get the candy?"

She looked up at Sam, "Luke got them for me. I think he got them from Emily's Delight's."

"Great, there you go Hank, while Lorie's getting your flowers ready, you can run down the street to Emily's and get the candy. The flowers will be ready by the time you get back, right?"

She nodded. "Will do, see you in a bit."

Lorie watched Hank walk out the door, then turned to Sam.

"What the hell got into us?"

"Now listen, let's not get upset. Really, no big thing."

She remained quiet.

"Okay, It's not our fault, what got into us was that damn sexy candy." Sam grinned.

He studied her face, "Come on Lorie, just a harmless kiss."

She finally smiled, "You're right, what's a kiss among friends?"

Sam breathed a sigh of relief. "Exactly, just friends. Do you need any help here?"

"No I'm good."

"Then I'll head out back. Let's go Tank."

Lorie watched Sam, tall, sexy, brown-eyed Sam, exit the back door with Tank. *God, he looks good in those jeans, and that kiss...*

The door bell jingled.

Damn that bell, "Hank that was fast!"

"When I walked into Emily's she was dipping strawberries—Rose loves chocolate covered berries. She's making up a box for me, so take your time. I'm going out back to get some perennials from Sam."

"I'll have your flowers ready in no time."

Lorie hurried to get started on his bouquet. *Let's see, roses, fern, and baby's breath.* She walked to the sink with her fragrant bounty and started snipping and arranging. Lorie glanced out the window and caught Sam looking at her. Embarrassed, she looked away.

⸺

Sam helped Hank with his plants and headed back to his seedlings.

Sam, Sam, what did you do? You've been so good these last four years.

Sam was surprised he hadn't lost it sooner, but he couldn't let it happen again. He had to respect Lorie's love for Luke. He was not a home wrecker.

Lorie was glad when Sam suggested she leave early. She still felt uncomfortable around him after that kiss and guilty that Luke never entered her mind all day. She was thankful it was Friday and had the weekend off. She needed a few days away from Sam.

Lorie opened the back door to the shop, saw the bulldog and Sam in the field, "Tank, time to go home." Sam waved and the dog came jogging toward her.

"See you Monday, Sam" she yelled.

As she turned onto her street, her cell rang.

"Lorie Madison."

"Hi, honey."

"Luke, I'm so glad you called. Are you on your way home?"

"No, sorry, I won't be back till Sunday."

"Oh no, this is my weekend off."

"I know, honey, I tried like hell to get out of here but no can do."

"You're not still mad at me, are you?"

"Lorie I don't want to get in to it on the phone, okay?"

"No, neither do I. Sorry, just glad you called."

"Okay, babe, I have a business dinner to get to. Give you a call tomorrow."

"Sure, and Luke…"

Damn, he hung up and I didn't get a chance to thank him for the candy. Oh well, I'll try calling him later.

"Let's go Tank, looks like another storm is brewing and you know how you hate to get wet."

Lorie had finished feeding the dog and pouring herself a glass of wine when the phone rang.

"Hi, Lorie, Patti. Don't panic, I'm not calling to say I can't work tomorrow, I wondered if you're free for dinner? I talked to Sam and he said Luke was out of town again."

"I don't know, Patti, I just got home and I'm tired."

"Then I'll have to go for the pity vote, it's my birthday. Sam's busy and I don't want to sit home alone."

"You asked Sam?"

"Yeah, that guy doesn't get out enough. I told him some day we're going to find him in the greenhouse sprouting roots."

"Sorry Sam couldn't go. I think you two would make a lovely couple."

"Lorie, really, Sam's waiting on his soul mate. He doesn't want an old work horse like me."

"Patti, you're beautiful."

"I appreciate that, but I told you, I married my soul mate and we had many happy years together, but losing him and my daughter a year later damaged my spirit. I'm not ready to get attached to anyone."

"Well, I can't have you sitting home alone on your birthday."

"Great, I'll pick you up in an hour."

Lorie sat down to finish her wine and thought of Patti. She hired her shortly after the shop opened and she fit in like a worn leather glove. Patti told them she had worked on a horse farm and had the muscles to prove it. Even though she was in her late forties she could run circles around them. They became best friends, they all had something in common, their own somber quests, Sam looking for his soul mate, Patti searching for peace, and Lorie longing for a child.

Lorie sipped the last of her wine and thought about calling Luke, but decided not to interrupt his dinner meeting.

Lorie found a good bottle of wine she had been saving for a special event and decided that event was Patti's birthday. She rushed upstairs to get ready.

Tank's bark announced Patti's arrival.

"Come in, Patti, and hush Tank. I just have to get my coat."

She knew as soon as the door closed Tank would head upstairs and make himself comfortable in her bed. He knew when Luke was gone, the bed was his.

"Thanks for calling me, Patti. This is much better than sitting home by myself."

"I'm glad you're coming. We're going to this wonderful restaurant in Old Town. It's a distance, but it's a beautiful night for a drive."

"Sound's great."

It took them almost two hours, but the drive was fun and they caught up on the entire town's gossip.

"I can't believe that Luke and I haven't been here," Lorie said, as Patti drove down Main Street.

"Look how beautiful this place is, one old Victorian after another. Wow, there's a magnificent house."

"Yes, it's a beauty. Remember the Muller's? They owned the cotton mill down by the river. The family sold it many years ago and that wonderful painted lady is now a Bed and Breakfast. If you want, we can walk over after dinner. We're eating at the restaurant right across the street."

"I'd love to."

As Lorie got out of the car, she noticed two large oak trees adorned with hundreds of twinkling lights flanking the restaurant.

"God, I can't wait to bring Luke here."

The inside proved to be just as outstanding, with its polished mahogany, crystal chandeliers, and ornate fireplaces. The icing on the cake had to be the waiters in tuxedos.

Lorie gave Pattie a hug, "This is wonderful. Let's get this party started with some champagne. How did you ever find this place?"

"Rhett's has been here for as long as I can remember. Now that Old Town is booming it's finally getting the recognition it deserves."

A seriously handsome waiter escorted them to their table. Lorie winked at Patti.

When the waiter brought their food, Lorie bumped Patti under the table.

"Stop messing around and eat your food, I'm not interested, but damn he is good looking."

"Ah huh, I knew you noticed."

They laughed.

Lorie leaned back in her chair, "What a delicious dinner. I propose a toast to yummy food and good friends. Happy Birthday."

"I'll drink to that."

"Let's do this every year for our birthdays, Patti!"

"I would love that, but I'm afraid I won't be here next year. I was planning on telling you on the way home."

"Oh, what's wrong? Do you need more money?"

"Lorie, please don't make this any harder on me than it is. It's been great, but I have to move on. It's been a joy working with you and Sam, but you're starting to feel like family and I can't have that happen."

"Where are you going?"

"I'm not sure—wherever the winds take me. Now, don't look so sad. It's my birthday, and besides, I promise to keep in touch."

Patti looked at her watch, "Whoa, look at the time!"

"Gosh, you're right. You have work in the morning. You are coming in tomorrow?"

"Thanks for reminding me, boss. Of course, I'll be around a few more days."

Lorie handed her the bottle of wine. "Well, it wouldn't be a party without a gift."

"I didn't expect this! Wait, I just remembered I have something for you. It was on the plant stand on your porch tonight. I put it in my purse when I rang the doorbell."

Patti pulled out a small, beautifully wrapped box. "If my sense of smell is accurate, I'd say that's a box of chocolates."

Lorie grinned "You would be right. Luke and I had a little disagreement before he left and it's his way of saying he's sorry."

Patti raised her eyebrows, "Really? I hoped it was from a mysterious admirer, you know, with Luke away so much."

Patti noticed Lorie's eyes mist, "Oh, Lorie I'm just kidding, I didn't mean anything."

"I know you are. I guess I miss him more than I realize."

She opened the box, "Here, let's have them for dessert with the rest of our champagne."

Patti popped one in her mouth and downed what was left in her glass.

"Delicious! Well, I hate to break up my own party, but it's getting late. Will you take this ticket for my car? I'm going to run to the restroom."

"Sure, see you outside."

Lorie stood by one of the trees to wait for the car and Patti.

A familiar voice caught her attention. *No, it couldn't be. She heard the laugh, there was no mistaking that laugh, Luke.* Her stomach knotted. There he was, across the street coming down the steps of the Bed and Breakfast with a beautiful redhead. Lorie stepped back into the shadows. Not that he would notice her—he couldn't take his eyes off the sweet young thing hanging on his arm. They got into his sleek, black car and drove off.

In a few seconds life as she knew it ended. Shock, anger, and sorrow poured over her like ice water. She put her hand on the tree to steady herself. She was frozen in time.

"Lorie, are you okay? Didn't you hear me calling you?"

Pattie shook Lorie by the shoulders, "Answer me, girl, and breathe. Did something happen? Were you robbed?"

"Uh, God no, I'm sorry, I don't know what got into me. I didn't hear you."

Patti studied her face, "You're very pale, too much of the bubbly?"

"Huh?" she finally looked at Patti, "Yeah, the champagne. I'm sure that's it."

"Do you feel up to checking out the B&B?"

"No, I'm a little dizzy. I think we should head home."

"Sure, Lorie, let me help you into the car. Close your eyes and take some deep breaths."

After a silent ride, Patti pulled into Lorie's driveway.

"Do you want me to come in with you?"

"Thanks, Patti, I'm fine, just a little tired and like you said, too much of the bubbly. I hope I didn't ruin your birthday?"

"Don't be silly. I had a great time, I'll call you tomorrow."

Lorie was just about to close the door, "Wait, don't forget your candy."

"The candy, right. I can't forget that."

Lorie closed her front door and slid to the floor. Tank came running down the steps. She gave him a hug.

"What a night, Tank," she said as he lay down on her lap. "I knew something wasn't right this past year—all those little signs I pretended not to see. What a fool I've been. I knew Luke was a player when I married him, but I thought he loved me enough to change. He made a fool out of me pretending to want children. Well, with age comes wisdom. I know a snake when I see one."

Tank barked.

"You knew it all the time, right?"

She got up and climbed the stairs. Even though a piece of her world shattered, there was still a solid chunk to build on, her business, for one. Yes, and Sam. Thoughts of Sam warmed her heart. She had to stay strong. She needed to replay this evening's events over in her head so she would be ready when Luke made light of what happened, and he would. She needed to drive that snake out of her Garden of Eden.

As she got ready for bed she noticed the box of chocolates in her purse. She unwrapped one expecting to read 'Passion' or 'Desire'.

"What the hell? 'Deceit'?" She opened another. "'Betrayal'?" She fell back on the bed. "This candy maker has a warped sense of humor."

She tried to work on Becky Abbot's wedding plans, but she couldn't keep focused.

Patti called as promised to see how she was feeling. After assuring her she was fine, Lorie asked "Did you break the news to Sam about your leaving?"

"I did, and he's in the greenhouse crying."

"Really, Patti, don't joke, we're going to miss you."

"Same here. Oh, there's that bell, see ya."

Lorie wished it was her weekend to work. She hated being alone waiting for Luke to call or God forbid, show up early. She wasn't ready to see or talk to him.

The day dragged on, and Lorie decided she would see if Sam or Patti needed help.

As Lorie pulled into the nursery, she noticed Sam's car was gone.

"Hi, Patti, where's Sam?"

"It was a slow day so he cut out early. He's going to pick up some boxes and help me pack. If you're up to it, why don't you come over?"

"Sounds like fun. I'm in."

"Okay, I just locked up. Follow me, it's just a few blocks away."

Sam was already there unloading boxes.

"Hey, Lorie, I didn't expect to see you today. Where's Luke?"

"He's not due back till tomorrow," Lorie said as she gathered up some boxes and followed behind Patti to the house.

The three packed, drank wine, and laughed till their sides hurt. Patti proved herself to be a true gypsy with very little to pack.

After Sam loaded the last box into Patti's trailer, she insisted on a group hug.

"I can't thank you two enough."

Sam yawned, "Yeah, yeah. See you Monday."

Patti watched Sam drive off as Lorie got in her car.

"Just a minute Lorie, I boxed up some books I thought you might like."

She carried them to Lorie's trunk and waved goodbye.

Lorie looked at her cell phone as she waited to pull out of Patti's driveway. She had missed a call from Luke. She listened to the message, "Sorry I missed you, babe, I should be home before dinner tomorrow. Love you."

"Sure," she hissed, "and that sweet thing who was hanging on your arm."

"Stop with the ringing, it can't be time to wake up."

Lorie looked at the clock, four a.m. She fumbled for the phone.

"Hello."

"Mrs. Lorie Madison?"

"Speaking."

"Mrs. Madison, this is police officer Hendricks."

"Just a minute, please." Lorie sat up in bed and reached for the light. "Yes, officer, what's wrong?" Her heart was pounding.

"I'm sorry, Mrs. Madison, but your husband has been injured in an accident. He's been taken to St. Clair hospital."

"Luke's been hurt?"

"Yes, Mrs. Madison. Do you have someone that can bring you to the hospital?"

"Uh, yes, thank you for calling. I'll be there as soon as possible. Officer Hendricks, was he alone?"

"No, he had a passenger. I'm sorry to say she was fatally injured."

"Oh, God!"

A month passed. Lorie still lived in a haze. She realized getting back to normal would never happen. She couldn't even remember what normal was. Thank God for Sam. He took charge the moment she called him for a ride to the hospital that fateful night.

She remembered being rushed in to see Luke, noise and chaos in the emergency room, and then as she entered his cubical, everything went quiet. Lorie stared at his face. He looked like he was sleeping. She took a deep breath. He was going to be all right.

Someone spoke. Lorie turned to the nurse.

"I'm sorry, Mrs. Madison, he's in a coma."

Lori had no response. She walked over to Luke and took his hand. She heard the nurse tell Sam they should say their goodbyes.

She spun around, fear in her eyes. "What did she mean, Sam?" He's going to be fine, isn't he? People come out of comas."

He put his arm around her.

The nightmare started. A police officer told her, "The car was badly damaged, it seems his brakes failed, the roads were wet, brake fluid leaked…"

She was questioned.

Did she know Miss Kellie Arnold, the young lady who died in the crash with her husband? Did she work with Luke? Were they having an affair? Did she know they were having an affair?

The next thing Lorie knew she, the discarded wife, was meeting the parents of her husband's dead mistress. She remembered the humiliation and grief she felt meeting Kellie's parents and saw the same reflected in their eyes.

It seemed the whole town turned out for the funeral. Everyone told her how lovely it was. How the hell can a funeral be lovely?"

"Lorie, Lorie."

She opened her eyes. She had no idea how long she had been sitting in her kitchen.

Tank barked and greeted Sam at the back door.

"I'm sorry, but I tried calling and when you didn't answer, I got worried."

"Come in Sam. Sorry I shut my phone off, needed some quiet time."

"I understand."

The haze was starting to clear and Lorie studied Sam's face, "You look God awful."

"Thanks." Sam sat down next to her with a sigh, "So, what's in the box, some of Luke's stuff?"

"No, that's the box Pattie gave me before she left."

"That's strange, I was thinking about her on the way over."

"What's strange is how she just disappeared."

"Yeah, I know. Now that I have some time, I want to try and find her. She would want to be here for you."

"Sam that would be wonderful. She was like a big sister."

He ran his hand over his unshaven face, "You know she never picked up her pay check."

"No, huh, maybe she didn't want to say goodbye again."

"Who knows? Who knows anything anymore?" Sam picked up the box and put it on his lap. "Let's see what she left for you", he said as he rummaged through the box. "Some old books, newspapers…"

"Sam, I bet Patti saved the ads that covered our grand opening."

She started scanning the papers as Sam empted the box.

"Lorie, if you don't mind, I'd like these two books, "Car Maintenance" and "Car Repair for Dummies."

"Sam," Lorie whispered.

"Hey, what's this doing in the box?"

"Shh. Sam, listen."

"Listen to what?"

"Me." The headline on this newspaper is about the suicide of a young girl."

"What? Why would Patti give that to you?"

Sam took the paper out of her hand, "Let me see."

"Damn, Patti's daughter killed herself. She said she died. No wonder she didn't talk about how." Sam continued to read. Finally he looked up, "Lorie, did you read the whole article?"

"No, why?"

Sam stared at her not knowing what to say. She grabbed for

the paper, but he held it out of her reach.

"Wait," he said as he held her hand. "Let me tell you, please." He turned his body toward her and took a deep breath.

"Sam please tell me what's going on, I can't take much more."

"Precisely."

"Sam."

"Okay, it seems that Patti's daughter, Meg, killed herself over a guy. They were to be married, a large wedding was planned, but he forgot to show up."

"Yeah, right, he forgot! How horrible for that poor girl."

"That's not all, Lorie. It seems the guy…was…well, he was Luke."

"My Luke?"

Sam stood up and started to pace, "How bizarre can this get? Yes, Lorie, you're Luke, your husband, what a freaking bastard!"

Lorie's eyes filled with tears.

"Lorie, I'm sorry, I didn't mean…"

"Stop, you did mean it and it's time I face it. Luke was a horrible person."

"What else did you find in that box?"

"Oh, hell, I can't."

"Damn it, Sam, what?"

He held up a small, beautifully wrapped box.

Lorie gasped, "You're kidding me, it can't be."

He lowered himself down on the couch next to Lorie as he slowly opened the box.

"Luke was sending candy to Patti? It makes no sense."

"Do you know for certain that Luke sent you the candy?'

"Well, I thought…but no, come to think of it, no, I don't have a clue who sent it."

They sat in silence. Sam finally opened a piece of the candy and read the wrapper. It dropped out of his hand. Lorie started to pick it up.

"No, don't touch it." Sam pulled her up. "Come with me, Lorie. You too, Tank."

"Sam what are you doing, where are we going?"

"To the police."

"The police? Are you crazy?"

"No, but I'm afraid Patti was. Lorie, the candy wrapper said 'Revenge'."

A Box of Texas Chocolates

The Cowboy's Rose
by Betty Gordon

It was a rainy Saturday when I pulled in front of Room 44 of the Round 'Em Up in Ft. Worth, Texas. Everything looked pretty much the same as the first time I stayed here. I was a newcomer to Ft. Worth's stock show and rodeo in those days and wanted to nest close to the rodeo grounds. The Round 'Em Up fit the bill.

When I first started riding buckin' bulls, I was dreaming the dreams of a small boy who wanted to be a cowboy more than anything else in the world. I endured all the jokes that I looked like a drugstore cowhand before I *really* started concentrating on what bull riding was all about—it was more than the crowds, more than the groupies that gathered at the nearest watering hole after the performances, more than being called a champion, if you were fortunate enough to become one—it was that special sense of accomplishment, that special feeling that settles inside you when you live your dream. After all, how many people spend their days and nights doing something they fantasized about as a youngster?

Anyway, back to the Round 'Em Up. The best thing I can say about it then and now—it's cheap, clean and companions can be had at a reasonable price if you want it. As I stepped into Number 44 and turned to flip on the light, everything exploded into blackness. When I came to, I stared down the barrel of a six-shooter aimed right between my eyes. It wasn't the first time I'd looked at a gun close range, but I didn't like being on this end of the barrel. I squinted, trying to focus on the man behind the gun.

"What the hell's going on?"

"Good question, cowboy. Why don't you tell *me* what's going on? I've been waiting to hear from you, Hank."

I grabbed the edge of the bed. "Gotta stand if you'll move that damn barrel out of my face." I pulled myself up. "You pack quite a wallop. Who are you? How do you know my name?"

The guy waved the gun in a circle. "Tell you what. I'm the one holding the gun, so I'll ask the questions."

"Shoot." The word escaped before I could stop it. "I don't mean *shoot*, I mean tell me what the hell you want."

The man hesitated, glancing toward the closet. "Come on out, sugar. Our man is here and ready for a visit from a pretty lady."

A woman exited the closet. Her long blondish hair called attention to lips painted bright red. Neither did anything for her face that had seen more than its share of hard times.

"Now, Hank, what do you think of my sugar baby? Ain't she sweet?"

"Sweet as candy, but what do the two of you want?"

"Don't you recognize me from the circuit, Hank ole man? I've done everything in Texas from bronco busting to bull riding. Think about it—don't I look familiar?" He pulled 'sugar' to him. "And how about this sweet piece of womanhood. Don't she look familiar?"

I tried to wrap my mind around these two but it didn't work. "I don't…"

"No harm in telling you my name. Those bulls you've been riding have scrambled your brain. My name is Jimmy, Jimbo to my friends. You are my friend, aren't you, Hank?"

"Tell me what you want and get out."

"Ahhh, sharp talk. What you think about this guy, sugar? I'm the one loaded for bear and he's talking trash." Sticking the muzzle back in my face, he growled. "You know what I want. I've gone to a lot of trouble to meet up with you tonight. My gal here,

Sally Mae, has too and we're tired, real tired of your games."

"Look, you have me mixed up with someone else. I don't have the slightest notion why you're here," he glanced at Sally, "or Sally either. Tell me what you want and maybe we can get this straightened out."

"Hank, Hank, Hank. Enough damn jabber. Give us what we want and we'll be on our way. I've got some serious messing around to do with my sweetie here and you're holding me up."

"For the last time, I don't have the slightest idea what you're talking about."

"Go ahead, play dumb. Tell you what, my gal and I will leave you alone to ponder the box. We'll be back tomorrow after the ride and don't think of going to the police or talking to anyone else about this. You're being watched and if you don't do what I say, you can tip your Stetson to Sweet Jesus. Get it?"

Ole Jimbo didn't leave any doubt about what he meant, but a box? What box? I nodded as he and his gal pal left my room.

After a long night of tossing, turning, smoking cigarettes that I swore off a month ago, and wearing my boots out walking around the motel parking lot, I reached for the phone at seven o'clock to call Rose. If ole Jimbo thought he had a sweet thing, he hadn't seen Rose. Her parents sure named her right. Her skin, soft and translucent as a white rose, combined with fragrant scents, made me heady every time I got close to her.

Rose's voice floated through the line.

"Hello, Hank."

"How did you know it was me?"

"Who else calls at seven in the morning?"

"Sorry, I thought you'd be up. Listen, I have some bad news."

"Stop right there—you don't want me to come to Ft. Worth?"

Hank hesitated. "It's not that I don't want you to come. Just talking to you makes me weak."

"How you do go on, sir."

"I mean it, darlin'. I miss you like hell and those old bulls will give me a lot of bruises you could soothe."

"Then, what's the problem?"

"The problem is I was greeted by a man holding a gun when I got in my motel room yesterday."

"What the… How'd he get in?"

"That's what I'd like to know, but the doors at the Round 'Em Up aren't exactly made to keep people out."

"Not that dump again?"

"It's good enough for me if you're not with me. Anyway, this guy waved a six-shooter in my face and said he wanted some box."

"What box?"

"I don't have a clue, but this guy, Jimbo, said I'd better hand it over and he meant business. He warned I was being watched and not to go to the police. He doesn't have to worry about that—the cops would think I was a total nut."

"This is why you don't want me to come?"

"Absolutely. This character is certifiable and I don't want you to get in his way. Comprendo?"

"Of course, but what are you going to do?"

Hank didn't say anything while vigorously rubbing the back of his neck.

"Hank, still there?"

"Yeah."

"I wish I was there to rub your neck for you."

Hank laughed. "You know me too well—that's exactly what I'm doing. I've got to figure out what the hell this guy is talking about and how I got in the middle of it. Anyway, I've got to ride later today, so for the time being, stay in Big D and I'll keep you posted."

When I checked the posts, I didn't pull good positions. It didn't matter—I'd have more time to ask around about Jimbo and figure this box shit out. No luck but didn't expect any. Rodeo folks are close-mouthed. So, that left The Branding Iron, a favorite hangout with the rodeo crowd after performances. Maybe a few beers would loosen some tongues.

After stepping into the saloon and before I could focus through the smoke and dark, I felt fingers running up my back, tickling the back of my neck before ending up with a squeeze on my backside. I spun around thinking Rose had come in spite of my warning. Instead, I gazed into the raccoon eyes of Jimbo's 'sugar.'

"What the hell?"

"You don't remember my name, cowboy? It's Sally Mae." She moved close, putting her hand inside my shirt letting it drift slowly across my chest. "You know, Jimbo won't be here for awhile. Why don't we sit at the bar and have a beer?"

I pushed her to arm's length. "I don't know what kind of game you and your boyfriend are playing, but I don't want any part of it. I told you yesterday I don't know what box you're talking about and today hasn't changed a thing."

Sally Mae pushed her bottom lip out while putting her index finger in her mouth. "I'm hurt, big man. I just want a friendly drink."

I looked around for Jimbo but couldn't spot him. Maybe I *should* have a drink with Sally Mae and pry some information out of her.

"Okay. Like you said, what's wrong with having a drink while we wait for your boyfriend."

Sally was three shades to the wind and it took some maneuvering to get her to one of the barstools.

"Tell me, Sally, y'all from around here?"

She wagged her finger at me. "No, no, no. I know what you're trying to do. Old Sally, here, ain't no fool. I want to talk about you, you good-looking, tall drink of water." She reached over and tousled my hair.

I grinned while putting my arm around her shoulders. "You're much more interesting, darlin'. What the hell do you see in that Jimbo fellow?"

"Can't tell you that, cowboy. Let's just say he satisfies me in lots of ways."

"You could do better, you know."

"I've heard that line more times than you've climbed on those old bulls. Men have twisted me from the inside out all my life." She looked in the mirror behind the bar scanning the crowd for Jimbo. Then, she rested her hand on my upper leg and started edging toward the center. I grabbed it and moved it back to the bar.

"Sally, I don't want any trouble here. You're a beautiful woman…"

"Aw, Hank, you really think so?"

"Yeah, but you're taken and I don't mess with other men's property. So, why don't you talk to me about the box?"

She strained to focus on my face. "The box. Right, the sweet box. Why don't you just hand it over and we'll leave you alone."

I took her hand, surprised at its roughness. "Sally, I'd give it to you right now if I knew what or where it is, but I don't. You two have the wrong man."

"No, Jimbo never gets anything wrong." She spun around on the stool looking again for her no good lover. "Seriously, bull riding man, if you hand over the box, we'll all be happy and you can get with your Rose."

Nausea swept into my stomach. "Rose? How do you know about her?"

"Baby, we know everything about you. Wouldn't you like your squeeze to be here?"

I grabbed Sally's wrist.

"Stop—that hurts."

"If you two go near Rose…"

Sally leaned her head back and laughed so loud it attracted everyone around us. "Oh, come on, man. Listen to Jimbo and do what he wants or you won't have to worry about Rose or anything else."

Jimbo came up behind us.

"Looks like you two are getting along. What did I miss?"

Sally Mae grabbed him around the neck as she slid off the stool. "I was just trying to help you, baby. He still claims he knows nothin'."

Jimbo lifted her up and deposited her on the stool. "Sit still, you sexy bitch. I know what you were doing, but I forgive you." He turned toward Hank. "Now, I've been patient with you, Hank, but my patience is gone. You wouldn't be planning to double-cross ole Jimbo, would you?"

I started to answer when he jabbed his fist into my midsection.

Straightening up, I mumbled something about trying to find out what the hell he wanted.

Jimbo took Sally Mae's hand. "Come on, sugar, we've got business to take care of."

I didn't expect him to leave. "Hold on. Your woman said something about Rose."

Jimbo's smile widened. "Sure 'nuff. She's real sweet and if I didn't have my Sally Mae here, I'd be looking twice at her."

I growled, "Leave her out of this madness. Deal with me."

"That's what I'm trying to do, but you're not cooperating. Listen up. I don't know what game you're playing, but you have thirty-six hours max to put the box in my hands. After that… well, no need to go into that now."

When I got back to the motel, I checked the office for calls. I didn't have any, but I did have a package with no return. I turned it over and over in my hands. It was light with something rattling inside.

The clerk acted nervous.

"Who left this?"

"I dunno know."

"You don't know?"

"That's what I said. This ain't a five star hotel, you know."

"You can say that again." I started out but stopped and turned back. "You have to know who left the package."

"So, what if I do?"

I pulled out a twenty. Jog your memory?"

"It was a kid."

"A kid? How old?"

"10 or 11." He frowned. "How the hell do I know how old he was?"

"Did someone drop him off?"

"Naw, don't think so."

I left. This was a dead-end. When I got to my room, I held the package to my ear half expecting to hear ticking. I shook my head before ripping off the wrapping and staring at a plain brown box. When I opened it, I wanted to toss it against the wall. It was a box of chocolates—some with red roses on top, some with yellow roses, and a large candy in the center with a white rose on it. There was a note taped to the inside of the lid.

"**THIS IS YOUR LAST WARNING BEFORE THAT PRETTY WHITE ROSE IS GOBBLED UP. THE CLOCK IS TICKING—TICK TOCK, TICK TOCK.**"

I called Rose and got her machine. "Call. It's important."

I didn't hear from her until six the next morning. She didn't sound like herself.

"Hank, cancel Ft. Worth and come to Dallas."

"Why?"

"Whatever's going on there…"

"Rose, stop. Is someone with you?"

Silence. "Baby, talk to me."

I heard shuffling and then nothing. I called back only to have the phone picked up and put down without a word. This was the final straw. Jimbo had gone too far. I went to the rodeo office to get in touch with the security guard—safer than the police. His name was Mark Coolidge. He wore plain clothes and only a few of the rodeo staff knew his identity. The gal in the office refused to give me his phone number at first, but when I convinced her it was a matter of life and death, she relented. I explained my problem to Mark and he agreed to meet, but whether Jimbo was watching me or not, he said it needed to be some place conspicuous, out in the open. He suggested The Branding Iron where we could strike up conversation and game of pool. If Jimbo *was* keeping track of me, he wouldn't think anything about this. Fortunately, the saloon was open 24/7.

I recognized Mark from his photograph and told him my problem in between shots at the pool table. He didn't act surprised. Red flags flew.

After the first game, I suggested we grab a beer and sit at one of the back tables.

"Mark, you don't seem surprised about this box thing."

"Tell you the truth, I'm not."

"What are you saying?"

"I'm not at liberty to say any more, but I will tell you this Jimbo guy has you mixed up with someone else."

I grinned sensing I had been granted a pardon from my problem. "So, how do I clear this up?"

"It's not that easy, Hank."

"Come again."

"I said, it's not that easy. I can tell you this much—you're only a small piece of what's going on here."

"Oh, that helps."

"I know it's not much, but it's all I can tell you now."

"So, in the meantime, this guy is doing who knows what to Rose and he's threatening to do more to me. Where do I go from here?"

"Keep your cool. Give me time to investigate."

"Sounds so simple when you put it like that, but how? Listen, I've got to call Rose again. Keep me posted?"

When I got back to the motel and called Rose, I caught her at the airport ready to wing it to Arizona.

"My God, baby, I was going to call the police if I didn't get you this time. What's going on there?"

"When I opened the door to my condo, a man ran from around the corner following close on my heels. He pushed something in my back. It felt like a gun, but he never brandished one, so maybe not. He told me nothing would happen if I played ball."

"What did he look like?"

"Short, built like a fire plug, sandy hair, no identifying marks I could see."

"Not Jimbo, that's for sure."

"What have you gotten yourself into, Hank?"

"Come on. You have to know I'm not involved in any of this. Whatever they're looking for is in somebody else's hands—not mine."

She sounded contrite. "Sorry, stressed out. I'm going to…"

"Don't say where, I know. That's good, baby. This thing has to be taken care of soon because I'm running out of time. Sweetheart, I'll be in touch."

When I hung up the phone, rage sliced through every part of my body. If they harmed one hair on Rose's head, there'd be hell to pay.

As soon as I got to Will Rogers Center before the matinee, I saw a crowd around one of the bull pens. Mark was on one side talking to a cop. I tried to push toward him but was stopped by another policeman.

"Hold it, Mister. You can't go in there."

I explained I was supposed to join Mark who looked over and motioned to let me in.

I looked down at what was left of Jimbo and a woman they called "an unidentified female."

I started to back off, but Mark crooked his finger to come closer.

"What's happened here?"

"I think that's pretty obvious. He introduced me to the chief investigating officer who, in turn, asked me if I knew the victims. I told him I didn't—not exactly a lie but enough of one to cause Mark to raise his eyebrows. I told the cop I was due to ride in 15 minutes and needed to go unless I could answer any more questions.

Mark nodded at the cop, took me by the arm, and moved me away from the activity.

"Okay, Hank. Where have you been since I saw you this morning?"

"I went back to The Branding Iron, called my girl, did some wash and here I am."

"All right. You didn't have anything to do with any of this?"

"Are you crazy? Of course not. I didn't want them dead, but I'm glad they're out of my hair."

"What makes you think they are?"

"Because they're dead, d-e-a-d."

Mark passed me a sympathetic look. "Yeah, Jimbo and Sally Mae are dead, but they had to be working with someone else and that someone else is not dead—that someone else still wants the box."

"I can't believe my ears. Once and for all, I don't know anything about any damn box."

"Calm down. Look, it won't be long before the cops find out you've been asking questions about Jimbo. Since you've said you don't know him, they'll be suspicious. Get ready for that."

"Thanks for the heads up. I hear my number—catch you later."

Mark shoved a piece of paper in my hand. "Come to my house after your rides."

The matinee was bursting at the seams with a deafening crowd which took my mind off my problems for a few minutes and forced me to focus on the beast under my body. The first time I sat on a mountain of bucking strength taught me to honor him with all my concentration, to think of nothing else, or it could be curtains. I had a great teacher when I started riding who told me I was lucky to have good control of my upper body and strong legs. He said I needed to keep my body forward at all times and the first time I didn't…let's just say, the lesson was enough that I didn't do it again. This same guy stressed the use of my free arm. I didn't get it until I finally imagined my free arm was like a trapeze artist's. After that, my balance improved. Every rider has to figure out how to maneuver his body and what works best for him. He also told me that even though spurring wasn't required, it would add points to my score. I thought this sounded preposterous—why make this giant animal mad? When I realized that half of the score is based on the contestant's performance and the other half on the animal's efforts, I understood. I also learned the rider would be disqualified for touching the animal or his equipment with his free hand. My mentor told me, if you stay on a bull for eight seconds, it will make a man out of you and believe me, eight seconds doesn't sound long, but it can be an eternity.

When the rides were finally over, I stashed my equipment and made my way to Mark's house. He lived about fifteen minutes from the Center, but it seemed more like an hour weaving in and out of traffic. I rang the bell. No answer. I knocked and heard Mark's call to come in—the door was unlocked. His living area was dimly lit, but I could make out his image sitting in a chair by the fireplace.

"Sorry for not greeting you at the door, Hank, but I have my hands full."

It wasn't difficult to see the 9 mm persuader in his hands.

"Why the gun?"

He twisted his lips sideways. "Guess it's the same as ole Jimbo's when he busted into your room."

"What do you mean? I don't get it."

"You're a smart man, Hank. It's simple—I want the box."

"Damn! For the umpteenth time, I don't have any box that doesn't belong to me."

"Ooops, ole boy. Maybe you think the box we're looking for belongs to you. Is that it?"

"I can't believe what I'm hearing. Listen, I don't have any box except for the one my new pair of boots is in. My boots, is that it?"

"Don't be absurd. No wonder Jimbo got exasperated with you. He sent you a box of chocolates, didn't he?"

"Yeah, but...?"

"C'mon, Hank. Where are the chocolates?"

"I threw them away."

He got up from the chair and hit me on the side of the face with his gun. "What the hell do you mean, you 'threw them away'?"

"I ate a couple of pieces and threw the rest away. It was a scare tactic to get to Rose."

"Ah, but it didn't work, did it?"

"Mark, can I sit?"

"Sit. I've got to figure out my next move."

"You're a lawman. What happened?"

Mark shook his head. "Guess it doesn't hurt to tell you. I've worked for peanuts all my life, but then a temptation came my way I couldn't ignore—a chance to get a bundle and a good chance of not getting caught."

"But murder?"

"Hold on there, bud. I didn't say anything about murder."

"Have it your way, but why me and Rose? How did we get involved in this damn business?"

Mark grinned. "Guess that's my fault. Jimbo didn't have a clue about me or how big this operation was. We had to dangle a carrot in front of him to find the box and you were the carrot."

"Why Rose?"

"Why not? She was the closest thing to you. Jimbo might have seemed like a fool, but he wasn't. He was trying to double-cross me and you know how that ended."

"You must think I have whatever Jimbo was looking for."

"Right. Look, Hank, I'm not a fool either. I've followed the trail of this box for awhile and it ended with you in Fort Worth."

"Don't know how."

"Through my organization's intelligence." Mark stopped enjoying his own words. "Intelligence—how do you like that? Anyway, we wanted a cowboy scheduled to ride in Ft. Worth for our own reasons. You were a smuck we could manipulate. You had a steady gal in Dallas and this was another way of manipulating you. So, we put the box in your hands. A package was sent to you at UPS' station in Mesquite, Texas—your last stop before Ft. Worth."

"But I didn't get it."

"We don't know that yet, do we?"

Hank shook his head. "I didn't pick up any package in Mesquite. Y'all are going to a lot of trouble for nothing."

"Don't think so."

"Go ahead, search my room although I'm sure Jimbo took care of that already. You can kill me, but where do you go from there? The way I see it there aren't any more options."

"Wrong, buddy. I've got some ideas of my own."

"And they are?"

"First, let's check out your motel. Jimbo was a little distracted with Sally Mae—God knows why. Then, we'll go from there. Come on, you drive and we'll get this over with."

As we walked out to my car, my mind raced to figure out how to overpower this guy. I came up with nothing. When we walked into my room, Mark positioned himself on one side and ordered me to remove the mattress from the bed and run my hands around the hem and top of the draperies. He ordered me to keep searching until I had completely dismantled the room. I managed to ask him what size box I was looking for and he said it was not large. That's all I got.

When he was finally satisfied my room was clean, he marched

me to the office to see if any more packages had been left for me. I knew any effort to alert the desk clerk was useless.

"Okay, Mark, where to now?"

"Rose's apartment."

"Dallas? You gotta be kidding."

Mark moved the gun in my ribs. "You don't really think I'm kidding, do you?"

"How do you propose we get into Rose's apartment?"

Mark chuckled. "I imagine you have a key, but if you don't, it's not a problem. Now, settle down, start driving, and we'll be there before you know it. Hank, one more thing, you should call the rodeo folks and cancel the rest of your rides."

"Why would I do that?"

"Don't be stupid. Just do it."

As soon as we got to Rose's apartment, I refused to give Mark the key burning a hole in my pocket, but his professional magic got us in anyway. He motioned me toward a chair I had relaxed in so many times with my Rose.

"Hank, call her…"

"I don't know where she is."

"Don't insult me. Of course, you know. This will save time. See if she's gotten any gifts or deliveries lately."

"No way."

Mark waved the gun again. "Don't make me find Rose myself—I can, you know."

I did what he said. Rose said she had gotten a delivery about a week ago with a Round 'Em Up return and a label not to open until Valentine's Day. She told me she put it in her lingerie drawer.

Mark smiled and motioned for me to say good-bye and whatever lovey-dovey words I wanted to close with. He pointed to the bedroom.

As we made our way to Rose's dresser, I could only hope Rose would contact the police.

"Open the drawer, Hank. Let's have a look-see."

I thought about yanking the drawer and knocking Mark out but knew the stops would prevent it. I looked around for another weapon. Nothing.

The package, neatly wrapped in brown paper and secured with tape, rested on top of Rose's lingerie. As Rose said, bold letters spelled out directions not to open until February 14th.

Mark grinned. "There's the prize, Hank. Unwrap it."

"Why don't you?"

"Do what I say."

When I ripped off the wrapping, I couldn't believe my eyes. "Another box of candy?"

"All right, Hank. Remove the top."

I lifted the lid and had to laugh in spite of the seriousness of the situation. "Oh, man, it's more chocolates with white roses."

"Take out a chocolate and put it on the dresser."

I did what he said. "Now what?"

Mark pulled out a small pocket knife. "Here. Cut it open."

"Why?"

Mark snarled, "Do it."

As soon as I cut into the chocolate, small, twinkling stones tumbled from the hollowed insides.

"My God. Are those what they look like?"

"You really work hard at being dumb, don't you? Now, put those sweet diamonds back in the box, close and tape it."

I fingered the pocket knife I had slipped in my pocket—my only chance. Mark was too distracted to think about the knife. As I handed him the box with one hand, I buried the small blade into his carotid artery. His hand flew to his neck. I grabbed his gun, pulled his hands behind his back and secured them with Rose's lingerie. Mark's eyes stared in surprise until death froze them for eternity.

It seemed like this agonizing problem was over until the cops arrived. They had a hard time believing my story. Who can blame them, and the fact that Mark was in the security business made it even worse. In the long run, Mark was right. This particular box of chocolates was only a small part of a crime puzzle that Texas law enforcement was trying to piece together. So, after my Rose and I agreed to testify at the proper time, we became chief characters against a ring of wrongdoers.

Rose and I still talk about how Jimbo and Sally Mae's greed fueled by Mark's fall from grace ended the trail of the chocolate roses.

A Box of Texas Chocolates

Books and Bon Bons
by Charlotte Phillips

Every time I meet a woman of a certain age, a woman who no longer cares what others think, a woman who says what she thinks when she thinks it, I indulge myself for a few brief seconds. I look forward to the day I no longer need to mind my tongue. Then I remember mean, old Mrs. Ruth and remind myself that I'll always need to guard my words. The universe is watching.

I was barely fourteen the year I met that old witch. Excuse me. I don't mean to speak ill of the dead. At least, I hope she stayed dead. If you told me she was back from Hell because the Devil kicked her out for excessive meanness, I'd believe you.

The event that has ruled my life took place in the summer—August—in Houston. I tell you this because the heat does crazy things to people, makes them do stuff they wouldn't normally consider. That's what I have told myself for the last twelve years. It's how I sleep at night.

I guess I should tell you, I grew up poor, food stamp poor, in the kind of place that didn't offer much hope for anything better in the future. But, I had an interest in writing. I may also have had a bit of talent. At least, I like to think that's why my ninth-grade English teacher took such an interest in me. She introduced me to her writing group. They adopted me, let me attend their functions as if I was a dues-paying member. One of them, Miss Weaver, even gave me a weekend job in her tearoom, Fiona's Café, so I could earn enough money to ride the bus to the meetings. I guess you could say that I became an expert at reading bus schedules, too, because a different member hosted the meeting each month and I had to figure out how to get all over town.

Anyway, by the time it was Miss Weaver's turn to host the meeting, I was working the tearoom full-time as my summer job. I had earned my way up to server. To get there, I had to learn a great deal—everything from grooming my fingernails, to gracious southern speech, to staying calm and pleasant no matter how rude the guests were. I also had to learn all the kitchen jobs from washing dishes, to making finger sandwiches without the crust, to dealing with vendors like the fresh-fruits lady. Please don't think I'm bragging. I just want you to understand why a young girl could be so proud about becoming a waitress. And I was proud. I think you need to understand that pride before you can understand why I was so upset over that witch's, I mean Mrs. Ruth's, behavior.

Ms. Weaver planned to surprise the group by unveiling her new desserts. We'd been playing with recipes all summer long, trying to meet her goal of coming up with one dessert that was more delicious than her prized To-Die-For Chocolate Cake. If you've ever had the pleasure of tasting one of those, you know just what we were up against. If you've never tasted Fiona's Café's To-Die-For Chocoloate Cake and you are anywhere near Houston, you need to drop what you're doing and make yourself a note to visit Fiona's Café real soon. This is an experience you do not want to miss.

Anyway, we'd been working all summer on the dessert recipes, and on the theme for the meeting. Miss Weaver went with Books and Bon Bons for a theme. That wasn't my favorite, but it was her meeting, so she got to pick. That year, the monthly hostess had to pick a theme, express the theme in alliteration, and include both something about writing and something about food. That's what they agreed on at the December meeting after dipping into the eggnog too many times. I thought for sure they'd come to their senses and change the rules, but Mrs. Barry started us off in January with Mysteries and Merlot. I couldn't take part in the wine tasting, but I did enjoy the talk from a local author about blended genres and putting a mystery in any story.

After the wine tasting, and after Mrs. Ruth had finished making a nuisance of herself and left, someone had suggested a contest: come up with a creative way to kill off Mrs. Ruth, fictionally of course. Everyone—except Mrs. Ruth, who didn't know about the contest—would write a short story where the victim had some form of Mrs. Ruth's name and came to a creative end. Every participant would submit their story before the December meeting, along with five dollars, which went into the pot for the winner. That was in January.

I am supposed to be telling you about August.

Miss Weaver and I spent a good part of August working out the decorations, preparing special handmade treats, and, of course, working on those dessert recipes. She really did include me in every part of preparing for the event. It was hard work, but fun—especially the tasting part—not to mention that Miss Weaver sent many great experimental desserts home with me that summer. Miss Weaver said I wasn't just learning about running a café, I was learning about event planning. We'd lined up a great speaker who we'd taken to calling The Hazardous Herbs Lady. I'd been looking forward to hearing the presentation because I was in the middle of writing a mystery novel in which the bad guy was poisoning people. I found out pretty quick that I needed to learn a lot more about plant poisons than I was finding at the library. I had a list of twenty-three questions for The Hazardous Herbs Lady—and that was before her presentation.

Arghhh! I'm off topic again.

The big day finally arrived. Miss Weaver picked me up at my house because the bus didn't run at five in the morning. We'd been working since five-thirty. We'd covered the tables in cloths ordered special for the event, put up decorations, used the different treats and candies we'd made and frozen in July and August to create artful displays on the buffet tables around the room. Miss Weaver's new dessert choices—the ones we'd be tasting and voting on—were displayed on a special table in the center of the room. Miss Weaver had worked on those desserts all week and she was both pleased and nervous. She had created five fantastic-looking choices and believed two of them would receive the "Better Than Fiona Café's To-Die-For Chocolate Cake" rating. At a little after noon we looked around and smiled. We were ready an hour ahead of schedule. We had time to sit and enjoy a few finger sandwiches with Miss Weaver's favorite tea. At least that's what we thought.

We took a moment to make sure we were ready for Mrs. Ruth. She had a nasty habit of showing up much earlier than she should, when the hostess would be frantically trying to take care of last-minute details. Most people who showed up so early would understand how rude that was and offer to help. Not Mrs. Ruth. She took pleasure in adding to the hostess's stress level. She'd mess up things that were already prepared, demand the hostess wait on her every want, make rude comments about anything that came to mind, and generally harass the poor hostess. And something would always disappear.

Once the group figured out she would do this every time, they started planning for it. Some sent special invitations to Mrs. Ruth giving her a different start time. Others had a second person on hand an hour early. That person had one duty—try to manage Mrs. Ruth, try to keep her from destroying the hostess's hard work. We'd learned the one thing you didn't want to do was ask her to not touch something specific because she'd just head straight for whatever that was and destroy it.

Miss Weaver had a brilliant plan. We put some stuff on the table where we wanted Mrs. Ruth to sit—some leftover decoration doo-dads, an assortment of treats, a chocolate-dipped Twinkie that Miss Weaver made special for Mrs. Ruth because we knew she could not resist. We were going to use her nasty tendencies to control her like a puppet.

Anyway, we satisfied ourselves that we were as ready as we could be, fixed a plate of sandwiches and some tea, and sat down for a little break. That's when our plans started to fall apart.

When the first phone rang, Miss Weaver took the call. I could tell from her side of the conversation that something was wrong. I wasn't trying to listen, but with just the two of us in the room, it was hard not to hear.

She was still on the first call when the second line started ringing, so I went to the hostess station to take that call. It was Angie, our scheduled hostess for the event. She was too sick to come to work. I told her not to worry, to take care of herself. I could fill in as hostess and still listen to The Hazardous Herbs Lady.

When I hung up, Miss Weaver told me the other call was Delores, our server for the day. She wasn't coming to work either. She had a good reason, but probably wouldn't like me to tell you she had to go downtown to bail her good-for-nothing father out of jail—again. Guess I shouldn't have said that. Please don't tell Delores.

Anyway, I could tell Miss Weaver didn't want to ask me to wait tables. She knew how much I'd been looking forward to this event. But we both knew that her asking was just a formality. I really didn't have a choice considering all she'd done for me. So I didn't make her ask. I simply said, "Sounds like I'm waiting tables and you're playing hostess."

Miss Weaver gave me a big hug and we headed for the kitchen to put on our uniforms—frilly dresses and gloves for both of us, and a white apron for me. She said we didn't have to wear the hats. Truth be told, Miss Weaver never required those dorky hats when she worked the dining room.

While we were changing, she suggested that perhaps the group would be so interested in the presentation that I wouldn't have much to do and would be able to sit down and listen. I smiled and said thanks, but we both knew who would put the kibosh on that plan.

We were still changing when the doorbell starting ringing—in a nonstop, annoying kind of way. We knew who it was and neither of us hurried to let her in. The sign on the door clearly said, "closed for a private event" and, "the doors will open at twelve-thirty."

I didn't want to open the door at all, but I knew Miss Weaver would expect me to use some of those southern manners she'd been hammering into me. She always said to me, "Sassy, anyone can be nice to pleasant people. The hard part is being pleasant to the ornery, but if you pull it off, it will sweeten them right up." It usually did, too. But some people enjoy being ornery and won't give it up no matter how you treat them.

Normally Miss Weaver would have been the one to greet guests as she loved that part of owning her own place, but I could tell she wasn't ready, and by that I mean she was hanging on to her own head looking like she thought it might explode. I told her I'd get the door.

I wanted to take my sweet time about it because I knew Mrs. Ruth would start ordering me around like she owned me as soon as I let her in. But that bell was still ringing, and I could see it was getting on Miss Weaver's nerves. So I hustled on out, opened the door, greeted Mrs. Ruth with, "Welcome! Come in, come in."

I used my best smile too, but it was wasted on the old crone, I mean Mrs. Ruth.

It would have been ever so gracious of her to at least cross the threshold before she started in on me. But then, she wouldn't be Mrs. Ruth, now, would she? She banged her cane on the step, and greeted me with, "It's about time, Girlee. Don't you know any better than to keep Mrs. Weaver's guests waiting on the sidewalk like commoners?"

She always called Miss Weaver "Mrs." I thought it was because she knew Miss Weaver never married and hated the title "Mrs." I found out later how wrong I was about that.

Anyway, Mrs. Ruth took a breath and stepped in before ordering me to the kitchen. "I'm parched from having to breathe all that dust. You should know by now not to leave your betters standing around on the street while you do God knows what. You hustle on into that kitchen and fetch me a large iced tea. Make it sweet and don't even think about charging me for it. It's your fault I'm so thirsty."

"Yes Ma'am," I said, "just let me show you to a table first."

"Do I look like an invalid?" She waved that cane around for emphasis. "I can find my own table. You stop sassing me and fetch that tea. I'm going to have to speak to Mrs. Weaver about getting you some proper training or replacing you with someone who knows the basics. She should know better than to employ the lower classes in a place like this. Why are you still standing here?" She pounded that cane on the floor one more time.

I knew she didn't need that thing. She was old, but strong as an ox. That cane was her weapon of choice. I half expected her to take a swing at me.

"Yes Ma'am," I said. "I just wanted to let you know, Miss Weaver says to sit anywhere except that one table near the kitchen." I pointed to be clear. "You can see we're still working on decorations. She wants to save that table in case The Hazardous Herbs Lady brings any friends with her."

"All right, you told me. Now get a move on. The tea can't walk out here on its own. And tell that woman she can't hide forever. I'll see to that." That last comment made me angry. I had no idea what she meant, but I understood she was threatening Miss Weaver—and I didn't take kindly to anyone trying to hurt Miss Weaver.

I headed for the kitchen, but took my time. I wanted to see if she'd sit at the forbidden table. I didn't have to wait long. She didn't even pretend to consider any of the other fourteen tables. She walked by the center display and used her finger to scoop some icing off the side of Miss Weaver's prized To-Die-For Chocolate Cake, then made a beeline to the forbidden zone and started clucking about the decorations. "What is this? Paper doo-dads? I hope this is not what you are calling decorations. Our speaker is a famous scientist. You need to show some class, Girlee..."

I tuned her out and headed for the kitchen where I found Miss Weaver downing some Goody's Extra Strength Headache

Powder. I guess Miss Weaver thought she was doing me a favor by having the tea already poured, but I would have preferred the extra time in the kitchen.

Miss Weaver wasn't looking so hot, so I tried joking around to make her feel better. "Too bad The Hazardous Herbs Lady isn't here with her kit. I could spice up the tea." Well, I thought it was funny, but Miss Weaver paled. "Please don't worry," I said, "It was just a joke. I hope you're not getting sick, too. Maybe you should go upstairs and lie down for a few minutes."

She nodded and headed for the stairs that led to a tiny attic space converted into Miss Weaver's private migraine recovery nook. I took a deep breath and headed back to the dining room with Mrs. Ruth's tea on a serving tray. I can't tell you how happy and relieved I was to see Miss Weaver's best friend, Miss Fiona Sullivan, coming through the front door. Fiona wasn't her real name of course. Miss Weaver named her Fiona, just like she named me Sassy, because it fit my unique personality, she said. I don't know why she picked a name like Fiona for Miss Sullivan. And I don't know if Miss Weaver named the tearoom after Miss Fiona, or Miss Fiona got her nickname from the tearoom, but Miss Weaver named them both.

Did you notice I'm off topic again? Guess by now you figured out why I never became a writer.

Anyway, Miss Fiona had volunteered to manage Mrs. Ruth, but the way the day was going, I half expected her to get a flat tire or something and show up late.

Mrs. Ruth didn't see me place her tea on the table because she was too busy gossiping to Miss Fiona, something about the great charade coming to an end. I ignored the old coot and walked over to greet Miss Fiona. I leaned in close to thank her for coming and to let her know a migraine was threatening Miss Weaver. I should have known better. Miss Fiona was too fond of Miss Weaver to let her suffer alone. Instead of rescuing me from Mrs. Ruth, she headed for Miss Weaver, said she wanted to see if she could do anything to help.

Mrs. Ruth started in on me again as soon as Miss Fiona disappeared into the kitchen, "Girlee, get over here and clean up this mess. What's wrong with you, dawdling over there when…"

I don't know about you, but I have a low threshold for bullies. I think it comes from growing up in the slums, surrounded by them. Miss Weaver had worked hard to teach me to smile at people like Mrs. Ruth and try to make their days just a little brighter. But in the slums, those of us who want to survive deal with bullies in a different way. I knew my actions would disappoint Miss Weaver, but I wasn't about to put up with that mouth focused only on me, nonstop, for another thirty minutes. I knew just what to do, too. I'd watched my tiny grandmother turn my big brothers into quivering blobs of Jell-O on more than one occasion.

I set my face on ugly, marched over to her, and slammed the tray down hard enough to make the table jump. Then I put one hand on the back of her chair and leaned over her is such a way that she had to lean back and look up at me. That was the trick my Grandma used.

I talked in a low voice so she would have to strain to hear me. I don't remember exactly what I said to her, but it was something like, "You listen to me you old witch. You are not going to spoil Miss Weaver's function, and you are not going to treat me like something the dog drug in, or I will show you how we deal with the likes of you where I come from." I tipped her chair back on two legs and said, "I hope we understand each other."

By then, Mrs. Ruth was looking a little pale and I didn't want to give her a heart attack or anything like that, at least I don't think I did. So, I let her chair fall back into place and told her to clean up the mess she'd made of the decorations and not to even think about going near Miss Weaver's desserts. Then I retreated to the kitchen to worry about what Miss Weaver would do once she heard about my poor behavior. And I had no doubt that she would hear an exaggerated version.

Not much happened for a while after that, although Mrs. Ruth did clean up the mess she'd made. The Hazardous Herbs Lady arrived and set up her presentation at the front of the room. She sure was pretty, by the way, not what I expected for an expert in murder. And she had a regular name, too—Mrs. Dolly Best, in case you ever need to know.

But that's not important right now.

The rest of the writers drifted in. Mrs. Ruth tried to complain about me to the other guests, but they ignored her. By the time Miss Weaver and Miss Fiona came back downstairs, Mrs. Ruth was back to bossing me around—first demanding hot tea because the room was too cold, then cold tea because it was too hot. I guess she felt safe with so many witnesses around, but she shouldn't have. Miss Fiona sat with Mrs. Ruth, finally, and the old bat, I mean Mrs. Ruth, calmed down. Miss Weaver checked on her other guests. The presentation started and I listened as best I could while running back and forth to the kitchen for this and that. Seems like everyone needed "just one more thing."

I was on my way back from the kitchen with yet another "clean" saucer for Mrs. Ruth and arrived just in time to see that old bat interrupt the proceedings by banging that cane on the table and shouting that she had an important announcement to make about our hostess. Mrs. Ruth tried to stand up, but by then I was behind her. I put my hand on her shoulder and squeezed real hard while leaning forward and whispering in her ear that she better sit down and be quiet.

She froze in place—half standing and half sitting. I figured she needed just a little more encouragement to behave, so I squeezed harder and pushed her back into her chair.

That's when she turned her attack on me with, "Girlee, you can't keep me from telling your boss about your poor skills. This tea is about the worst excuse for tea I've ever tasted."

Miss Fiona, who is always quiet and likes to stay in the background, surprised everyone by speaking up in my defense. She said Mrs. Ruth shouldn't try to blame me for the tea. She said Mrs. Ruth had poured salt into the cup and ought to know better then that.

Miss Weaver, who was sitting across the room, stood and said, "That's okay, Fiona. Everyone makes mistakes. Sassy knows the customer is always right. Isn't that so, Sassy?"

Well I can tell you, I thought no such thing. But I would never contradict Miss Weaver, especially in public, so I put on one of those smiles she'd taught me and said, "Yes, Ma'am."

"Thank you, Dear. Would you mind fetching a fresh cup of tea for Mrs. Ruth?"

"No Ma'am. I'll be happy to make a special cup of tea for her," I said.

Then I whispered to Mrs. Ruth that she better behave while I was gone, or else. I picked up the cup of ruined tea and "accidentally" spilled just enough of it on her dress so she would know I meant business. I apologized, of course, and hustled back to the kitchen.

Somewhere between the dining room and the kitchen I thought up a bad idea and convinced myself it was the right thing to do. I decided to make a very special cup of tea. Miss Weaver had taught me several different ways to make what she called antimonials and I called barf syrups.

Sometime I'll tell why we had that particular lesson, but that's a different story. Right now I need to finish telling you about Mrs. Ruth.

I made that special cup of tea and delivered it to the table. As soon as I put it down, I pictured myself going to jail. I decided to take that cup back to the kitchen and do what Miss Weaver had asked. Mrs. Ruth and I reached for the cup at that same time and she got there first. I watched in horror as she gulped down a good half.

I still planned to take the tea away as soon as she set it down, but just then Miss Weaver waved me to the other side of the room. When I reached her, she motioned for me to sit next to her and told me it was time to take a break. I just couldn't believe her timing.

And what was wrong with Mrs. Ruth? She kept drinking that

stuff. It couldn't have tasted anything like tea.

Any normal person who suddenly felt ill in a public place would rush off to a rest room to suffer in private. By now you know that Mrs. Ruth was far from normal. When the brew took effect, she stood up and started shouting. She pointed that cane right at me and said, "She killed me! She killed an innocent old woman, just to keep her evil secret." I didn't know what evil secret she meant and she didn't get a chance to say.

Just as she reached the center display table, the one with all the special desserts, she started heaving. She ruined everything on that table before she let Miss Fiona lead her off to the rest room.

I can't begin to tell you how bad I felt about ruining Miss Weaver's hard work like that, and of course for making Mrs. Ruth so sick. Mostly, though, I tried not to tremble. I didn't want to go to jail and I didn't want Miss Weaver to hate me. The room stayed dead quiet for a long time. No one moved, they just all stared at me and waited.

Finally, Miss Weaver did what she always did in bad moments. She patted my hands and said, "Chin up, Sassy. The world hasn't come to an end."

That's when one of the other ladies spoke up. She said, "Take your own advice, Lila. I can tell you, your deep, dark secret is the worst kept secret this side of the Mississippi. Don't you know your friends love you just the way you are?"

I was stunned. I had no idea Miss Weaver could have a dark secret, and I sure didn't know what it was, but I was relieved to have all those attentive eyes move from me to Miss Weaver. Then I felt guilty for being so selfish and announced that I'd get the mess cleaned up. That got everyone moving as most of the ladies jumped up to help me. I guess everyone needed something to do. I figured Miss Weaver was angry with me, though, because instead of heading for the main buffet table like everyone else, she headed to Mrs. Ruth's table and cleaned it up by herself. She even dumped out Mrs. Ruth's purse and cleaned up the mess inside. I don't know why Mrs. Ruth shoved all those chocolate treats in there, but it made a huge mess and Miss Weaver cleaned it all for her, threw away the ruined treats, and replaced them with a to-go container of replacements from one of the side tables.

While we were cleaning, Mrs. Ruth emerged from the bathroom to hurl some more accusations. She shouted for someone to call the police, said Miss Weaver had poisoned her and she would have satisfaction.

The Hazardous Herbs Lady spoke up then. She said, "You might want to think that through. Filing a false police report is a serious offense."

"What do you mean false? You saw how sick she made me! Are you in on this?"

"Ma'am, I think you did it to yourself when you put that salt in your tea. Don't you know saltwater has that effect on people? Why did you put salt in tea?"

Mrs. Ruth responded, but I couldn't hear what she said because so many of the ladies burst into laughter. I think they enjoyed the idea that one of Mrs. Ruth's stunts finally caught up with her. Miss Weaver and Miss Fiona didn't join in. They sat off in a corner with their heads together. I figured Miss Fiona was trying to make Miss Weaver feel better. Miss Fiona was good at that.

Mrs. Ruth left in disgrace and the Herbs Lady followed her out the door.

I couldn't believe my good fortune. Just as I was beginning to believe I would get away with it, someone yelled from the kitchen, "Y'all need to come in here! You're not going to believe this."

Most of the ladies hustled on in. I didn't follow. I knew what they had found. All my ingredients were on display on the kitchen counter. I could only imagine what they'd do with this new information. I wanted to run, but knew I couldn't. Instead, I went over and apologized to Miss Weaver for ruining her function. I could tell she didn't know what I meant, but I didn't have to explain because all the ladies came out of the kitchen to do it for me.

Mrs. Barry stepped forward and said, "Sassy, would you come over here please?"

I took a deep breath and dragged myself across the room.

"Sassy, did you have anything to do with Mrs. Ruth's condition?"

I hung my head and nodded. The ladies roared with laughter. Mrs. Barry shushed everyone.

"Well then, Sassy, the group has agreed that you are the winner of the December writing contest." Someone else stepped forward and handed me a "trophy" they'd made from a teacup. Mrs. Barry handed me a check.

"I don't understand," I said. "It's only August and I didn't even write a story for the contest."

Mrs. Barry grinned and said, "That may be, but we've decided no one can top what you pulled off today." The ladies laughed then. Well, not laughed so much as hooted and hollered. They went back to cleaning the place up, but kept laughing the whole time.

I didn't know what to think, so I went back to sit with Miss Weaver and Miss Fiona.

I can't tell you if I was more stunned that day, last week when I learned I'd lost Miss Weaver and Miss Fiona to a drunk driver, or yesterday when I received the letter. I can tell you that this has been the saddest week in my life.

In the days and weeks that followed the Books and Bon Bons event, much changed at Fiona's Café. The whole place became more relaxed, less formal. Those dorky hats went to Goodwill. Miss Fiona spent more time with us. She took good care of Miss Weaver, gave her encouraging hugs, made sure she put the migraine recovery area to good use, and filled in where ever needed.

You probably already figured out why Mrs. Ruth was threatening Miss Weaver. It took me a long time to understand. More than a year after the tea incident, I figured out Miss Weaver and Miss Fiona lived in the same house. Sometime after that, I figured out they were a couple. I guess you could say I was a dumb kid.

Miss Weaver and I never talked about that day, and I eventually stopped feeling so guilty about ruining her event. But I've never forgotten what I did to Mrs. Ruth, never stopped thinking the universe would get me back one day. The event has ruled my life, kept me on the straight and narrow when many of my peers drifted astray.

So I can tell you it was a real kick in the pants yesterday when Miss Weaver's lawyer came to visit. He delivered a sealed letter from Miss Weaver. I've read that letter at least ten times now and I still can't quite believe any of it. Miss Weaver wrote that I may have saved the old bat's, I mean, Mrs. Ruth's, life with that tea. May have saved Miss Weaver's life, too.

It seems Miss Weaver didn't care much for Mrs. Ruth's threats either and had decided to put an end to it. Remember that chocolate-dipped Twinkie? Turns out, that was even more special than the tea I prepared. Without the effects of that tea, Mrs. Ruth would not have survived the week, and Miss Weaver may have been the one to go to jail. According to the letter, I had saved Miss Weaver from her own actions. She had also forgiven Mrs. Ruth. She said Mrs. Ruth saved Miss Weaver and Miss Fiona from a life of fear and hiding, and because of my tea, they were able to enjoy their new-found freedom. Miss Weaver thanked me and said I was her heroine. More than that, she made me the sole heir to her estate.

Like I said—a real kick in the pants. You are talking to the new owner of Fiona's Café. I don't yet know when I'll be able to open the café. I'm not yet ready to face it without Miss Weaver. But when I do, I hope you'll stop by for some To-Die-For Chocolate Cake—original recipe. I promise, I won't prepare any special teas. And I'll mind my tongue. I know the universe is watching.

A Box of Texas Chocolates

Valentine's Day
by Diana L. Driver

February 13th

"*Last hired, first fired.*" Erin Whittier shifted in her chair as she picked at her salad. Those four words were on everyone's lips, but she knew they weren't always true. Among her co-workers she had the least amount of seniority, but so far management had only reduced her work week from five days to three. Even though that still hurt, she hoped it was enough to keep her neck off the chopping block.

To save money, Erin brown bagged her lunch and ate it in the company dining room with her office-mates, Crystal and Molly. Usually, the three of them ignored the subject of corporate downsizing, but today snippets of conversation floated over from the other tables.

"If they're going to lay me off, I wish they'd go ahead and do it," Crystal said. "Waiting for the axe to fall is driving me crazy. It's difficult to plan anything. We were going to take a cruise this summer, but we cancelled that idea."

"I know I'm afraid to spend any money," Molly said. "My car just rolled over 100,000 miles on the odometer. We're going to have to spend major money in the near future just to keep it going. I really want a new car."

Erin set down her fork, leaving her lettuce and tomato salad unfinished and took a sip from her water bottle. She wasn't bothered by not having the big things. She really didn't care that she and Larry drove older cars or that they couldn't afford their own home right now. After all, they were newly married and these large purchases would come with time.

She hoped.

Feeling like she couldn't afford the little things bothered her. The water in her Evian bottle came from the kitchen faucet and the plastic bowl she used every day for her salad was so old it had yellowed. Feeling like she couldn't afford regular bottled water and a new Tupperware container made her feel *poor*.

"So Erin," Crystal asked, breaking her reverie. "Have any plans for Valentine's Day?"

"Not really." Erin picked up her fork and fiddled with her salad. "We might watch a movie. Larry's company is also downsizing so we can't spend any money. I told him not to make a fuss." She paused before adding, "Valentine's Day is way overdone. I know Larry loves me. I don't need any chocolates."

"Girl," Crystal's voice went up half an octave. "That is so lame. This is your first Valentine's Day as a married couple. It's one of those special days that you'll remember for the rest of your life."

Erin suspected Crystal might be right.

"Don't let it be a bust. Let your man know what you expect," Crystal continued. "Make him deliver. Men are like dogs—you can't let them backslide or they'll poop all over your heart. Harry knows to treat me right or he'll be on the couch for six months." She laughed. "And, you *know* what I mean!"

"You haven't seen Erin's husband," Molly said. "That man's a gift all by himself. If I had someone like him at home, I'd forget the movie and just slide in-between the sheets—Valentine's Day or not."

Erin visualized the black lace nightgown she'd be wearing on Valentine's night and flushed all the way to her ears.

"Look at her," Crystal said. "Erin's going to take that clip out of her hair and let it down. The girl has plans!" She got up from the table and patted Erin on the shoulder. "Good for you."

Erin watched Crystal sashay out of the lunchroom.

"You don't really believe that bull you said about not expecting a present on Valentine's Day, do you?" Molly asked. "I know you better than that."

She was a new bride and of course Valentine's Day was a special day for her, but she wasn't going to admit it to anyone. Their bank account balance was so low they were afraid of an overdraft if they made even the smallest withdrawal.

"They've cut Larry's pay twice in the last sixty days," she said. "He's doing the best he can. I'm not going to put any extra pressure on him. Although, I wish Valentine's Day came the day after payday, instead of the day before." She sighed. "Besides, I'm on a diet. Heaven knows, I don't need any chocolates."

"You're just trying to convince yourself." Molly smiled. "All women need chocolate—and Valentine's Day is a tradition."

Larry set the phone receiver back in its cradle and waved his younger brother into the office. "Sorry to keep you waiting." The kid sure looked grim. "What's up? Problems at school?"

"School's good." Paul plopped in the chair in front of the desk and shook his head. "No, it's Monica. I was going to give her a ring for Valentine's Day, but I'm still tapped out from tuition and books. I can't even get her a box of candy. Personally, I think the whole day's a crock, but you know how women are about these things."

Larry nodded. He knew how some women were. Women like Monica tended to be high maintenance. "Don't let it get you down. It's hard times for all of us."

"When I show up empty handed she's going to tell me to take a hike."

"You think she'll break up with you over a stupid box of candy?"

Paul nodded and leaned forward. "Anyway, that's why I'm here. I was wondering if you could help me out."

"I'm sorry," Larry said. "I'm flat broke myself."

"Don't worry about it," Paul sighed. "I just thought I'd ask."

There was nothing like a woman to make a guy feel like a loser. From the look in his brother's eyes, Larry knew that was exactly how Paul felt. "Wait a minute. Don't go."

Larry swiveled around in his chair, slid back the door on the credenza and took out two boxes covered in velvet—one red and one black. The red one was heart-shaped and had a satin rose embossed on lid and the other was an elongated jeweler's box. He set them side by side on the desk. "Here, give these to her."

Paul's eyes widened when he opened the black velvet box and saw the diamond bracelet inside. He snapped the box shut and set it down. "No, man I can't. You bought these for Erin."

"Take them. Erin won't care. She even told me that she thought Valentine's Day was too commercialized and she didn't want me to spend any money. The candy wasn't that much and I got the bracelet on sale right after Christmas. I'd front you the money so you could get Monica your own presents, but I just don't have it."

"I don't know."

"Take them," Larry grinned. "They might just save your ass. And, like I said, Valentine's Day doesn't mean that much to Erin."

February 14th –Valentine's Day

Mrs. Peggy Whittier squeezed the clippers and the rose cane fell to the ground. She picked it up and cut it into little bits, dropping them into the black plastic bag. Pruning the rose bushes wasn't her favorite job, but it needed to be done and on this particular day she needed to keep busy. This was her first Valentine's Day since her husband's death and she missed him very much. She smiled remembering the multitude of flowers, jewelry, and chocolates she'd been given over the years on February 14th.

"Mom?" Paul's voice rang out from the side of the house.

"Back here," Peggy answered. The side gate squeaked and Paul came around the corner of the house. She laid the shears down on top of the garbage sack, pulled off her gardening gloves, and smiled. "What a nice surprise."

Paul looked at the huge bag of cuttings. "You shouldn't be doing that. Let me take care of it."

"Thank you, but I think I'll do it myself. It keeps me busy."

"Rough day?"

She nodded. "It's really bad today. Valentine's Day, you know." She looked up and saw the sadness in his eyes. "What's wrong?"

He glanced away. "Monica dumped me."

She reached up and pushed a lock of hair away from his eyes. "I'm sorry."

"Yeah, we were supposed to go out tonight. She sent me a message that we were through and she had *another* date."

"She broke up with you today? With a text message?" She couldn't think of anything worse.

Paul forced a laugh. "Is that lame or what?"

"I'd say it's very lame." She took his arm. "Come on in. I'll put on the coffee pot and we can sit and chat. I even have a pecan pie."

His eyes brightened at the mention of pie. "Be there in a second. I have something to get out of the car."

Peggy had the pie on the table and two cups filled with coffee when Larry came in carrying a large heart-shaped box. He set it on the table then took a jeweler's box from his pocket and handed it to her. "These are for you," he said, giving her a kiss on the cheek. "Happy Valentine's Day, Mom."

She looked at the heart shaped box and traced the outline of the red satin rose with her finger. Then, she opened the jeweler's box and stared at the diamond bracelet.

"Goodness!" She studied his face. "Did you buy these for Monica?"

He shook his head. "Not really. Larry got them for Erin. He

gave them to me so I could give them to Monica, but I didn't get the chance. I hope you don't mind."

Peggy closed the lid and set the box down beside the chocolates. "Larry gave you Erin's gifts?"

"It's okay," he said. "He was just trying to help me out and Erin doesn't care about Valentine's Day anyway. She even told Larry not to bother buying her anything—that as far as she's concerned, Valentine's Day is just another commercial holiday."

Peggy nodded. "I understand." Both her sons had a lot to learn about women. Every year she'd told their father the very same thing.

Yes, she understood completely.

Larry's Valentine Day was off to a bad start. First of all, he'd overslept and nearly missed his morning goodbye kiss with Erin. Then there'd been a wreck on the freeway which added extra time to his commute. By the time he walked into his office he was almost ninety minutes late. That was ninety minutes he'd have to make up before he could leave in the evening.

He waited until mid-afternoon to pick up the phone and give Erin the bad news. "Hi sweetie," he said. "I'm not going to be able to leave the office until 6 at the earliest. To save time, why don't you go ahead and pick out a movie for us?"

"You can't get out of it? After all, it's…"

"I can't. I came in late and need to make up my hours." He felt like a heel, but he couldn't jeopardize his job or lose out on the money. "I wish I could. I'm sorry."

"You were *late*?" He heard the disappointment in her voice.

"You know that romantic comedy you wanted to see? The one called *Pig in a Poke*?"

"*Pig in a Park*," she said, but her voice was lighter now. "Oh, you *are* good. I forgive you."

He laughed, knowing that it wasn't much of a concession. "Thanks for being so understanding."

"I have to go," she said. "I have another call."

"See you tonight. Love you."
"Love you right back."

It had been threatening to rain all day, but held back until Larry was on his way home. The wind blew the sheets of rain sideways and the wipers were barely able to keep up. High water rose on the freeway access roads and some of the underpasses were completely flooded. Several times Larry had to find an alternate route or risk ruining the engine.

Even on streets clear of flood water, the traffic backed up and he found himself sitting through cycle after cycle before he reached the intersection and was given the green light to move ahead. He tried not to feel frustrated, but he was anxious to get home. A nagging voice in the back of his head kept warning him that maybe he'd been wrong to accept Erin's assertions about Valentine's Day. Perhaps she protested a little too much. Perhaps he should have held on to the chocolates and bracelet.

It was close to 10pm before he finally turned into his driveway. The house looked completely dark. Apparently, Erin had given up and gone to bed. He heaved a sigh of relief tinged with sadness. Valentine's Day really didn't hold any special meaning to her. And, now he kind of wished it did. She'd sat by herself watching a romantic comedy and hadn't missed him enough to wait up. He certainly didn't relish going into a dark house and spending the rest of the evening alone in front of the television. Not on Valentine's Day.

He let himself in through the garage door and as soon as he entered the house the thick aroma of roast beef seasoned with garlic and onions surrounded him. There were other fascinating scents as well and while the kitchen, itself, was shrouded in darkness, the soft glow of flickering candlelight emanated from the formal dining room.

He stood in the doorway between the two rooms and took it all in. The dining room table was covered with a black satin table cloth and centered on top, between two red tapered candles, was a bouquet of two dozen red roses.

Place settings of their wedding china, crystal glasses, and silverware were at both ends of the table and the delicious aromas came from silver warming dishes on the sideboard.

His heart sunk. Erin had gone to a lot of trouble for a day she'd sloughed off as an unnecessary expense.

"Larry! You're home!' She grabbed him from behind and slid her arms around his chest. "Isn't it beautiful?"

He turned to face her. She was wearing a black laced peignoir and feathered black satin boudoir slippers with slim, narrow heels. Her auburn hair hung in loose curls around her shoulders, highlighted by the candle flames. He drank in the very sight of her.

She rose up on her toes, wrapped her arms around his neck, and he caught a glimpse of an all too familiar sparkle encircling her right wrist. Her kiss was deep and passionate as she ran her hands through his hair. He got chills when she brought the tips of her fingers down the back of his neck and to the sides of his face.

"Wow!" he said when she released him.

"Now, that's even better than chocolate," she whispered. "You are the most wonderful husband in the world." She smiled shyly and looked down at the bracelet. "I know I told you not to bother with Valentine's Day, but I'm so glad you didn't listen to me!"

"What? How?" He stared at the diamond bracelet then noticed the red heart shaped box on the table right by the bouquet of red roses. He didn't know how he'd missed it earlier.

"Your mom called this afternoon and I'm afraid I complained about you having to stay late. So, right after supper she came by with the bracelet and the chocolates that you'd left with her for safekeeping. She thought it would cheer me up." She gave him another deep, passionate kiss. "Which it did."

"But, the roses?"

"Oh, those are a present from her," Erin giggled. "She called you clueless for forgetting the flowers, but hoped you'd understand and forgive her for stepping in and helping you out this *one* time."

Larry understood completely. He might be a slow learner, but once he caught on he knew he wouldn't make the same mistake again.

A Box of Texas Chocolates

Jadead
by Iona McAvoy

"Mother, these brown lights make The Stonehouse look like some giant dog pooped all over it." Camellia ignored the regal whining from her phone.

"Look, you moved this 'Chocolate Jewels Rule' gala to the Stonehouse at the last minute. I understand, it's not your fault the gallery owner got indicted for insider trading. Whatever." Camellia frowned. "Do I care that your chairwomen gave up their golf games to notify gala guests about the location change? Listen mother, I'm just seriously annoyed that you volunteered The Stonehouse without checking with me first."

Camellia held the oddly shaped lights against the front gable and dismissed them in disgust. She tossed them back into the bin she'd found that morning on her front porch.

"OK fine, so they have some sort of good luck legend, blah blah, blah. I can't believe the Chinese Embassy would ask us to put up lights that look like mutated cow patties. End of discussion. They are ugly, they look like poo, and worst yet Mother, they don't match your dress."

Camellia snapped the phone closed with a sharp goodbye, and a flash of the Italian temper she'd inherited from her grandfather. Leo Nordin, or Papa Leo as folks called him, had spent a lifetime amassing a rock collection and mineral store of international repute. The Stonehouse had been home to Camellia and her brother Phillip when their parents were globe trotting for her father's law firm. After Papa Leo died, it became theirs to own and love.

Congratulating herself that the combination of her laziness and the absence of her brother had allowed the holiday white lights to remain up on the house's gables, Camellia plugged in the switch, sighing in pleasure as they twinkled bright white against the dark trim.

"You know, maybe we'll keep them on all year" she announced. "What do you think Jasper? They'd give you some light when you do your perimeter checks." She looked over to the gate and met the pitiful stare of her hundred pound German Shepherd. He usually got free roam, but remained sequestered for the party. He grunted his displeasure.

"Oh, not you too Jasper. I've had enough whining for today. I don't care how famous those chocolate jade dragons are, Mother will not force those ugly lights on me. Why, I bet you two dog biscuits they're actually meant to attract a trust fund husband. Yuk!"

Jasper barked suddenly, announcing "Intruder Intruder." Turning, Camellia stumbled straight into a muscled chest. She stared up into amused almond shaped eyes as an arm reached out to steady her. Long legs in designer jeans, the guy looked a bit like that tall Houston Rocket's player from China, but with some Brad Pitt thrown in. Camellia usually went for the Johnny Depp type, but her heart still fluttered when he smiled at her.

He shifted the case he held and stuck out his right hand. "I'm Paul Yu. My father's the Chinese Ambassador to Houston. There was an emergency, so he asked me to bring the statues over until his assistant is free to relieve me of guard duty. You must be Camellia Nordin. Your mother's told me about you, and this place."

Camellia shook his hand, grumbling "Please, ignore whatever she said, she's never been fond of The Stonehouse and isn't particularly pleased I'm here. She thinks I should follow her on the charity ball circuit, or pop out grandchildren so she can have bragging rights at her Country Club." Camellia stopped before she could put her foot further into her mouth.

Paul grinned. "Gotcha. Hey, about those lights, I don't remember any trust fund legends. I think they're just supposed to resemble candles used when the Emperor married his princess. The chocolate jade dragons were a wedding gift." He picked up one of the brown light strings, and grimaced. "Whoa, you're right, they *are* seriously ugly."

Camellia chuckled, "Thanks for the vote. Come on in. See if you approve of the display for the statutes." She led him across the massive porch and into the main showroom. It took up most of the front of the house. Stones and fossils filled all the nooks and crannies—heaven to mineral lovers. Between two tables set out for the party, stood the flared column she used for special displays. Standing under a spotlight, it was the prize find from the last field trip she'd taken with her grandfather, a few months before his fatal heart attack. She'd climbed over debris from the old federal building being demolished in Beaumont, pointing out this one massive column with glee.

Paul nodded. "That's totally awesome!" As she told him the history, he took out two large pieces of brown stone and placed them on the column stand. At first glance they were just awkward rectangles of polished brown rock. Then the jade stones actually seemed to melt as she watched. The umber dragons shone with bronzed tipped wings, steadied by short stocky brown legs. Rows of russet pointed teeth gleamed darkly inside their gaping jaws. Camellia's expert eyes took in the green undertone of hazel eyes casting an eerie effect. They were almost identical, carved by the hand of a chosen royal artisan thousands of years ago.

Camellia picked up one of the dragons, tracing the strong jaws and front breast plate. She touched the front teeth, eyes widening as a shock of heat flashed through her finger. Strange, even though she was accustomed to the physical properties stones could create, with varying energy fields and temperatures.

She set the dragon by its mate, trying to hide her surprise.

"So what's the story behind these dragons?" Camellia inspected her finger for burn marks.

"They are symbols of love and protection, presented to…" but before he continued there was a shout from the door. Her helper, Tommy, stood there with his mouth open in dismay.

Tommy pointed at the dragons, "Miss Melli what are those things doing here? I've seen them before, back when me and my wife went to China, during my Navy tour. Miss Melli, them things are killers." He turned his rheumy eyes on her. "We saw them at this museum and my wife, well, she got scared, said they were looking straight at her. Later that night at our hotel, we heard that a museum guard was killed when he tried to steal them. They said the dragons done killed him. There was blood everywhere, even on the statues." Tommy coughed. "This one fella told us that they were cursed. Please, you've gotta get them out of here."

Camellia took Tommy's arm and led him into the hall. "Now Tommy, I bet those aren't even the same dragons you saw." she lowered her voice "They have a lot of dragons over there you know. And didn't Papa Leo tell you about the stories folks make up, just to protect things like those dragons from thieves? I bet the police killed the thief, and then spread that rumor to keep other robbers away."

But Tommy refused to agree, shaking his head. "No Miss Melli, them are cursed dragons and really bad."

Camellia sought a diversion. "Hey do you smell that? Jim Benton is catering this event for mother, and I think he's made chocolate fudge cupcakes, yum, I know you like them." Tommy looked to the kitchen, where the caterer to Houston's elite stood prepping. Tommy licked his lips at the smells wafting down the hall. "Yeah I guess I could see if Mr. Jim needs my help. But Miss Melli, you gotta get rid of them statues. You just gotta." Camellia watched him shuffle to the kitchen, and then turned back to the showroom.

Paul Yu stood at one of the jewelry displays, not meeting her eyes.

"Sorry about that. Tommy's getting old, but he's like family and I promised Papa Leo we'd look after him."

Paul hesitated, "Yeah, um. Listen, you should probably know, some of what he said is true. There's a legend about the chocolate jade dragons. If anyone tries to steal them, they are doomed, usually ending up dead. I know it's crazy, but that's the emergency my Dad's working on. The dragons were flown over a couple of days ago, and one of the crew members arrived really sick. They took her to the hospital, but she died within a couple of hours."

Camellia gasped "You're kidding right?"

Paul shook his head. "Nope. At first they thought it was food poisoning, but since everyone ate the same things on the plane, and no one else got sick, well, the staff started talking about the dragons being cursed." He shook his head again. "It gets worse. They went through her things to see if there was anything to explain her illness. Get this, they found a note she'd written. She was going to steal the dragons and meet up with someone to ransom them off. Between keeping the rumors, and her death, below the media radar, my Dad's been going nuts. He doesn't want to ruin your mother's party, or freak out the Houston business community. He's got some intense negotiations going on right now."

Camellia walked around the display. Tommy was right, the dragons did stare straight at her. She shook off her doubts, just a trick of a skilled artisan.

"No worries, tons of rocks have similar legends, it doesn't mean anything. I'm sure your Dad will get things handled." She noticed him holding a dainty pendant. "Hey, I see you found one of the pieces for tonight's party. It will definitely make any girl happy." Camellia sighed. The thought of some girl in his life sure wasn't making her happy though.

"What, oh no, I mean, the girl is my mother, I thought she'd like this for her outfit tonight. Any chance I can buy it now?"

Camellia smiled in relief, "Of course! The mahogany obsidian is not only for strength and protection, it looks like dark and milk chocolate swirled together, good enough to eat."

She laughed as she wrapped the pendant for him, "You do realize that all this hoopla is just an excuse for my mother, and her closest three hundred friends, to show off the latest fashion, share spa secrets, and make sure they get jewelry for Valentine's Day? But since thirty percent of the profits goes to our favorite animal charity, it's all good. Still, with my brother out of town, I'm slammed here."

Paul laughed, "I know that one. How do you think I got drafted to be here instead of at the gym? I'm glad now though, I mean, it's been wonderful to meet you. You'll be here tonight, won't you?"

She rolled her eyes, "Oh please. You don't think Mother would allow me to escape when she has the chance to make me an indentured servant?" Just then a dark suited man entered the shop.

"Looks like my relief is here. Chocolate jade is rare, but the legend makes them appealing to thrill seekers. I'm going to get in a short run before my father realizes I'm free. See ya in a few." Taking his purchase, he grinned at her as he left.

Camellia sighed, and then gave herself a mental slap. *Focus here girl, he's just a man, a tall, charming, good looking one, but you know your luck with handsome men. As in none.* She set to work, putting out the rest of the brown quartz and stone art she'd volunteered for the show. Maybe calling brown stones "chocolate" was a marketing gimmick, but she remembered how brown jade was also a favorite of the Aztecs. And, wasn't one of her favorite treats Aztec Fantasy? Hey, if it helped the gala's charity, the animal shelter, she was on board. Camellia mused that animal welfare was one of the few passions she and her mother shared. It certainly wasn't a love of overpriced shoes, with five inch killer heels.

Almost done, Camellia giggled as she filled a crystal bowl with the round "chocolate marbles" she discovered from an Arizona mine. She couldn't help herself, the round stones were actually mud balls, frozen in time by hot lava. Just tiny balls of fun. Their happy energy guaranteed good revenues for the gala. Only when she glanced at the dragons did Camellia feel unsettled. She told herself it was just the lighting that made their teeth bloodstained daggers, not Tommy's warnings.

Her cell phone vibrated, startling her. Her grandmother, 81 and vibrant, boomed, "Where is your brother? I left him a message to come get me, but he never returned my calls. I had to find my own way over to help with your Mother's latest extravaganza. Luckily, I found a ride with that nice widower, Pierre. You tell Phillip I am not happy with him."

"Go easy on him Nonna," Camellia managed to cut in. "He's hiding from Mother. She keeps trying to get him back with Sandra, even after the bimbette dumped him for that new partner in Daddy's law firm. Phillip probably couldn't get through to you on his cell phone, it was pretty choppy when I talked to him earlier this morning. His flight back from Colorado got delayed by a snow storm, but he's promised to make it back before the party."

"I guess. Tell me Camellia, what do your brother and mother see in that Sandra? How can he sleep next to someone who's puffed up like Barbie on steroids? And, aren't they worried she'll just start leaking one day? Your mother only likes her daddy's oil money and, oh, there's the bell. Pierre is here." She hung up without giving Camellia a chance to say goodbye.

Chuckling at her Nonna's spunk, she gave the room a final check and ran upstairs. She showered then slipped into the designer dress her mother had sent with orders to "wear it, or else." Her mother's approval rating did not extend to Camellia's closet, full of work boots, cargo pants, and rock tools. Clearly her mother had traded any maternal instincts for fashion savvy. Still, she loved how the rich brown velvet fit her curves, and for once the neckline did not shout "For Sale." Her mother must have been distracted when she picked it out. Tonight, Camellia didn't feel the need for a shawl to cover up her "assets".

Camellia pulled strands of her dark, curly hair back with jeweled combs, and went downstairs. As she doled out Jasper's doggie dinner, Camellia denied that the extra spritz of perfume had anything to do with Paul Yu. Jasper sneezed in her face as his response. With no word from her brother, she reluctantly braved the maternal onslaught alone, and trudged to the front room.

Yep, the troops had arrived. At the helm, her mother floated into the room, brown silk sculpting her size zero body. She gave Camellia the usual inspection, but before she could start her criticism, one of the chairwomen waylaid her with a problem.

On her pricey heels, towered the dreaded Sandra. Tall, thin, blonde. Pretty much everything Camellia wasn't. A part-time paralegal at her father's firm, due mostly to her daddy's oil wells, Sandra had managed to worm her way into Camellia's family. Carrying more plastic inside her body than in her credit cards, she'd even stayed in favor after she dumped Phillip, for an odious lawyer in her dad's firm, Kirkland Smith. It annoyed Camellia that Sandra was more her Mother's daughter than she, but before she could analyze that thought, something even more annoying distracted her.

"Now how the heck did those get there?" Somehow the ugly brown lights were now draped on both serving tables, dully twinkling. She was about to remove them when Sandra marched up to her, seriously violating every law of personal space known to mankind.

"Camellia, how are you darling? I suppose you've heard Phillip and I are officially over haven't you?" Sandra waved her left hand insuring Camellia, and everyone in the room, could see the bling on her ring finger. Camellia had to duck the huge rock, as Sandra included the entire room in her beauty pageant wave.

Camellia raised an eyebrow at her. "So, you finally took Mr. Elmhurst's offer? You'll be what? Trophy wife number ten?" Camellia referred to an ancient client of her father's who'd gone through nine decades and as many wives.

Sandra sputtered, "Ewww, of course not! I'm engaged to

Kirkland!" She nodded at the beefy man stuffed into his tuxedo, talking to Camellia's father. Camellia wondered if Sandra's ring was as fake as Kirkland. Where was her jeweler's loupe when she needed it?

"Ewww is right" thought Camellia. Kirkland Smith, just before he was up for partner, had suggested he and Camellia hook up but "solely to enhance his career." He insisted that he would live his own life. Her purpose—to guarantee social clout by bearing his children. Camellia refused his offer, delivering a tirade that instructed him where to put his "let's make a deal" proposal. He'd just shrugged and moved on to another society victim, Phillip's girlfriend Sandra. That it broke Phillip's heart or infuriated their father, his boss, meant nothing to Kirkland Smith.

"Well good for you Sandy. I'm sure you are perfect together." She tried to wave at Paul Yu as he walked in, looking ever so hunky in his tuxedo. She turned to go to say hi, when nails dug into her arm.

"Wait, have you heard from Phillip?" Sandra pulled at Camellia. "I thought he'd be here by now. Your mother said that his plane had landed, and he was driving in from the airport."

Camellia rubbed her arm, just then noticing Sandra's chipmunk cheeks. "Mother is the ultimate source of news Sandra, you know that. I thought he'd be here by now." Between pondering Sandra's cheek implants, and the background noise, she missed hearing the ring tone identifying her brother's call, 'Rock Around the Clock'.

Sandra snatched the cell from her hand, "Why hello Phillip dear, why aren't you here yet? I have a surprise. No, if you are that close, it can wait. Oh I will just tell you, Kirkland and I are engaged! What did you say?" One of her fake nails hit the phone's speaker button and suddenly the entire room could hear Phillip screaming at her.

"You what? You idiot! I thought you wanted me back. Last night you said you were leaving him, and today you're engaged to that jerk? I've seen the bruises Sandra, he hit you. You promised to file charges. You make no sense, he's bad news." The room fell silent, everyone frozen in place. Camellia tried grabbing her phone back, but Socialite Barbie kept it just out of her reach.

"But Phillip, darling..."

"Don't darling me Sandra, I've been in an airport or on a plane all day just to get back to mother's party, and to help you. Now you tell me you're engaged to Kirkland? Do you know what you're doing? He only wants you for your trust fund. I'm five minutes away, don't do anything until I get there, you hear? No way will you be marrying him, I'll kill him first." Phillip hung up after a series of expletives.

Sporting a satisfied smile Sandra clicked the phone closed and handed it back. She sashayed over to her fiancée, enjoying the limelight. Despite knowing her as she did, Camellia could not fathom how Sandra could give up her brother for someone as sleazy as Kirkland Smith.

Sandra got her own back as Smith grabbed her arm, whispering angrily. He ignored her tears, pushing her away, and slamming out the side door. Sandra rushed outside after him, nearly knocking over the harpist on the way out.

Camellia's mother broke the moment, giving a sharp clap, snapping everyone back to reality, and back to preparing for the party. She marched over to Camellia, her grimace as frozen as the stone dragons. "What do you know about this Camellia? Your father mentioned some trouble at the firm and now this embarrassment. I will not allow these shenanigans to ruin my gala."

Even a mountain of happy chocolate marbles couldn't stop Camellia's temper from flaring. Matching her mother's snide whisper, she said, "You know what Mother, I have no clue, none, niente, zippo. I work here, and do not keep tabs on the Nordin psychodramas. If you hadn't insisted on pushing that botoxed bimbo back on Phillip, he'd have moved on to a girl with real body parts. But not my mother, total control freak. Tell me, aren't you just a little afraid your grandchildren will be born with Mick Jagger lips?" She stormed out to the front porch where a cool breeze greeted her. As she sank into a wicker chair she realized Paul had followed her out. He watched her, chuckling.

"I've always heard about Italian tempers, but dang girl, remind me to never get on your bad side!"

"Yeah, but I can't manage to stay mad, that's my real problem. People just get to irritate me, again and again and, well, you get the picture. I need to work on that, I guess." Camellia wrapped her arms around herself and shivered as the air turned suddenly cold. The porch lights dimmed.

"Wait, do you hear something?" An eerie shriek shook the very stones of the house—terrifying screeches carried by the force of a bitter north wind.

"That almost sounds like a hawk or eagle, but no way, not here in the Heights?" They both listened as screams scrambled through the night, and Jasper howled. The sharp slam of a car door startled Camellia. The wind stopped as suddenly as it started. The air became heavy, as if they were in the eye of a hurricane, the calm only momentary.

Before either of them could move, her brother Phillip stood on the porch. He stared blankly at Camellia, as he held one of the chocolate jade dragons, blood dripping from its teeth.

Phillip looked down at the dragon in shock. He mumbled, "I think he's dead!"

Paul found Kirkland lying on the driveway, still breathing, but blood spilled everywhere. Paul called 911 while Camellia sent Phillip into the house to find their father. Soon red and blue lights flashed. Paramedics loaded Kirkland into the ambulance, while HPD's Sgt. Timmons took down names. A canine team searched the area, frustrating Jasper who wanted in on the action.

Despite the brass at the scene, Camellia's mother took control of the chaos. She ordered everyone back to their assignments, and then commandeered Camellia's office for Sgt. Timmons and his team. She even provided them cappuccino and truffles. No donuts allowed at *her* gala.

The party was now in full force. Gossip flowed, insinuating

that the police were actually security for a possible visit by Number 41, code for the former President and Houston resident. Chocolate martinis kept pace with the jewelry sales. Camellia shook her head as she watched the money flow for the charity. Her mother either had real talent, or was one powerful witch. Not everyone could turn a potential disaster into such a success. Still, the attack on Kirkland worried her. She wondered how the dragon got outside and what made that terrifying shriek? She saw Paul staring out a window, watching the police search the driveway.

She touched his arm, "Hey, any idea how the dragon statue got past your guard?"

"No, my father's asking the same question. Our guard says the dragons were never out of his sight, but suddenly there was only one on the column, and I believe him."

He glanced at the solitary dragon on display. "Have you heard anything about Smith's condition?"

"Nothing yet. I'm terrified for my brother. Some thirty people heard him threaten to kill Kirkland. It's bad if he dies, and if he lives, he'll probably sue us all. He's such a jerk."

Paul gave a slight smile, "Tell you what, I'll go check with my father, see if he's had word from the Embassy. Maybe you can talk to that ditzy blond. Find out what happened?"

Camellia agreed, pleased they shared distaste for Sandra. She found her in the bathroom, hands shaking as she tried to apply lip gloss. In the light, bruises shined on her cheeks, tears having washed away any masking cover. "Whoa, Sandra. Kirkland really did hit you?"

"What? Oh it's just you. Yeah, I bet you're thrilled aren't you? I know you detest me," Sandra snapped, tears trickling down her face. "You should hate me for being so horrid to Phillip on the phone. I was just trying to make Kirkland jealous. He came in tonight in an obnoxious mood, hinting he was going to call off our engagement. And I'd just gotten my ring! We argued outside and it was nasty. He bragged he'd found someone else, someone richer and more 'real', whatever that means." She shrugged.

"Then what happened Sandra, who hit Kirkland?"

"Oh I don't know. I was trying to find out about this woman he was seeing, but Camellia, she's just some tramp, some common stewardess he met on a trip to China. He said she'd done something spectacular, something that would make him even richer than my Daddy." She paused. "Then there was this awful screeching. It hurt my ears. Kirkland fell to the ground and that dreadful dragon lay by his head. My life is ruined, I may never get married."

Camellia bit back a sarcastic comment. "Get a hold of yourself Sandra, this isn't all about you. Was Kirkland on the ground before or after you heard Phillip's car?"

Sandra wailed, "How should I know? I'd drunk two chocolate martinis by then, besides, I had more important things on my mind."

Camellia thought "Seriously, what mind?" She left Sandra to mourn the demise of her engagement, only to bump into her mother outside the door.

"Shouldn't you be selling jewelry for the charity, instead of gossiping with Sandra?"

"Oh don't even go there mother. If it weren't for you and your silly Chocolate Jewels Rule party, none of this would have happened!" Camellia fought back tears.

Her mother frowned. "You don't get it do you? It's not just about this one charity. It's how we spread the donations amongst all the needy in Houston. We have to make it fun, Camellia, not every wealthy person is naturally altruistic. Some need to be entertained into donating." her mother pushed one of Camellia's curls behind her ear, almost tenderly. "Plus we help a lot of businesses, and keep people employed. It may seem like fluff to you, but money flows both to charities and to the local economy." Camellia begrudgingly accepted her mother's words, acknowledging that many hospital wings were built over champagne fountains. "I do see your point, but Mother, what about Phillip? He could be in serious trouble."

"I know. Go talk to your father, he's in the kitchen with Ambassador Yu. Maybe they can give you answers." Ignoring Camellia's puzzled look, she greeted Judge Nile Copeland with a smile and went to introduce him to the Ambassador's wife. Camellia wandered back to the kitchen. Sure enough, the Ambassador and her father sat talking, while Paul paced the room.

"Did you learn anything Camellia?" Paul asked.

The older Yu looked at Camellia with interest. "Ah, the young lady my son told me about."

Camellia answered Paul, "Sandra doesn't know anything that isn't about her. She babbled something about Kirkland calling off the engagement and leaving her for some stewardess that was... Oh wait, Paul, didn't a crew member, from the plane bringing the statues from China, die? Could there be a connection?"

Ambassador Yu interrupted, "Lovely and smart. May I enlighten you dear?" Camellia nodded.

"Special treasures have been stolen in the last few years. Not ordinary art pieces, just those with some sort of curse. The thefts are always timed to coincide with major international business deals, making any bad publicity a possible jinx." He took a sip of brandy and continued.

"The FBI was alerted to large fund transfers made by Mr. Smith. They contacted your father's law firm, when they discovered that Kirkland was using the firm's international business as a cover. He'd locate these special artifacts, such as the chocolate jade dragons, when the firm was negotiating important deals between countries. Then he'd arrange to ransom the statues back for a very hefty price."

Paul interrupted "But, how did the stewardess get involved?"

"It seems they met when Smith first started traveling for the firm. Her father was an art thief that died in prison. She convinced Kirkland to help her take over the family trade, and he came up with this clever plan. They knew that the countries would want to avoid the authorities and the press, given the sensitive business transactions."

Before Camellia could digest the Ambassador's explanation, Sgt. Timmons marched in and looked at her father.

"Mr. Nordin, I've got bad news. Your law partner is not going to be rejoining you at the firm."

"Oh my gosh, is he dead?" Camellia cried out. Paul moved to her side, putting his arm around her shoulders.

"No ma'am, he's fine. He's hurting, but he'll live. The problem is, he's been arrested. Between the art thefts and other illegal activities, Mr. Smith is going to be occupied answering a lot of questions. It seems that he has made some enemies, here and abroad."

"Yes, but who hit him?"

"We don't know, it is really strange. We've taken everyone's statements. Mr. Smith's fiancée was no help, she just babbled. The guard didn't see anyone move the statue, he says it just disappeared right in front of his eyes. Your helper, Tommy, was watching Sandra and Kirkland arguing from the back shed. He says he saw the statue come flying out, straight at Kirkland's head. He swears Phillip drove up after that happened. Our canine team couldn't find any scent either." Sgt. Timmons stared down at his notes.

"But here's the clincher, Kirkland himself keeps swearing that the dragon flew at him out of nowhere. Said it was screaming curses at him. He says your brother driving up saved his life. He's begged us to protect him, to keep him in jail where the dragons can't get him. I tell you, that's one freaked out man."

Camellia and Paul followed him out of the kitchen. The party was winding down. They were startled to see both statues back together, on the column. Even more startling, they no longer glared. Instead, the swirls of chocolate jade blended together, glowing from the brown lights still on the tables.

"This is one of the strangest nights in my life. You probably think my father's crazy to believe in the curse of the chocolate jade dragons. Until tonight I doubted his sanity on this one. I figured the curses were as real as those news stories about three headed aliens running the stock market. Now, I'm not sure what to believe."

Camellia stopped him. "Paul, really, it's fine. I'm used to weirdness, remember, I grew up in a superstitious Italian family. The curses that come with some of the stones would curl even the dragon's toes."

"Seriously? That rocks. I mean, well, you know what I mean." Paul hesitated, "So is there any chance you'd catch a movie with me this weekend? As long you promise none of those rocks will turn me into a frog."

Camellia grinned, "Sounds like a plan, but only if *you* promise to take back those ugly brown lights." Laughing they went to see if any chocolate martinis remained.

Neither of them saw her mother smiling at them from the hall. Nor could they see the string of brown lights she held—images of the candles fabled to have lit a path guiding the Emperor to his one and only true love.

Stones aren't the only treasures with legends.

Deep in the Heart of Texas
by Autumn Storm

The embers of his hand-rolled cigarette glowed bright as he stood in the shadows and watched. The smoke, layer upon layer, lingered and then dissipated into the night air. He inhaled the last little bit of his cigarette, dropped the burning butt to the ground, and extinguished it with his shoe.

He had watched her every move. He knew where she lived, what time she went to work and what time she returned home each night. He knew where she shopped and what she had eaten for dinner the night before.

This had been a long time in coming and he sensed his time was drawing nigh. He'd make her pay and if everything went his way, he'd make her pay big, because everyone knew, revenge was a dish best served cold.

Stepping outside *The Chocolate Cove* as she did every day about this time, Megan took a moment to relax, stretch her legs and appreciate all of the movement around her. Late afternoon, and many of the chic little shops along the Kemah boardwalk were closing for the day. This was what her friends called the *transition twilight*, a small period of time when the day ended and the night came out to play; a time to be one within the two worlds.

For Megan, it meant beauty beyond words, and her favorite time of day. Brilliant red streaks filled the sky as the sun descended towards the bay and kissed the water's edge. For one brief moment, Megan smiled and allowed the memory of her father to enter her thoughts. They had stood in this very spot, just before the wedding, watching the sun go down and the boats drift by.

She took a deep breath, filled her lungs with air, and held it for a moment then felt the tiredness and pent up tension of the last few days leave her body as she released it. The museum opening in Chocolate Bayou was fast approaching and while it had already been a long grueling week, she knew the worst was yet to come.

Outside her door stood a statue of the pirate Jean Lafitte; giving him a quick little wink, she walked back inside repeating the ditty her father had taught her so many years before.

Red sky at night, a sailor's delight. Red sky in the morning, sailors take warning.

Megan glanced at the clock on the wall. She had a customer coming in late, still more than an hour away. At her desk, she turned up her stereo and sang along as Jimmy Buffett talked about finding his lost shaker of salt. One of her favorite singers, she found it easy to relate to the songs he sang, but the truth was, the only thing she worried about right now, was losing time. Megan opened her daily planner, her eyes drifting down her overwhelming list of things to do. She appreciated the value of her list; it was the backbone of her day and the one thing that she contributed to her success. She flipped the page and prioritized the events scheduled for the next day. Once she completed her list, she set about gathering the supplies for the morning's body casting project: strips of casting material pre-cut and ready to use, saran wrap for the hair, her long sleeve black unitard, petroleum jelly, a bowl for cold water and plastic sheeting for the floor and tables. With the project set up and ready to go, Megan took a deep breath and thought to herself—ahh breathing—and added straws to the stack.

The familiar sound of the bell ringing above the door told her that someone had arrived. She pulled aside the red and black striped curtain that separated the workroom from the shop, and collided with her best friend, Sarah.

"I should have known I'd find you here! I thought we were

meeting for drinks—I swear Megan, you need to get a life."

With a wave of her hand she replied laughing. "I have a life—there's this and in a couple of weeks I'll have the museum and the amusement park as well."

Sarah let loose with an exasperated sigh. "Megan! You know that's not what I was talking about."

"Yeah, I know, but I'll have to wait until both of these projects are off the ground before I can think of anything else."

Sarah reached out and gave her a hug. "While I might agree with that right now, it's been almost two years, and it's time to put the death of Scott and your parents to rest. You're my best friend Megan, and I worry about you."

Megan felt the makings of a tear form and quickly brushed it away. "I'll make a deal with you. Let me finish getting some things ready for tomorrow and as soon as Ron comes in for his anniversary cake we'll leave and go have a couple of drinks at the Cadillac Bar."

Megan removed two Dr Pepper's from the refrigerator and handed one to her friend. "Here, make yourself comfortable and I'll join you in a minute. If you want something to read while we're waiting, I think there's a newspaper somewhere on my desk."

Once she knew that Sarah had the Houston Chronicle, Megan continued on to the second item on her list and began her prep. No sooner had Sarah picked up the paper when Megan heard her give an audible gasp.

"Oh, my God—Megan—the headlines; *Missing Woman's Mutilated Body Found in Chocolate Bayou.*" Before Megan had a chance to respond, her movements caught Sarah's eye and she glanced up from the paper. "What on earth are you doing with all those body parts?"

Megan laughed. "These, my dear friend, are the makings of my chocolate people. This will be like working on a life size puzzle, only better, because once they are reassembled and covered with gesso; we'll dip them in the chocolate and then move them into position at the museum."

"And pray tell, where did you find anyone who wanted to be immortalized in chocolate?"

"It's amazing Sarah what you can find when you do a search on the Internet."

"You ran an ad on your blog? I bet that posting had all the tweeters twittering."

Megan, now sitting cross-legged on the floor, laughed at her friend's inexperience with the computer. "No—in all sincerity, I got a local Girl Scout troop working on their art badge and a few of their families to come in and pose for me. The whole body casting experience went pretty smooth, but I'm sure that's because Matt and a couple of his friends came in to help."

"Matt? Now there's a name I haven't heard in a while. Who called who?"

"I called him, but before you get any wild and crazy ideas—he came in to help with the body casting project and nothing more."

"Yeah, yeah—I hear you sister, but I predict, by the time this is all said and done, you two will be dating again."

Megan sighed. "Sarah, you're just a hopeless romantic. I wouldn't say one date classified us as dating, and I know for a fact, that I won't be going out with him again any time soon. I called him because of his expertise. I know lots of people that have done the body casting thing, but Matt is the only one I know that has actually studied under the master, George Segal."

"Well I've seen you do some pretty amazing things in the past, but the only word that comes to mind right now is freaky. You hear me Megan…freaky!" Sarah started singing the theme from the Twilight Zone.

"You need to stop. There's nothing freaky about my people here, they're just unique. Now if you really want to see something that will give you the willies, go take a look at all the masks I finished yesterday. Even I'm surprised at how real they look and I could have sworn they were whispering to me last night."

The bell above the door rang again. "That'll be Ron—be right back."

"Hey Megan, sorry I'm late. I ran a little late getting to the restaurant and then had a hard time breaking away from the boys."

"No problem Ron. I know this is a really big night for you and I can't think of a better night to celebrate your retirement from HPD than on your wedding anniversary? Have you given Sharon her surprise yet?"

"No, I thought I would wait until I had the cake in place and then wow her with that and the tickets to Paris."

Megan reached for two boxes on the back counter and put them down in front of Ron. "Since you pretty much gave me free reign on the cake, I took the liberties of designing you a very unique topper and nothing says Paris like the Eiffel Tower. I wanted it to be completely edible, so I used a waffle cone base and double dipped it in chocolate."

"That's what makes your shop so special Megan. You put thought into your designs, and everything you do comes straight from the heart."

Megan placed her hand on Ron's arm. "Springtime in Paris; I can't think of a better place to celebrate twenty-five years of marriage. A marvelous trip, an elegant dinner at the restaurant La Tour d'Argent on the river Seine; what on earth are you going to do for your fiftieth?"

"Well speaking of romance—Sharon has invited a guy from work and wants the two of you to meet. She tells me he's a really nice guy, smart as a whip and like you, he's just fun to be around."

"A blind date—has she lost her mind? I'll meet her half way on this one, but I've never been crazy about any of my friends setting me up. I'm just guessing—but I have a sinking feeling, that words like, really nice, smart, and fun to be with, are the code words for an ugly duckling. Am I right?"

"I don't know Megan. I'm a guy and that's not my area of expertise, but I do know if we don't get back to the party, they'll do what detectives do best, and come looking for us."

"Give me a minute and we'll be all set to go. I just need to make sure the back door is secured, grab my purse, and get Sarah."

Megan, with Ron not far behind, started towards the back of the shop. She pulled the curtains back, and Sarah waved her over. "Megan, come see! I thought you were just being funny a little while ago, but listen—they *are* whispering—I can hear them."

Megan nudged her friend as Ron looked over their shoulder to see what they were talking about. He touched one of the masks. "Megan, these are really good, so lifelike, but what are they for?"

"I'm working on a wall in the museum that highlights all the people that have influenced the growth of Texas. I'm hoping to include everyone from the First Lady to the pirate Jean Lafitte."

"And what does a pirate have to do with Texas?" Sarah asked.

"Well, if memory serves me right—he smuggled in slaves for Jim Bowie and Stephen F. Austin, both of which are here."

Pointing to another one of the masks on her worktable, Ron continued. "Now I can't say that I recognize this one. Who is she?"

"Let's see—that would be Emily Perry. She was the sister of Stephen F. Austin and she was instrumental in developing the colonies around Chocolate Bayou."

Sarah picked one up from the back of the table. "I may not have been able to guess the others, but this has to be Scott."

Taking the mask from her friend's hand, Megan threw it in the trash. "It is—or I guess I should say it was supposed to be. It was perfect up to a point, and then it was like it took on a life of its own. No matter what I did, I just couldn't seem to get it right."

Megan cleared her throat. "Hey guys, I think it's margarita time."

The music of the Cadillac Bar and the laughter of the crowd called to her. Built in the fashion of a Mexican adobe, its casual enviroment said—come—stay—relax—have a good time— and a quick calculation in her mind told her that it had been well over a year since she had enjoyed a real night out. Megan reached for the cake and headed towards the elevator. "How about I drop these off in the kitchen, get us a couple of drinks, and I'll meet up with you downstairs on the broadwalk level." Pointing to Sarah, Megan continued. "Find us a good table by the water and I'll be there shortly."

Megan approached the bar and studied the liquor bottles that lined the wall. She was in the mood for something different instead of the usual beer she had every now and then. She leaned against the laquered wood bar; smooth and cool to her touch, smiling as the bartenter approached.

"What'll you have hon?"

Megan made her decision. "I'll have a Kamikaze and two Patron Margaritas on the rocks; one with salt and one without."

Since she had decided to loosen up a little bit, the Kamikaze was a total impulse and she downed it in one fluid move.

"Megan? Megan Montgomery? I just can't believe my eyes."

With her empty glass in mid air, Megan froze. She'd recognize that voice anywhere, and on some occasions in the past, she had even yearned for it. Megan placed her glass on the bar and spun around, a huge smile bursting across her face. "Phillip? Oh my God—what are you doing here?"

Without even thinking, she threw her arms around him, pulled him close and held on like there was no tomorrow. Megan pulled back to get a better look and then hugged him again.

"Way to go Megan! We've been looking all over for you and here you are picking up strange men at the bar—and to think, we were worried about you." Sarah turned to Ron and wrapped her arm around his. "I'd say your instincts were way off—I don't think we're needed here after all."

"No wait! I can explain. This is an old friend of mine. In fact

I guess you could say we were high school sweethearts."

Sarah grinned. "And would this be the cousin of the boy next door?"

Phillip raised his hand and waved. "Guilty—that's me. We drifted apart and lost touch after my Aunt died and Megan went away to college."

Ron patted Megan on the back and extended his hand to Phillip. "It's good to see you again. I've been hearing some pretty good things from Sharon, so I guess this means you're all settled in. Now if you will excuse me, I really need to get back to my lovely bride and mingle or we may have a homicide investigation on our hands."

Megan winked at Ron and smiled. "Tell Sharon I'll come see her in a bit and if you will, let her know she got lucky *this* time."

Megan, bubbling over with excitement, took Phillip's hand. "Come on, let's find a table outside and talk; you can fill me in on what's been happening."

"What about your friend Sarah?"

"She'll find us when she ready—right now she's making the rounds."

Megan leaned across the table. "You haven't changed a bit; you are just as I remember."

"Wish I could say the same Megan." Taken aback by her look of surprise, Phillip added. "Well take a good look at yourself—you're all grown up now and you've traded in your shorts and halter tops for blue jeans and boots. Never in my wildest dreams did I ever picture you as a country girl."

With each passing minute, Megan felt the chains of her self-imposed confinement breaking away. It had been a long time since she relaxed and let down her guard. Might've been the drinks, but Megan believed it was just being in the company of a man—a long lost friend—with no hidden agendas.

"You never answered my question Phillip. You're a long ways from Georgia, so what are you doing in Houston?"

"It's work. An associate made me an offer I couldn't refuse; managing editor for the media company Sharon owns. It's giving me the opportunity to work in a lot of different areas so I'm pretty excited about my new job and talk about a promotion; it was a good jump in pay as well. I'm in charge of all the editorial pieces and photography that comes through my office. I have an interview on Tuesday and if you can get away I'd like for you to come with me. It should be a lot of fun. They're opening a new museum in a place called Chocolate Bayou and if my notes are correct, the owner, Megan Hunt, is filling it with chocolate people."

"No kidding? That's me!"

"Of course, how could I have been so dense? Nothing is ever as simple as it seems and here I was just thanking the cosmic Gods for bringing us back together."

She smiled. "I've been a widow for almost two years now and yes I would like to think that fate had a hand in all of this."

Once Megan got the attention of the waitress, she ordered a second round of drinks.

Eager to fill in the gaps of their lives, Phillip said, "Tell me about this husband of yours."

"There's not much to tell. We dated a couple of years during college and then decided to tie the knot. We were married less than a week when he was hit by a drunk driver going the wrong way on the Hardy Toll Road."

"I'm so sorry Megan. I didn't mean to be so insensitive. You had already mentioned you were a widow. I should have left it at that. Let's talk about something else. How are your parents. Are they still living in Florida?"

Megan struggled to maintain her composure as she jumped up from the table. Going to the boardwalk railing she faced the water.

Phillip walked up behind her and placed his hand flat against the back of her waist. "Megan? Are you okay?"

Tears welled up and spilled over onto her cheek, her voice cracking as she wept. "They died in the crash with Scott."

Warmth and compassion radiated through his hands as he took her in his arms. "Oh God Megan—talk about jumping out of the frying pan and into the fire. I can't imagine what you must have gone through, losing both your parents and your husband in the same crash. I drove through Pensacola on my way out here to see David, but the only thing he was able to tell me was that your parent's house had been sold. I had no idea Megan, or I wouldn't have brought it up."

She turned, wrapping her arms around his waist. He pulled her closer, guiding her head to his chest. She had forgotten how good it felt. "How could you have known, Phillip? We haven't seen each other in years." She sighed and continued, "I passed out a couple of days before the wedding, and wrote it off as pre-wedding fatigue. Scott insisted that I lay down to get some rest, but I had so much to do, it was like telling Santa to hold off on Christmas for a couple days. For a while, everything seemed to be okay, but then it happened again during the reception. Never could pinpoint any one thing, but Mom was afraid it was a relapse of the mono I had in college. They stayed a few extra days to make sure everything was okay, and they were on their way to the airport when they got killed."

Megan, struggling to keep her emotions at bay, pushed away from Phillip and walked back to their table. Picking up her glass, she swirled the light green liquid and downed the last little bit in one gulp.

"Megan, I'm sorry. Take a walk with me, show me the sights and maybe ride a few rides."

"Okay—but I need to let my friends know I'm leaving."

Megan looked for and found her friends. After telling them good night and sharing a few hugs, she and Phillip walked out of the restaurant, past the fountain and into the heartbeat of the waterfront community.

"How long have you known Ron and Sharon?" Phillip asked.

"I know it's hard to believe, but I have only known them for a couple of years. Ron was the lead investigator on Scott's accident, and Sharon helped me through a really tough time. I don't think I would have made it without her. Now they are like my adoptive parents."

"Sharon was telling me that Ron has worked for the HPD going on thirty years."

Megan nodded her head. "Yeah and as soon as they get back from Paris, he will be working for me. He's coming in, setting up and running my entire security department."

Much of the easy going banter had returned by the time they made their way to the amusement park. Feeling better, they stopped for an ice cream cone and then headed for the rides. As they approached the carousel Phillip told Megan. "If you will ride that fine looking stead over there, then I will take the white one over here and we can pretend."

"Oh in other words, I am going to be the damsel in distress and you are going to be my knight in shining armor, eh?"

Laughing, Phillip pretended to remove his hat. With a big sweeping gesture of his hand, he bowed and replied, "Prince Charming at ye service, m'lady."

By the time they rode the Boardwalk Bullet and the Pharaoh's Fury, Megan was ready for something a little quieter. They stood in line and then waited as the Ferris wheel handler filled all of his empty seats. A cool breeze blew in from the bay forcing her to raise her hand and brush hair away from her face. "You know at one time this little community used to be called Evergreen, but they were forced to change their name when they applied for a post office. After some consideration they took an Indian word that meant *wind in face* and that's how Kemah got its name."

"Oh really—that's interesting."

"I could tell you had something on your mind and I'm sure that was one of the things you were just dying to know."

"As a matter of fact Megan, I was just sitting up here thinking how beautiful you are, right now at this very moment."

Megan blushed as she gazed into his eyes and he into hers.

For one brief moment, time stood still. A current of electricity passed between them, transporting them back to the days of their youth and back to a time when their love was new.

"This makes me think of the swing in your Aunt's backyard."

"You're right it does. Know what else this reminds me of?"

Megan thought a minute and replied, "No—what?"

Phillip grinned, "Our first kiss." Placing his arm around her shoulder, he pulled her close. He nuzzled her ear and when his lips touched hers, passion burned within. The familiarity of his kiss left her wanting more, and she had not felt that in a very long time. Megan closed her eyes, savoring the moment, wanting to remember it all.

The Ferris wheel jerked back into motion, pulling them back to the present. With the moment gone Megan forced herself to look away from Phillip's gorgeous blue eyes.

The walk from the amusement park to the Chocolate Cove was relaxing and filled with easy going conversation. The tension Megan felt earlier had dissipated and she enjoyed the company of her childhood sweetheart.

"I've been wondering—why build a chocolate museum, Megan?"

"Why not?" She laughed. "I wanted something that people could relate to, something that was fun and interactive for the kids and besides, who in their right mind doesn't like chocolate? Did you know that at one time the cocoa bean was so valuable that people used them to barter with? And did you know that Hernando Cortez was the first European to use chocolate when he invaded Mexico and the Aztec Indians had already discovered it?"

"I really can't say that I did."

"I can't wait for you to see the museum. We're lucky enough to have a cyclorama and it's the coolest thing I have ever seen. It starts off with the growing of the tree and then highlights all the different ways man has incorporated chocolate into our lives. I can't think of a better way to educate the public and still make it fun.

"Sharon did tell me that you've got some pretty unique ideas."

"I'd like to think so. The gateway to the museum is based on the trading of the beans. Everyone has to barter their way in. Right now I only have the three permanent displays but I have several on loan from artists around the world, and I think the people around here will really enjoy them."

"This really seems like old times."

"What do you mean?" Megan asked.

"This reminds me of all those walks around the neighborhood and the trips to the corner store we used to make. The only thing missing is a soda and two straws."

Just outside the shop, Megan stopped. Looking around she asked, "Can you hear that?"

"Hear what? Wait I do hear something. It sounds like…"

Before he could finish his sentence Megan inserted, "It sounds like someone whispering. I can't quite make it out but it sounds like—he's here, he's here, he's here."

She heard the click of the knife moments before she felt the hard cold metal pressed against the skin of her throat. "Nobody move—I have her exactly where I want her."

"Don't hurt her—whatever you want, we can work this out." Removing his wallet, Phillip offered it to the attacker. "Here, take my wallet. It's got cash and credit cards. If that's not enough, we can get more."

"I'm not interested in your money. It's vengeance I demand!"

Megan, frozen with fear, was barely able to ask. "Why do you want revenge? I don't even know you."

"How could you not know me? It's because of you that I lost him. He was my only friend, the only person who came to see me, the only person who cared about me and you took him away.

I need to make you pay for what you did."

Megan stated. "I don't know who you are talking about."

"You idiot—I'm talking about my brother Scott!"

Shocked beyond words, Megan exclaimed. "Scott had a brother! I never knew! He never said anything about you."

"Yes he had a brother! He came to see me every Christmas and most of my birthdays. My brother, Scott, loved only me until you came along. He was all I had. You took him away from me, and then you killed him."

Megan made eye contact with Phillip trying to reassure him that everything would be okay. "Let's don't be rash—if you give me half a chance, I think we could be friends. What can I call you?" Her voice sounded much calmer than she felt.

"Not that it matters, but my name is Steve."

"Well Steve, it doesn't have to be like this. Let's go inside, find something to drink and see if we can't work this out."

"Feeling the pressure increase along the side of her neck, Megan followed along as the attacker made his way to the door. The whispering appeared to get louder as he reached behind the statue and pulled out a key.

"How did you know about the key? I haven't used it in months."

I've been watching you for a while. I've gone over this moment, time and time again. I had this all planned out; every last detail down to the second." Removing the knife from her throat, he waved it in Phillip's general direction. "Everything was going great, until you showed up. Now what am I suppose to do with you?"

With the knife away from Megan's neck Phillip saw it as an opportunity to make his move. He rushed forward, closing the gap between them, and grabbed for the knife.

The attacker's reaction was quick. He avoided Phillip's lunge and jerked the knife back toward Megan's neck. She cried out in pain as the blade of the knife sliced into the upper part of her arm.

The sleeve on Megan's shirt changed color as the blood worked its way down her arm. The attacker yelled at Phillip. "Now look what you made me do! You're ruining everything—it's just not supposed to be happening this way."

The attacker's hold on Megan tightened as he started mumbling. "You killed my brother. You killed my brother."

Megan's anxiety continued to build and fear raced through her veins. She pleaded with her attacker. "Please let me go—it wasn't my fault. Scott was killed in an accident."

All of a sudden, a shot rang out. The attacker's hold loosened as he fell to the ground moaning. Phillip rushed to Megan's side, pulling her to safety. In an effort to stop the bleeding he removed his shirt and tied it around her arm.

Within minutes, Megan's corner of the world was filled with flashing lights and police cars. Once the attacker was secured, paramedics moved in to look at her bloody arm.

Megan reached for Phillip's hand and pulled him close. "This is the most excitement I've had in months and I can't thank you enough for being here with me."

Ron made his way over to Megan gave her a hug. "Thank God I got here when I did."

With a blank look on her face, Megan asked. "How did you know I needed help?"

"At first I didn't. I was looking for you so that I could give you your purse, which you left behind at the bar. I saw the perp holding you at knifepoint so I stepped back into the shadows and called for backup. When Phillip made a grab for the knife and the assailant stabbed you in the arm I knew I had to act."

"He's hurt pretty bad Ron. He is going to be okay, isn't he?"

"He'll be fine Megan, but I'm pretty sure the bullet has shattered his knee, so I'm not sure that he will ever walk the same again."

"I didn't see a whole lot of resemblance but he kept saying that he was Scott's brother. Any truth to that?"

"I know this comes as a surprise, but yes it's true. He is Scott's younger brother. I did some checking and turns out there was a missing persons report filed a few months back. Funny thing is, when I talked with the facility in Austin they said he might be delusional, but that he had never shown any signs of being violent. They'll be down in a few days to get him. Right now young lady, it's time to get you to the hospital and have your arm looked at."

Megan looked up at Phillip. "It appears my plans have been changed for the weekend. I still have a lot of work that needs to be done, but now it appears I will be limited in what I can do. If you would like to come to dinner, I'm pretty sure that I can still cook, and I promise the evening will be a whole lot less exciting."

Phillip kneeled down, looked Megan in the eye and squeezed her hand. "I have a better idea. Tonight showed me that everything I've been looking for could be taken away in the blink of an eye. What about I come over and take care of you. I can do whatever needs to be done and one of the first things on my honey-do list will be to replace that noisy fan motor in your air conditioner unit."

Truffles of Doom
by Mark H. Phillips

I held a pair of twos when the phone rang.

"Don't answer." Herbert sat cross-legged across the faux bear rug, bronze skin glowing in the flickering light of the faux wood fire. I wondered how much of his admittedly hunky physique was faux too. You can never be sure with plastic surgeons. I ached to search thoroughly for tiny scars.

"I've got to." I recognized Shade's ring. When I gave him his cell phone, I insisted that he only use it in true emergencies. I groaned as I carefully put my cards face down. I had just discarded three aces to get my current hand. Why did Shade have to call when I was down to just one article of clothing and had promised with all my heart to be a very good loser? I love strip poker. Herbert groaned too as I got up and padded out of the warm circle of light.

Shade was just this side of hysterical. "Eva! Crazy Wilma, Tio, and Captain Sam are sick. They were puking. Now they can't even stand up. They can't breathe right. Tio's lips are turning blue. I don't know what to do."

"I'll get ambulances there as soon as possible." I confirmed the location and hung up.

Herbert had heard my end of the conversation and turned on the lights. He sighed and pulled on his pants. I gave him my most apologetic smile while I phoned first for ambulances and then Kate Ramirez. Herbert had dressed and had his car keys out by the time I was stuffing my feet into warm boots. "Sweater?" I smiled sweetly and held out my hand.

He sighed and pulled off his warm cable knit. I pulled it on. He's six foot three and I barely pass five feet even in high heel boots. The sweater came down to my knees and the V neck made him groan again. I pulled on a coat to keep him focused and me warm. It was in the mid-twenties outside, and we Houstonians aren't used to such bitter cold.

Pynchon's was only six streets away from my Montrose house. Shade's little group of homeless friends had a cold-weather hangout in a back alley courtyard formed by Pynchon's and two other gourmet restaurants. The exhaust vents from all three kitchens made the little courtyard rather warm. The owners fed them regularly. In return, Shade's group had promised not to dumpster dive, not to harass the customers, and to sound the alarm when drug peddlers wanted to utilize the prime location.

Herbert parked his BMW on the street. We hurried on foot through a dingy alley. We had beaten the ambulances and could hear their sirens in the distance. When we turned into the well-lit courtyard, the smell of fresh-baked bread and roasting meat wafted over us in a warm, damp mist. Shade stood beside a cluster of shanties made of cardboard and damaged warehouse palettes. Mr. Kiatsu from the Sushi Stop and Lou, the youngest son of Mr. Pynchon, stood beside Shade with worried expressions.

Herbert ducked into the first occupied structure. He emerged and ducked into the next and then the next. The paramedics bustled in about then. Herbert announced that he was a doctor and started them on Tio, who appeared the worst. He rattled off some of what he'd found, left them to their work, and returned to where I was talking with Shade and the restaurateurs.

Herbert whispered, "I think it's botulism. I'm familiar with the symptoms because I work with Botox. Overdoses and other complications occasionally happen." Lou Pynchon let out a curse, and Mr. Kiatsu turned a sickly shade of green. They grabbed their phones almost immediately. To their credit they phoned the health inspector first and their lawyers second.

Kate showed up soon after. For years she and I had shared in the role of Shade's guardian angel. We both owed him a great deal, but he stubbornly thwarted most of our attempts to help him. Currently Kate and I barely spoke to each another, which wasn't helping my private detective business any. I had been depending on her as a source of inside information. One of my investigations had landed her in hot water with her bosses at HPD. She wasn't catty or mean about it, but I was the one who had screwed up and it would take a while to work my way back into her good graces.

Now, to make matters worse, she had a wracking cough and a voice so hoarse as to be barely audible. She took me aside and whispered that she was too sick to conduct interviews, but wanted to take the case anyway. Though it killed her to ask me for a favor, it was obvious that she needed me to be her voice. I was happy for the chance to get on her good side.

The paramedics wheeled Tio to one of the ambulances. They had intubated Tio and were pumping air into him. Captain Sam's stretcher was next. Wheezing desperately he made them stop so he could talk to us. Sam could barely whisper. "I don't think it was the food from the restaurants. We all ate the same food and Shade and Grady aren't sick. I think it was the box of chocolates we ate. They came out of Wilma's Christmas stocking, and she was sharing them with me and Tio. Tio had the most."

I knew that Captain Sam had been a medic during the first Gulf War and mentioned this to the paramedics. They wrote down approximately when he ate the candy, while Kate and I went to search Wilma's lean-to for the box. We found it stuffed back into a large, felt, Christmas stocking full of sweets, wool socks, a miniature sewing kit, toiletries, and other small gifts from a local shelter. The empty box of chocolates had held about a dozen truffles. Kate pulled on some latex gloves to handle the box.

I borrowed a pair of latex gloves from a paramedic before he wheeled Crazy Wilma away. I searched through the detritus covering the floor of Wilma's lean-to until I collected the shrink-wrap and the bright red wrappers for all twelve of the chocolates. I took the shrink-wrap and wrappers outside so I could silhouette them against the sodium floodlight above the courtyard. Pinpricks of light shone through the wrappers and there were minuscule holes in the shrink-wrap.

Kate duplicated my actions and found the tiny pinpricks in the bottom of the box. Someone had injected something into the sealed candies with a needle. Kate carefully bagged everything as evidence. She handed me her cell and I phoned in her request for more officers, both to secure the crime scene and to get to the shelter to prevent any more tainted candy from going out in Christmas stockings. I notified the restaurateurs not to assume that it was their good deeds that had gone astray.

I gave Herbert a very thorough goodnight kiss. He picked me up and kissed me back until my toes curled in my boots. I whispered into his ear, "I concede our poker match. You have no idea how well I intend to pay off my debts."

He squeezed the breath out of me and growled, "I intend to collect with interest."

I waved to him as he drove away, and Kate and I drove off towards the local shelter. Kate's heater wasn't working, and I shivered. I got my mind back on the poisoning. Someone had poisoned candy and hurt my friends. Fury made me warm again.

The Salvation Trails Shelter was full because of the cold. The director, Mrs. Jamison, led us through a busy cafeteria and then down a hall beside a large gym area that now served as a dormitory with bunks stacked three and four tiers high. We finally entered a backroom where volunteers were busy stuffing more stockings.

Fortunately only a few stockings had gone out early and only Crazy Wilma's had had chocolates in it. We went through a stack of candy boxes until we found a second that had the same needle marks. It was a different brand. No disgruntled worker at a candy factory had done this. A lab tech carefully opened the box and another officer took a sample of the candy off to the hospital for testing. Acting as Kate's proxy I ordered some other detectives to interview the volunteers. I enjoyed having minions.

Kate took notes again while I interviewed a rail-thin, recovering junky named Raoul. He had worked kitchen staff three days before when a large donation of candies had come in. Now he shook like a leaf because he had eaten a box of the candy soon after the man had left. I said we would have a squad car take him to the hospital for testing as soon as I finished interviewing him.

Raoul calmed down enough to tell us what he remembered. "The dude was old, white, maybe fifty. He was average height, fat, and had short gray hair. He had on a red and white check farmer's jacket over a weird looking sweatshirt. The sweatshirt had one of those science jokes on it, but it didn't make no sense. Anyway, the dude brings in a shopping bag full of candy, mostly boxes of chocolates, all different kinds. He asks if we can use it, and I say we do stocking stuffing at Christmas, and he says that's perfect."

I had a uniformed officer take Raoul in for testing.

Kate and I went to the Main Street campus of Memorial Hermann hospital next. Dr. Martinez was in charge of the case. He was in his 60s, only a little taller than me. He reeked of cigarette smoke.

In a hoarse voice he said, "It's botulism all right. The toxin interferes with nerve firings, paralyzing the victims. Death usually occurs from suffocation when it hits the lungs. We've got two of the patients on ventilators. We've flushed their systems and administered the antitoxin. The prognosis is good for all three, though they may need months of physical therapy to get back full use of their muscles."

I asked, "What about Shade, Grady, and Raoul?"

"Everyone else checks out clean. Shade and Mr. Dixon are down the hall in the waiting room. Mr. Fuentes is in my office with your forensic artist trying to come up with a sketch of the maniac who did this."

"How hard would it be to acquire this toxin?" I asked.

"If it's a commercial brand, you could steal it from any plastic surgeon's office. But it's probably less trouble to just to grow the stuff. Any semi-competent chemist, biologist, or botanist could easily culture it. The bacteria grow all over. It's in the soil. It grows in any anaerobic environment and then the toxin comes from the spores."

The doctor walked us down to his office. Lois Gibson, HPD's brilliant forensic artist was inside using her magic to coax detail after detail from Raoul. We stopped Dr. Martinez from knocking on the door. Both Kate and I had worked with Lois before and we knew she always worked with witnesses alone. She would never let anyone disturb the intense one-on-one concentration and rapport she established with a witness. Dr. Martinez left us outside his door while he went down the hall to make a telephone call.

Lois finally emerged and handed us her amazingly lifelike sketch. Although it was in black and white, she'd managed to get just the right gray tone to suggest the red in his check coat. She had even given a partial reconstruction of the cartoon on the sweatshirt beneath the jacket, something involving a couple of scientists in a lab. Kate took it down to the nurses' station and ran off some copies.

In the waiting room I told Shade and Grady that Wilma and the others were going to be okay, but they would have to stay in the hospital for some time. Shade was all concern, but Grady was as furious as I was. His face turned red. He growled, "You're going to get the bastard that did this, right?"

Kate showed him the sketch. I told him that we thought this was the man who donated the poisoned chocolates.

Grady got a puzzled look on his face. "I know this guy. I wouldn't think he'd have done something like that." Grady handed back the sketch. "I met him a couple of weeks ago. I volunteered to help out that Angel-for-a-Day charity at Toys 'R' Us. Teachers from all around Houston make up lists of poor, deserving students and then people buy gifts at Toys 'R' Us and we wrapped 'em up and put stickers on 'em and whatnot. I remember this guy coming in and buying a bunch of toys. We got to talking. See, he'd bought all of these educational toys. I told him that kids liked army men, and Tonka trucks, and video games, and such. But he insisted that they might as well learn something useful from their holiday gifts. I'm sure it's the same guy in the drawing. He even had a t-shirt with some Math joke on it. I forget the punch line, but it started, 'There are only 10 kinds of people in the world…'"

"Those who know binary and those who don't." Everyone looked at me. I shrugged. "I dated a numbers geek last month." Kate just grinned. Damn. She must have heard about my IRS audit and what I had had to do to get out of the auditor's clutches.

After I arranged to get Raoul, Shade, and Grady back to their residences, I started thinking out loud, "Could we be looking for a teacher or University professor? What if he's a high school teacher? He could have sent out poisoned chocolates to hundreds of kids." The thought of it sent shudders up and down my spine.

Kate was on the same page. She whispered, "Everyone will be on vacation, but we can find someone to give us access to faculty photos. We should start with the largest employer, Houston Independent School District, and then work our way down the list by size."

Dr. Martinez returned in a hurry. He said, "I contacted other hospitals to check their supplies of antitoxin, just in case this madman has poisoned a lot more people. Ben Taub hospital has a case of botulism. Theirs is a case of infant intestinal botulism, so it's probably unrelated. But I thought you should know."

I asked, "What is intestinal botulism?"

Dr. Martinez went into teacher mode. "There are three types of botulism cases. The rarest is wound botulism where the bacteria grow in a cut and the spores release toxin. Then there are cases of direct adult ingestion of the toxin, usually from tainted canned foods. But infant cases of ingestion of the bacteria are much more common. Infants are particularly susceptible because they have low acid levels in their intestines, and if the botulinum ends up there it can multiply prodigiously. Children beyond a year are safe because they have enough acidity in their guts to kill the bacteria. Infants can get infections from unprocessed honey, corn syrup, or even eating dirt. The child's name is..." He looked down at a note in his hand. "Crystal Jasperic, eleven months old."

At Ben Taub, we met with Mrs. Jasperic and her daughter's doctor in a waiting room not very different from the one at Memorial Hermann. She was a thin woman with bleached blond hair and large green eyes now red from crying. Dr. Wilson was a devastatingly handsome young man with a cleft chin and tousled brown hair that just begged me to tousle it even more.

With Mrs. Jasperic's permission, he gave us a breakdown on Crystal's progress. "It's definitely intestinal botulism. We've flushed out her intestines and administered BabyBIG®. She has the beginnings of descending paralysis. She can't hold her head up. Her oxygen levels were low so we've got her on a respirator as a precaution. The paralysis will wear off gradually in a few weeks. Is it true that Dr. Martinez's cases are deliberate acts of poisoning?"

I answered. "Maybe. Are there indications that your case connects to ours? The mode of delivery in the other cases is chocolates."

"We're still running tests but most of the time we never find out where the bacteria originated."

I turned to Mrs. Jasperic. "Would Crystal have had access to any chocolate candy?"

"No. We're very careful of what she gets into because she's allergic to eggs."

The doctor excused himself to return to his duties. Kate led Mrs. Jasperic back to a couch. We pulled up a couple of chairs. Mrs.

Jasperic's voice quavered. "My husband, John, is in Afghanistan. The Army says they won't be able to get a message to him for days. He's never even seen Crystal except in photos. Did someone intentionally poison my baby?"

I tried to sound neutral. "We're not sure that there's any connection. We have a person we need to question, but we haven't identified him yet." Kate pulled a photocopy of Lois's sketch out of her briefcase and showed it to Mrs. Jasperic.

Mrs. Jasperic's face took on an expression of profound shock. "That's Mr. Hoskins. He is my other daughter, Helena's, biology teacher at Bellaire High School. Is she in danger? She's at home baby-sitting her brother."

I said, "Phone your daughter and tell her you're on your way home. I'll have a squad car keep an eye on your house until we get there. Tell the nurse you're going home for a little while. We'll take you directly there, since we'll need to talk to Helena anyway."

While Mrs. Jasperic made her call and then talked to the nurse, I was on Kate's phone calling for the squad car and assigning a detective to get the HISD employee files on Hoskins. Kate drove while I arranged to get a search warrant. Getting used to wielding police power was all too easy. It would be hard to go back to being just a private detective once we captured this sick bastard.

The Jasperic residence was a two-story Victorian set in a small yard in a backstreet of Bellaire. As we pulled into the driveway, the daughter, Helena, was standing at the door holding the hand of a grumpy ten-year-old boy. She was a nubile teenager with dishwater blond hair worn in a long ponytail and had the same overlarge green eyes as her mother. Her eyelids looked puffy and drooped. She looked physically and emotionally exhausted. When she stepped aside to let us enter she was visibly shaking and looked like she was about to cry. But she said nothing.

As we entered, a fluffy white cat sauntered between my legs.

I reached down to pet it and snatched my hand back just in time to avoid a scratch. The cat hissed at me and then ran farther into the house.

The young boy grinned and said, "She'll tear your arm off. Miss Snugglebunny is psycho." He sounded proud that his cat was so vicious.

Mrs. Jasperic bundled her grumpy son off to his room and returned. She indicated that Helena should sit down and answer our questions. I pulled out the sketch. "Do you recognize this man?"

Helena's voice was a timid whisper. "Yes. It's Mr. Hoskins, my biology teacher."

"How well do you get along with Mr. Hoskins?" I asked gently.

"Okay, I guess." She didn't sound convincing.

"Is there anything you can remember that might indicate that he had any bad feelings towards you?" Helena just sat there. She drew her knees up and held them tight to her chest with her left arm while her right arm hung limp. She rocked slightly, but said nothing. I let the uncomfortable silence continue a long time. "Do you feel that he might be hostile? Did he make a threat?"

Helena shook her head but still said nothing. Alarm bells were going off in my head. Mrs. Jasperic blurted out, "Oh God, did he do anything to you?" Helena started to cry and hid her face behind her knees.

Kate got up and took Mrs. Jasperic into another room. The mother, outraged and devastated, was overprotective and would hinder our interview. Kate would have to convince the mother that Helena might be too embarrassed to reveal what had really happened with her mother in the room. I stayed with Helena, listening to her muffled sobs. I wanted to hold her, but wasn't sure it was the right thing to do. Kate finally returned and nodded for me to continue.

"Helena, look at me." Helena's red, puffy, half-closed eyes peeked out at me from behind her knees. "It's better to just get it out. Tell us about Hoskins. You tell me, and I'll tell your mother only what she needs to know. Okay?"

Helena stared at me for what seemed a long time. Then she dropped her legs to the floor and wiped the tears from her eyes. "My sister. Is she going to be all right?"

"The doctor thinks she has a good chance."

"It was poison, wasn't it? That's why you're asking about Mr. Hoskins."

"It's a real possibility. Did Mr. Hoskins give you any chocolates or other candy? Could Crystal have gotten into a present meant for you?" Kate kicked my chair. Damn. I didn't mean to lead the witness.

"Oh, God. This is my fault. I never thought…" Helena's voice was a whisper that trailed off into an almost inaudible groan. She wiped her eyes furiously. "You think Mr. Hoskins was trying to poison me? I think you're right. He did send me chocolates. I threw them away just like I threw away all his other gifts, but maybe Crystal got to them. She gets into lots of stuff she's not supposed to."

Helena sat up straighter. Her voice became louder, more forceful. "Mr. Hoskins raped me, right in his classroom after school. I never told anyone because I had kind of flirted with him, and I thought maybe it was my fault. But then he said he was in love with me and kept sending gifts and threatening me. He said if he couldn't have me, no one would. Stuff like that." She broke down and wept again, soon sobbing so loud that her mother came back in.

When everyone had calmed down a bit, I said, "I'm going to have a detective come over in a little while to take a formal statement. We're already tracking Hoskins down. Until we make an arrest, I'll keep the squad car posted outside." I gave them Kate's phone number.

Outside in the car, Kate whispered, "It still gets me every time, even though I've handled dozens of these types of cases. The poor kid is beating herself up because she thinks it's her fault that he raped her and her fault that her sister is in the hospital. A monster rapes and poisons and the poor victim thinks it's somehow her fault. It always makes me angry."

I reached over and patted her hand. She turned and smiled, then started the car. Just then a call came in. I listened and then said we'd be right there. They had found Hoskins' residence and we had our search warrant.

Hoskins had a two-story townhouse apartment on the far west side. Once we established that Hoskins wasn't home, the crime lab investigators went to work sweeping the place for evidence of bacterial cultures, botulinum spores, or chocolates. They found nothing.

Kate loaned me another pair of latex gloves and we commenced a thorough search. She knew I was good at searches and had no fear that I would corrupt evidence. Her trust felt good.

Hoskins seemed a neat bachelor with a simple life style. He had a modest library downstairs, about equally divided between science books and 19th century English literature. A leather reading chair sat beneath a Tiffany-style floor lamp. The table next to it held a humidor for cigars and a cut glass bottle half-full of brandy. He didn't have a TV anywhere in his apartment.

In the kitchen I looked over the shoulder of a lab tech who was carefully bagging containers of leftovers that might contain bacteria. He pointed at three small glass bottles. Two had small metal caps, while the third, half-full bottle had part of the cap removed to reveal a rubber circle. The bottles contained insulin. The lab tech bagged the open bottle as possible evidence. I found a package of disposable needles and a blood sugar testing kit in the cabinet beside the fridge. I handed the lab tech one of the needles. Perhaps they could match the needle type to the punctures on the wrappers and boxes of poisoned chocolates.

Kate didn't need help searching the downstairs living room, so I went upstairs and began on the master bedroom. Big king-sized bed carefully made. A large suitcase-sized empty space in the closet and a bunch of empty hangers suggested that he had packed for a trip. I found two whole drawers of his dresser full of science and math joke t-shirts including both the one mentioned by Raoul and the one mentioned by Grady. I marked the drawers with post-its so cops could correctly bag the clothes as evidence. Bizarrely enough he kept his underwear and socks in duplicate drawers; underwear, socks, then underwear again, and socks again. The duplication didn't make any sense.

Next to the bed above the nightstand Hoskins had tacked a calendar to the wall. I grinned. It was the same calendar tacked next to my bed. Then I stopped grinning. I looked back at the duplicate drawers of his dresser and back at the calendar. Why did he have a calendar with photos of nearly naked and extremely muscular male firefighters tacked to his wall? I went through the drawers of his nightstand. One drawer was full of condoms, while the other contained two cheap pornographic books and a smutty magazine, all with blatantly obvious male homosexual focus.

I hurried downstairs. Kate held up a stack of gift cards, perhaps two dozen, some in envelopes, some just the gift identifying tags. I started reading. "Thanks, Mr. Hoskins. Your biology class is the best science class I've ever had. I baked these sugar cookies myself. Have a wonderful break, Cindy." All were similar. One was from Helena Jasperic. "Sorry we argued. I'll do better next semester. Merry Christmas."

Hoskins was a teacher. The students gave him gifts before the Christmas break. Many of them would have given him chocolates, not knowing that he was a diabetic. What would a diabetic do with all that chocolate? Regift of course. And if he was charitable, which we knew Hoskins was, he might donate the chocolates to a shelter. And Hoskins was gay. The duplicate drawers were for someone special who stayed over regularly, someone male.

I told Kate about the insulin and took her upstairs to show her what I had found. I didn't even have to explain anything. She whispered to me, and I relayed instructions to the patrolman outside the Jasperic house. "Get inside and hold the fort until we get there. Make sure that no one destroys any evidence. Try to keep a poker face, but the daughter, Helena, is now our prime suspect."

Kate drove us back to the Jasperic house while I called the D.A. and urged him to expedite a new search warrant. He seemed greatly amused that I was Kate's proxy. I wisely refrained from asking him how his wife was doing—the wife he had neglected to mention before our one-night stand last Halloween.

As soon as I hung up, her phone rang again. I listened for a while and then summarized for Kate. "Sgt. Kamble says he contacted Hoskins' sister who gave him details of Hoskins' trip to Canada to visit with old college buddies. The Mounties found Hoskins and advised him of his rights. He's waived extradition and they will fly him back to Houston tomorrow morning with a Mountie escort."

As we pulled into the Jasperics' street we saw that two more squad cars were on the scene, lights flashing blue and red. Officers set up a perimeter blocking curious neighbors. Kate and I rushed up to find Mrs. Jasperic sitting on her front stoop, a uniformed officer standing over her. She cried into her hands, but she looked up at the prostrate form in the middle of their yard and screamed, "Bitch!"

An ornate gas lamp lit the yard, and I could see another uniformed officer inspecting Helena's injury. Helena struggled to prop herself into a sitting position with her right arm, but it folded uselessly beneath her and she fell back to the grass. As I stepped closer, I saw that Helena had a broken and copiously bleeding nose. I noticed the odd droop of her eyelids was even more pronounced.

Helena spit blood and then screamed back at her mother. "You're the one who made me give him chocolates! Even after I told you what that bastard really did to me. It's just as bad as rape."

Mrs. Jasperic would have gone after her daughter if the officer hadn't caught her from behind. "As bad as rape? He gave you a B!"

"I deserved an A," Helena screamed. "I'm an A student, damn it. The only B's were from that fucker Hoskins. He knows how good I am at biology. My IB biology project was better than anything he's ever done. I'm going to be a real scientist, not some damn wanna-be science teacher. My semester average came out to be an 89.48% and the bastard wouldn't bump me up to the A! I've never made a B until his stupid class. It's his fault, I tell you."

Mrs. Jasperic suddenly came out of her rage. She looked at Kate and all the other officers standing around. She looked at her neighbors who were gawking from behind the crime scene tape. When she cried out again to her daughter her voice was full of panic. "Don't say anything more. Don't say anything to anyone until I get you a lawyer."

The daughter wasn't listening. Enraged far beyond linguistic expression, she just sat there and howled. When Helena came up for air, Kate instructed the officer to Mirandize her. Better late than never.

We heard an approaching ambulance. I pulled Kate aside. "Tell the EMTs to check her right arm."

"You noticed it, too?" Kate whispered.

I nodded. "She's carrying around the incriminating evidence inside her paralyzed right arm. Did you see how her eyelids droop? I'd bet anything she has wound botulism. Maybe that damned cat scratched her while she was harvesting spores. And if she was that sloppy, there's probably any number of ways the baby could've become infected. They'll have to sterilize the whole house."

A month later I was visiting Crazy Wilma in the hospital. Captain Sam and Tio had fully recovered and moved back behind Pynchon's. The doctor would release Wilma soon. I was explaining yet again why she was in the hospital. Wilma could never quite keep it all straight and I patiently went through the whole story.

Wilma's response was full of indignation. "It ain't right that schoolgirl should go to jail for twenty-five years. She didn't mean to hurt Tio and Sam and me. And to get her own sister sick, and to have her arm all cut up and operated on. Well, that seems like punishment enough."

"I'm not sure Mr. Hoskins would agree. If he had eaten all the candy, he would almost certainly have died. Mr. Hoskins is coming by today to see you."

"I don't remember no Hoskins."

I sighed and patiently reminded her. "He's been here every week with flowers." I pointed to the roses on the table. "He and a bunch of his teacher friends are helping the shelter build an annex, so maybe you won't have to live behind Pynchon's next winter."

"I won't live in no shelter. I's a free spirit. You tell this Hoskins fella I don't like roses neither. I like 'tunias." She looked down at her empty lunch tray. "Or maybe something good to eat. Maybe some chocolates." Her little bird-bright eyes lit up, but then she thought a moment and shook her head forcefully. "Nope. No chocolates. I's had enough of his pisoned chocolates. I want 'tunias, and no pisoned 'tunias, neither."

I nodded and said I would do all I could to see that no one poisoned her again.

A Bona Fide Quirk in the Law
by Cash Anthony

Not because she expected her face to be plastered on wanted posters as a stone-cold killer, nor on billboards as a celebrity, but out of general prudence Jessie Carr reminded herself to obey the law in Liberty County.

Within yards of crossing the county line, she rolled off the throttle on her Road King and watched her speedometer needle drop to a discreet 65. She had plenty of time, and though the temperature was in the 60s, her riding gear and gloves kept her warm from the wind chill. The sun tried to help, but its efforts were stymied by drifting clouds. Still, the February afternoon would stay mostly fair.

Her ultimate destination was Houston and the Sweets for Sweethearts Ball, a day away. No doubt it would be populated with a few true benefactors to the city, along with a host of greedy show-offs and randy recently-divorced professionals, forced by their notoriety to give to a charity now and then. These sweethearts were sick kids, who couldn't afford to quibble over the secret intentions of people underwriting hospital wings and research.

Recognizing her cynical streak and a tendency to judge others by standards way too high—what she defended as "calling a spade a spade"—Jessie considered how hard it was to break out of her solitary, drifter ways, even when she only had to make one phone call to wangle a ticket to the hottest Valentine's Day gala in town.

She liked being on her own, having no one to please but

herself. In a way she wanted to be more than a dot in the cosmos, a nameless biker on the road of life. But she wrote plays and weekend "entertainments", transitory things without a cover to bear her name in ink.

And she was only a detective by happenstance, which allowed her a limited sideline that grew out of her crime-solving abilities. As to that part of her life, she kept her reputation pristine and restricted. She might come up for a look-see at the rich and famous, in disguise, but she would go right back underground.

Jessie's Harley purred along a rural highway through fields of black soil awaiting the Spring application of seed. A pleasant odor of wild flowers with a hint of cow manure enveloped her. One of her grandmother's sayings came to mind: "Grow where you're planted." For Jessie, that was in the saddle of her Harley. When she rode, she could let her mind relax, grow quiet, embrace the moment where she, and only she, chose which road to take, without reference to anyone else's journey.

Tomorrow night, it would be exactly the opposite: Saturday night in the Big City. She had to clean up for the River Oaks social set in order to show them she still existed, even thrived, and wanted to keep their business. Her work needed support from wealthy clients, but she had no doubt that she earned her money. They never complained.

The real satisfaction came elsewhere, though. She could scarcely resist a direct Call for Help. Something in her felt a moment's glee, mixed with paranoia, at the thought of putting herself out there in the tumultuous world of other people, on behalf of another. She was so happy, at first she did it anonymously. Now she enjoyed the cash flow, too.

She let her mind wander to the job she'd just finished successfully. That guy wouldn't beat his grandmother or rape his nieces again…

His victims wanted to smother Jessie in gratitude, to the point that she had to smile at them and grow deaf to their entreaties to stay with them longer. One of the nieces had gone around with a beat-up straw hat with a sweat-stained band, into which each of the women in the family threw a twenty or a five or a one, but Jessie had accepted the hat and its contents from the grandmother as if it were The Order of the Garter, presented by the Queen herself.

Later than planned, she had mounted up and left Jasper on her Road King. A quick dash through East Texas on a Friday afternoon, going against the weekend traffic, would get Jessie into downtown Houston and the Four Seasons Hotel around dusk. There was a mixer at the bar tonight, and a chance she might hear some juicy gossip or twig to shady dealings in town. It could be good filler conversation for the ball.

In the earliest days of her career as an unhyphenated writer, Jessie found that one benefit of doing a good deed was that it broke the isolation of her day-to-day work. When it became a real sideline, she realized her work must remain solitary, but she made sure the community benefited by more than her contribution to art.

Whenever Jessie received such a Call in the past, she responded with alacrity and without assistants; and since she had no formal training in detection, law enforcement or outlaw life, it was only by dint of bouncing off the world's rough edges and rougher people that the heroine in her could shine through.

Eventually she realized she had a marketable specialty. A pro bono case now and then was fine, but these days, to be independent, a gal had to have a cash stream. Still, part of her wished the world would just leave her alone to indulge her fun, creative side and go ride her Harley whenever she pleased.

But the world just kept on coming…and she could duck it only for so long. For Jessie, standing idle and passive, watching the Screwers have their way with the Screwees, was now left behind in the mystery of Before—before buying a bike, before taking herself off the grid that consisted of "address, telephone, job, work number, credit cards, social circles—gym rats, bartenders, informants," and so forth. Before becoming the watcher, the wraithlike avenger, the unexpectedly expert righter of wrongs.

Along with restrictions and prohibitions, Jessie had also discarded the tedious habit of studying her past in too much detail. If she needed someone's expertise, she pulled a name out of her resource list, but otherwise she had few friends. She was a writer, a wanderer, and maybe a sometime heroine, and that was enough. Until Beau.

She didn't want to think about Beau. He was still a confusion in her life, even if the idea of a partner was a welcome development. Maybe. Instead, she remembered the last time she'd been on this road on her bike. It was on a Sunday the previous summer...

A line of thunderheads butted their anvil heads against the troposphere that afternoon, but they looked far away when Jessie arrived at a picnic and swap meet near Cut N Shoot. The day's heat was livable, the skies above were blue; so afterwards, on a whim and without studying the weather forecast, she rode east on 105—and unknowingly into Liberty County, Texas.

On her helmet was a sticker that read, "I've got PMS and a .45. Do you feel lucky?" It was always good for a laugh among fellow riders. She carried a mere .38.

She'd just turned south on 770 toward Daisetta when a deputy sheriff for Liberty County rolled up behind her in an unmarked patrol car.

At first she saw him as part of the local scenery. She was more concerned about the darkening clouds that were chasing her, the intensifying gusts of wind, and the fingers of lightning that reached for her from the sky. Though she could handle it if necessary, riding through a strong thunderstorm was not Jessie's idea of fun. She began looking for shelter and slowed down.

The off-white Crown Victoria behind her pulled up close to her rear fender. It bore no painted insignia, nor reflective stripes, but it did have a light bar. The driver appeared to be burly and his hair was short. After following Jessie 10 minutes, he switched the bubble lights on, signaling her to stop.

Jessie scanned the highway ahead for a pull-off wide and deep enough to hold a bike and a car. Huge drops of rain hit her helmet and tank and arms and legs, plopping with noisy force and stinging after their long fall from the dark clouds. Leaves and dirt picked up by the wind tumbled through the air, and the ditches to her right began to fill.

The road glistened like a creeping silver snake in her headlights as the big drops hit the hot asphalt and spread. The afternoon became murky night when the thunderheads arrived. She slowed to a crawl. The storm was almost on top of them, and it pissed her off that some jerkwater lawman would delay her search for shelter now.

She debated for a moment whether to stop: was he a real lawman, or a wannabe? It was hard to tell in a county so poor that the lawmen had only their gussied-up private vehicles to drive for work. She could outrun him on dry pavement, but she wouldn't risk it in this.

When she spotted a paved slip of road over a culvert, she put on her turn signal and pulled off. Obviously the man behind her didn't need to blip the siren, but he did anyway, and she nearly jumped out of her leathers at its shriek. By the time she put the kickstand down, Jessie was trembling with anger and adrenaline.

She pursed her lips and rolled her eyes in a private commentary to the heavens, waiting for an accusation that she knew would be a lie. She was meticulous about obeying traffic laws on her bike, and there were no equipment violations for him to find.

Jessie watched the patrol car in her mirror as the driver climber out. He appeared to be alone, which could cut either way in terms of being a threat. He wore a black Stetson cowboy hat and a yellow rain slicker with "Deputy" across one side and "Sheriff" across the other. No name-tag or jurisdiction patch was in sight, not an outline of Texas, nor a five-pointed star. His face was full and jowly, and he sported sideburns and a dark Wyatt

Earp mustache, which at the moment glistened from sweat, or snot, or rain.

Jessie took her helmet off. She fruitlessly swept raindrops off its visor with a gloved hand while the deputy wrote down her license plate number, his big flashlight wobbling where he'd tucked it under his arm. When he finally sauntered up to her, she looked him in the eye.

Or rather, she tried to. He flicked the beam into her face, blinding her, then surveyed the bike. He kept his eyes down, the brim of the black Stetson hiding his face.

She glimpsed thick lips pulling back to expose crooked yellow teeth before he moved to a point behind her left shoulder, out of view. From his position, the sticker on her wet helmet shone brightly, its words visible in reflective ink.

"Think that's funny, do you?" was the first thing he said. "You got a .45?"

"No."

"Didn't think so. License and registration." The deputy wiped his nose and mustache off on the back of his hand.

Jessie asked permission to go into an inside pocket of her jacket to pull them out. She also announced, per Texas law, that she was the owner of a concealed carry permit for a handgun, and that her pistol was currently loaded and residing in her tank bag, within arm's reach. She handed her papers and her permit to the deputy.

"You trying to be aggravating? I ast you about that already. Little woman out alone on a Harley, packing heat." He sneered, "What are you, Bandido bait?"

If you only knew, Jessie thought.

This was the point where the officer was supposed to tell her why he had stopped her. Here in Liberty County, it would be something plausible and inarguable, she knew.

His probable cause turned out to be a headlight that wasn't on—it was—perhaps because of a loose wire—plausible and nearly impossible to check on the spot, especially when the unit appeared now to be working fine; so, inarguable.

As the storm thundered overhead, the deputy ignored it. He insisted she dismount.

"Aw, come on. We're both gonna get soaked."

"You want me to take you in?"

"Don't mess with my bike," Jessie said in a flat voice. She slid out of the saddle.

"Go stand over there, and look the other away."

"Why? You gotta pee?"

"Watch my car."

The deputy gave Jessie a shove to move her away from her bike. She stood near the shoulder in front of his car, looking north, as the rain began to pour.

This gave Officer Snotnose full access to everything she carried, while her head and face were soaked. He rummaged through Jessie's tank bag, pocketing her pretty chromed Springfield .38 Super. Finding nothing else of value, he planted a wet baggie containing a skimpy amount of pot inside a small map book, then zipped the tank bag shut.

Later, Jessie realized he must have done it when an oncoming 18-wheeler passed, buffeting her with wind and road spray. She threw an arm over her face by reflex, but the headlights left her seeing white spots before her eyes, forgetting the cop for a moment.

A squeal, some garbled words and a loud squawk from the radio inside his car suddenly drew the deputy's attention.

"Car 52, what's your 20?"

He ran to pick up the dispatcher's message. Then, without a word to Jessie, he tossed his Stetson into the front seat, jumped in, slammed the door and peeled out onto the slick highway headed south, light bar flashing.

Jessie made herself breathe deep. She refused to drown in the emotional floodgates the encounter had opened, though her desire to follow him, take him down and crush him under her heel was a terrible urge. Instead, she scrummaged up a flashlight from one of her saddlebags.

The rain was letting up, and the temperature dropped 18 degrees on the back side of the summer storm. Jessie shivered, scrunching up her wet hair to squeeze as much water out as she could, while she did a walk-around before she got going again. It was only by observing her unbreakable routine, and turning her head at just the right time to the side, that she discovered the deputy had screwed the valve cap off and let the air out of her back tire. When she fished in the tank bag for her tire gauge, to check whether she might be able to limp to help, she saw that her weapon was gone, too.

Jessie stomped the ground, furious. She shook both fists at the dripping sky and yelled to the long-gone patrol car, "Bully! Thief!"

For an instant, she wanted to plop down on the shoulder and have a good cry. But she immediately told herself, "That's just adrenaline, and you'll do no such thing, Jessie Carr."

Instead she pulled out her cell phone and called a specialty towing service for help. She waited for the tow, alone and wet and unarmed in the dark. She wanted to enjoy the good luck that had protected her so far, but she was far from certain she could afford to let down her guard. The Man had meant for her to stay there until he came back to finish whatever his first intentions were.

Half an hour later, a tow truck arrived, driven by a geezer who loaded the Road King onto his flat bed with care and confidence. Once she got to a fleabag motel in Hardin that night via taxi, drenched and disgusted, Jessie reviewed everything she had just been through…everything she'd seen and heard that was related to patrol car #52 and The Man who had stopped her for fun.

With concentration, she brought back the details of his face in every angle she'd seen them; and she slid into his body in her mind, to feel his walk and the way he stood.

She didn't know his name, but she'd find a way to even the score. She always did.

The ride to Houston this afternoon no longer felt so pleasant to Jessie. Her hands were cold from the wind, her back stiff from the highway miles. She raised herself up to let a whiff of air move under her jeans, to readjust her muscles before she settled back into the padded seat. Now she wished she hadn't recalled that ride last May.

Leaving Jasper, the road was a feast for her eyes, with lacy white dogwood blossoms dotted amid the pine tree forests to either side of the road. She had soaked up the smell of freshly mowed grass in the median, too. But here, down on the coastal plains near Daisetta, the odor of crude oil and marshy bogs seeped into the mix, until every sweet fragrance was obliterated by molecules of stink.

Thinking about The Man and her nasty encounter in Liberty County last summer killed the buzz of her ride, for sure. She'd attempted to track him down through her various law enforcement contacts, without success. Her description fit too many men.

Jessie clucked her tongue, exasperated with herself. All this dwelling on the past might even bring a nightmare, the kind where she was an invisible spectator trying to puzzle out what the dream was about, knowing all along that something dreadful was going to happen, and soon.

She intended to get to metropolitan Houston and its four million people tonight, but now decided to go no further than hamlet Dayton, first called West Liberty, and its five thousand. She felt frazzled, and had a headache coming on.

By 7:20, it was well dark, and she was happy to pull in at a tiny bed & breakfast on the Houston side of town run by a friend of a friend—Nina Marie Fillett, a throw-back to the naturalism of her hippy days. An aging nudism devotee, Nina Marie liked to party and kept late hours, but she always had a bed free. Only two cars sat in the weed-dominated driveway this evening, one of them the innkeeper's '66 VW Bug. Jessie turned off the key on the Road King and pulled out her cell phone. She gave Beau a quick call to say she'd arrive in Houston a day late, unloaded her gear, then checked in.

After a chat over two wonderful cups of hot chocolate spiked with white chocolate liqueur, during which Nina Marie insisted on showing her guest pictures from a recent family reunion—no way to complain that the tattoos hadn't held up since the 60s, though the supporting structures had, alas, given way—Jessie made her way to a simple room, created by enclosing the back porch and furnishing it with a bed and a nightstand.

She undressed and lay on her back under a cone of yellow light coming from a single bulb screwed into the ceiling. The temperature was dropping into the 50s—it was mid-February after all—and in a moment, she reached over and pulled the bed's quilt-top spread over her. She wished the room were dimmer, but Jessie felt disinclined to get up and find the wall switch to turn off the light. Her unbrushed teeth tasted of cocoa and the bite of alcohol. She knew she ought to get up and go clean her face. Too tired to argue with herself about anything, she rolled over and drifted into a deep sleep.

In the early morning hours, the predicted nightmare began. As always, The Man's face was almost exposed to her.

Naked and sweaty, Jessie tossed and squinched up her eyes in the dream, the better to see him. She *would* see his face this time! The Man was poised, ready to face her, ready to sneer at her again. His shoulders shifted, his name tag was about to slip from under his rain slicker, if only he'd turn her way—

And then Jessie's cell phone rang. She awoke groggy, blinded by the yellow light overhead. Where was she? Was she caught in a raid?

The she registered the theme from "Superman" that trilled in her ear at high volume. She groped for the cell phone that should have been under her pillow, and knocked it off her bedside stand, along with her keys.

When she had retrieved it from under the bed, "Jessie Carr," she mumbled. She used her toes to fish for the key chain, not quite able to bring it near enough to pick up.

"Hold on a sec." The voice was female and breathy into the phone. Then it cut like a chain saw as the speaker blasted someone nearby. "Get out of my space, bitch! Me and my lawyer are talking. What are you, blind?"

The thump of competing radio stations, the clatter of metal bars, and the jumble of voices in the background could only have one source: the call was coming from a place of incarceration. Nothing else sounded like people locked up by a government and made to put up with each other at close range.

Jessie blinked her sticky eyelids—in February the pollen count started climbing along the Gulf Coast. She wondered who was in jail and seeking her services at—she consulted the window on her cell—was that 5:37 a.m.?

She pulled a sweatshirt on. In the eaves of the porch, a bird twittered, ready to greet the dawn, or disturbed by the call and subsequent movement. Jessie pressed her ear tighter to the speaker, and a shiver of excitement cleared her head. It was—it had to be—a Call for Help!

"Aunt Jessie? It's Laurie. Laura Voyaczic. I'm sorry to bother you, but I'm in jail. In Houston. The police…"

A Voyaczic in jail? My, my. Had someone provoked her out of her well-mannered Rich Girl daze? Why wasn't she on Spring Break in Martinique, or skiing in Gstaad?

"Do you have a lawyer?"

"Yes, he's right here. It's his cell phone—"

"Put him on." Jessie pulled on her jeans. She opened the door from the porch into the house and padded, barefoot, inside, which put her mercifully in the kitchen. It was 25 degrees warmer there, except for the floor. A tenor voice spoke.

"Is this Miss Carr?"

"Jessie Carr. Lots of mileage, but she still rolls."

"Er. I represent your niece? No, your cousin's daughter-in-law? Well, I…"

"I know who she is. Who are you?"

"Randy Hudson. I'm an associate of Will Farlow. He said to have my client call you."

"Got it. What's the charge?" The cell phone clamped between her shoulder and chin like a violin, Jessie drew a cup of water, unwrapped a tea bag, dropped it in and stuck the cup in the microwave. As she pushed the On button, her mind moved into a higher gear.

"And what's the jurisdiction?"

"Houston. HPD. Possession of more than six obscene devices for the purpose of promotion or distribution. You're a writer?"

"Yep. Ah. Her party stuff?"

"Yeah. Why did he think a writer…"

"Have you seen it?"

"Yeah. Well, not this specifically. She was picking up a new order, just sitting there." Hudson's voice rose with indignation.

That was because he was young, Jessie thought. Unjaded as he was, he could still get fired up. What his pinched voice suggested to Jessie was emotional outrage. Not a good trait for a defense lawyer, except in front of a jury, she thought. Especially when the client was hysterical herself.

The microwave oven gave a ding, and Jessie removed her cup of tea. She threw the bag away.

"I presume the police took everything into custody when she was arrested?"

"I guess so."

Jessie sipped at the tea, then wrinkled her nose. It was barely tepid. She set it down. Nina Marie wasn't big on capital expenses, so no telling how long the microwave had been on the blink.

"Okay, Mr. Hudson, suppose you track down that evidence, just in case we need to get a look at it, pre-trial. Always good to know exactly what you're dealing with, you know."

"Trial? Good luck. I know exactly what it was, Miss Carr. It was a sexually oriented business, in this case a warehouse like Fort Knox of fancy lingerie for Miss Voyaczic to buy and resell. It's all right here on the list she gave the police, dammit."

Jessie could see the problem: Laurie's inventory trouble was both broad and deep. For giving her bachelorette parties, Laurie might wind up having to register as a sex offender for the rest of her life. Really, really not good for a recent debutante.

Without thinking, Jessie lifted the cup and sipped again, then drank half its contents.

"So where are you taking her now?"

"As soon as they process her out, we'll head to Joe Henry's Bail. She's not an employee of the store, but the owner asked me to handle it as a favor."

The dregs in Jessie's cup delivered their message, whatever it was, and she let these facts swirl around in her mind.

From past dealings, Jessie knew that Laurie Voyaczic and Family had plenty of assets and community ties sufficient to have her back on the street within a few hours—and to pay Jessie's modest fee.

From Dayton to Houston was roughly 40 miles. Jessie allowed a generous two hours for travel time. On Highway 90, she'd have to go through a bunch of little towns, each of which had its own brand of hick cop whom she surely didn't want to rile. Plus she needed to eat and to top off the tank on her Road King. If she left at 8:30 a.m., that would put her into Houston before the Saturday shoppers got into gear.

She could check in at the hotel, clean up, and get a cab to a meeting with Laurie before the gala, which began at 7 p.m. "Tell her to meet me at the Chocolate Bar," she said. "At two o'clock sharp. And tell her to come alone."

Jessie moved a wool scarf to one side in her thick, waterproof duffel bag. She closed her sketchpad and tucked it in, then picked up a collection of snapshots one by one, which had been spread in a series across the quilt. They showed strangers' faces to be used as flash cards, so that she could practice drawing the characteristics that caught her newly-trained eye at once. She focused on emotional content, sometimes catching an expression on the nose and satisfying even her hypercritical mind.

Her goal was to learn how to detect hostility and deception, and she had practiced with her collection an hour this morning, as she did everyday. Now she put them on top of a pile of her folded clothes and slid them all into the bag that would be stowed behind her on the bike. Her formal gown and accoutrements for tomorrow evening's shindig were being Fed-Ex'd in to the hotel.

Jessie noticed how the silver latch on the bag's oversized lock captured her image. Her face shifted and distorted as she moved away from it, like a reflection in a haunted house mirror. That she should be epic in any way perplexed the reclusive part of her, since she was short, mousy and nosey, bookish, and prone to compulsive disorders.

Middle-aged, dry of skin and gray of temple, her mental alacrity and acrobatic skills no longer supported a sleuth's or assassin's lifestyle, if one was thinking of every Tom Cruise spy movie ever made. And she'd become a little accident-prone around the house. But she could still think on her feet, and her reflexes, when it came to sizing up truly bad people, were still right on. Had to be, actually. She checked to see that the magazine for her new 9mm was full. The Yukon was a great pistol, but once it was taken away from her, she'd never own another one.

Bang! A car door slammed shut, followed by repeated "rrrr-clunk" attempts to start the engine. The driver didn't know how to start a standard, apparently.

In a moment, the innkeeper came through the kitchen naked, boobs swinging and flaccid butt all a-jiggle. She carried a tire iron in her hand and a wild-eyed expression that was closed and intent and shrewish all at the same time.

Glad I'm moving on, Jessie thought. Nina Marie, a cougar before the term existed, had brought home a man last night—her niece Persephone was entertaining him while Jessie drank cocoa and traveled with Nina Marie down mammary lane. Jessie surmised that he either didn't pay or didn't perform as desired, and now he was trying to flee.

He wasn't making a Call for Help to Jessie, though; and she didn't want to be around when Nina Marie decided what kind of punishment he should get.

The Chocolate Bar reflected the kookiness of Montrose, Jessie observed. Besides its two dozen flavors of chocolate ice creams, it offered fudge, brownies, chocolate cheese cakes, a purple lava lamp, and huge, wooden cut-out reminders to customers that the word of the day was "INDULGE."

She drank in the fragrance of cocoa and sugar, her long nose twitching like the proboscis of an oversized mouse. Laurie, a thoroughly modern version of a Southern belle, had gone over her story twice now, and Jessie felt she had sniffed out the pertinent facts.

"It's a weird little piece of the law," she told the distraught young woman. "Apparently you can possess a dildo, but you can't sell one."

"That's the dumbest thing I ever heard. You telling me the State of Texas expects everyone to make their own?"

"Oh, it doesn't stop there. I said *a* dildo. If you possess six or more, the law presumes you must have them only to sell, so you're guilty before you start."

Laurie truly was floored. "So much for getting the government off our backs. That means every store that sells vibrators could be targeted. And I didn't even work there!" Laurie nibbled a broken nail and threatened to weep again. "Everybody goes to lingerie parties. We always have them if there's a big social event, like the afternoon before. There has to be an exception."

"Hard to argue against solid, if rubbery, evidence."

"Oh, Aunt Jessie, they took my picture, too! When I got to the jail. I've never been so embarrassed in my life." Laurie rummaged in her purse and came out with an article and photograph torn from the Chronicle. "Read it!"

The story was below the fold, but still front page. "Oilman's daughter arrested on sex charge," it said.

"Oooo." Jessie snagged a piece of chocolate marbled layer cake from the counter and shoved it in front of her client. She handed her a fork. "Your daddy must have made somebody mad."

Laurie shrugged and dug in. She had no clue what her father's work entailed, or why a Houston oilman might not be so popular, given the recent record profits his industry was enjoying, while 2008 gas prices went sky-high.

Jessie sipped on her hot chocolate while she examined the black-and-white photograph accompanying it.

A police officer had a big paw on Laurie's arm, yanking her out of a patrol car into a crowd of photographers and media. Laurie looked scared and wishing she could hide. And there was something shockingly familiar about the cop's face.

Jessie shook her head. She looked more closely, then took out a pair of cheaters that she despised, and perched them on her nose. Had to be sure she wasn't making a connection that wasn't there.

No. Those lips, that mustache, that jaw, those sideburns, the ears with no lobes—it was The Man. Jessie made a gurgling sound.

"Are you all right?" Laurie asked.

"Who is he?"

"That's the cop. Right there." Laurie pointed. "He came in where I was eating."

"The arresting officer in your case?"

"Right."

"Do you know his name?"

"Spinner, Spiner, something like that. He told me he was new on the force here, transferred in from Liberty. The weird thing is, I see him around here all the time. Guess he likes chocolate better than doughnuts."

"Really." And just like that, The Man from Jessie's dream suddenly had a complete face and a name. And Jessie had a cause of her own. Revenge!

She pushed her cup of hot chocolate away and handed the article back to the young woman. Her mind raced ahead, considering and discarding possible tactics.

"Well, there's no question you have to go to trial," she announced. "That's the first thing. It'll buy some time because the dockets are so full. Solving this kind of problem isn't my forte', but we'll get you off the hook. Have Hudson get you a trial date and call me."

By now Laurie was wiping the last of the dark chocolate icing off her plate with a much-licked finger. She seemed to be recovering her equanimity. "I feel so much better. All those reporters and flash bulbs made me so nervous. They kept yelling at me! I felt like a celebrity. Wonder how they knew I'd been arrested?"

"I have an idea." Jessie flagged down Gil Johnson, one of the shop owners. "Let me ask you about special orders," she said.

Jessie spent the late afternoon devising a plan. At the Four Seasons she went to the business center, but all the computers were in use. She went back to her room, took a nap, and showered for the ball.

Hanging behind her in the bathroom steam, the long red satin gown, a one-shoulder number, was decorated with crystals on the skirt. Beneath the dress sat a pair of red Louboutin signature pumps. Jessie restyled a long red wig and put it on. With quick brush strokes she had it wrapped neatly around her head. She pinned it into place, her own mousy brown hair entirely covered.

Once she had applied make-up, spritzed on something fragrant, and slipped into the dress, no one would ever guess she'd lived the life of a biker chick for most of the last three months. She knew that an old friend, a former criminal district judge, would be at the gala—he never missed it—and Jessie meant to fit in.

Ten minutes later Jessie entered the hotel ballroom. Gigantic flower arrangements in pink and red heralded Cupid's holiday, coming up next week. To her right, the little orchestra tuned its instruments in a corner of the huge chamber, next to a tiny section of wood parquet floor. Clusters of rich and formally-dressed members of Houston society sipped their second cocktails of the night and chatted in low tones.

Jessie noted round tables and chairs in the area furthest from the music. There, near the drapes, would be the best location for the chat she hoped to have.

Her intentions were stymied, however, for as she soon spotted her target, an elderly man in black tie, of portly build and Late Einstein hair, she saw that he chatted up the singer in the band, quite close by. This person, an unlikely choice for the occasion, was a young woman dressed in layers of sheer silver tatters over black tights, with black nail polish and make-up a la Alice Cooper. The judge had her trapped in an arrangement of gigantic speakers on which some idiot had taped over-size valentines.

As her suitor leaned in, one arm on the wall behind her, she shrank away. From the way her gaze roamed the room and her arms hugged her body, Jessie guessed that the musician was hearing an authority-laden lecture, or an unimaginable pick-up line.

Jessie teetered over to them in the outrageously high, haute couture red heels. "Would you like me to help you out of an embarrassing public display of excess testosterone?" She faked a tiny slur of her words, and made her question deliberately vague as to its intended recipient.

The gentleman glanced Jessie's way with a scowl, followed by a late realization that she had complimented his hormones in an oblique fashion. Meanwhile, the singer slunk away into the shadows toward the nearest open bar. Then, it clicked.

"Jessie McGonegal! Whah, Honey, ain't you a vision, I do declare! Never thought I'd see ya again, 'specially not looking like this." Judge Graham Forbiss snatched Jessie off her feet in a bear-hug and gave a roar of delight that had other partygoers craning to see the stunning lady in red in the judge's arms.

After a moment's catch-up conversation between them, the

judge, who had retired from a criminal district court, snagged Jessie a tulip glass of champagne from a waitress's tray and took her to an empty table, adequately far from the singer's vocals, to sit for a chat.

Forbiss looked at his empty glass and waved another waitress over. He held up his glass and said, "I'll have another Piece of Ass."

The waitress looked at the judge with a wary eye. "For how much?" she asked.

Jessie tapped on the judge's arm. "You'll have to tell her what's in it."

"Ah. Em, well, it's Southern Comfort, and it's, aw, sweet stuff. Peaches."

"It's one shot of Southern, one shot of Amaretto, and fill the glass with sweet and sour." Jessie waved the waitress along. "Go, before you forget."

"Kind of you to remember, Jessie, very kind." He patted Jessie's scarlet-clad knee and let it linger there.

Jessie got down to business. She removed his hand with a friendly shake of the head "no." Sipping her champagne, she casually asked the judge about the statute involved in Laurie's case, Section 43.21 of the Penal Code.

A different waitress arrived with Judge Forbiss's deep pink-amber drink. He slugged down half of it, then leaned back and assumed a storyteller's mien. "Oh, hell yes, that one's famous—maybe infamous—around the law schools. They all enjoy debating the Dildo Statute."

"Are there any exceptions?"

"One, but it probably don't apply to your gal. In 1993, the Texas Legislature amended the act. Now it allows for an affirmative defense, to protect folks promotin' an obscene device for 'a bona fide medical, psychiatric, judicial, legislative, or law enforcement purpose.' Now Ah can't tell ya what's a bona fide use of a dildo for a judge, but there's a few Leggies who maybe needed that law changed. God knows what they'll promote next."

"Gives a whole new meaning to the term 'legislative staff,' I agree."

"But if ya want to attack the statute itself, ya might oughta look to the definition of 'obscene device' they used. Could end up with a jury nullification, based on just how reediculous that law is. Those're rare as hen's teeth these days, but that might work."

Later that night, after she shed the wig and fancy dress and donned a sweatsuit, Jessie went back to the hotel's business center to spend a few moments online. She found that "obscene device" in Texas law meant "a device designed or marketed as useful *primarily* for the stimulation of human genital organs."

Forbiss had been right—this might be her best bet to help Hudson get Laurie off.

The morning of Laurie's trial, Jessie pushed her large leather briefcase across the belt of the X-ray machine in the lobby of the Harris County Criminal Courthouse. Her trusty 9mm was safely stashed in her hotel room, and she gave an expansive smile to the deputies running the screening process.

She stepped through the metal detector's empty doorway and collected the case, then trotted to the elevator bank alongside a steady stream of attorneys. A large crowd waited there, as usual, for the next empty car to the courtrooms several stories above. Many were going to be late, because a raft of reporters had gotten there first.

Jessie spotted the heads of Laurie Voyaczic and Randy Hudson bobbing far ahead of her. Laurie was near an opening elevator door, but Jessie didn't call them out by name. She didn't want to start a riot, as she was pretty sure she knew which case they were there to cover.

"Go ahead, I'll meet you there," she shouted over the din, and waved them onward.

She found the deserted staircase and ran up to meet them outside County Criminal Court No. 23, where Judge Salvio Fortunato presided. Jessie always enjoyed Judge Lucky Sal. She was excited and eager for the fun.

Outside the courtroom, Laurie and Hudson conferred, trying to find privacy in a corner of the hall. Jessie saw that the young woman had dressed like a secretary out of *Mad Men* in a 60's-style dress and bolero jacket that covered her arms, teased at her cleavage, and flirted with her legs. Should work fine when the press wakes up to who she is, Jessie thought.

Hudson looked anxious, but his client had done as much as she could to distract the judge. The defendant was allowed to waive a jury, and Laurie probably had, as was customary in these embarrassing cases.

"Have you inspected the evidence?" Jessie's manner with Hudson was brusque. She didn't have much time before court would convene.

"I looked at it a while ago. I couldn't see anything that would help."

"Take me to it. Laurie, go to the ladies' room. Never pass up a chance to go pee before a trial, in case—" Jessie stopped explaining, struck with the insensitivity of her world view, however practical. She waved Laurie away.

Hudson led her around the hallways of the sixteenth floor and back to a small conference room. The prosecutors had rolled a cardboard box of some size into one corner.

Hudson lifted a flap and exposed the contents to Jessie. "I don't get it. These are perfectly harmless. Why criminalize this?"

Row upon row, six across and eight or ten layers deep, the packing box held smaller ones reminding Jessie of how fancy dolls, like collectible Barbie's, were displayed. The top layer was pink, and each box had one side open to view, the merchandise visible inside through a cellophane panel that ran most of its length.

The printed logo on each box was the same: they were all "Mister Squiggledy's." Jessie dug past the top layer, which were all the yellow-pink of cheap flesh-color. All the boxes in the second row were tan, and their contents were a dark brown.

Knock, knock! The door pushed open. It was Laurie, nearly

hysterical. "The bailiff's calling everybody in! It's time, come on!" Hudson rushed out to join his client.

Jessie quickly locked the door behind him.

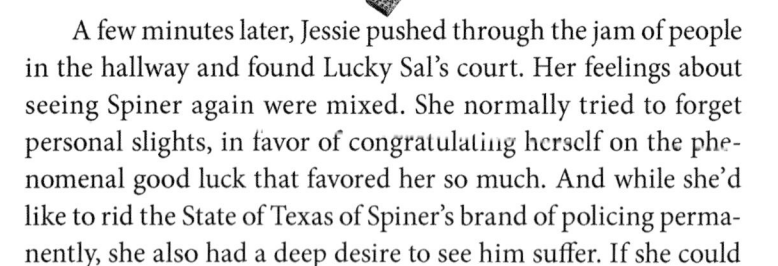

A few minutes later, Jessie pushed through the jam of people in the hallway and found Lucky Sal's court. Her feelings about seeing Spiner again were mixed. She normally tried to forget personal slights, in favor of congratulating herself on the phenomenal good luck that favored her so much. And while she'd like to rid the State of Texas of Spiner's brand of policing permanently, she also had a deep desire to see him suffer. If she could strip him of credibility and his macho mask, too, she might get a good night's sleep again.

Now that she'd found him, it was only that personal interest in ongoing revenge that kept her from killing him outright.

To find her seat in the second row, she had to pass near where he sat behind the prosecutor's table. She smiled at him in a friendly, absent-minded way, then waved to someone behind him. The attorney whose eye she caught didn't object to the greeting from a stranger, even making a half-hearted attempt to wave back. Ignoring him, Jessie made sure she could see Spiner's face with her peripheral vision.

Her dream hadn't lied. The lips, the mustache and yellowing teeth, the sideburns—it was The Man, all right.

The bailiff intoned, "All rise!" and everyone stood while Lucky Sal took the bench. He motioned them to be seated and called the first case on the day's trial docket. The prosecutor made a quick opening statement to the court, and Hudson reserved his for later. The D.A. called only one witness to the stand: Spiner.

It took only minutes for the D.A. to establish that on one recent Thursday, Officer Snotnose saw Laurie Voyaczic in the back room of the Montrose Total Satisfaction book store, a place that sold adult and X-rated movies and books, and 'other things.'

Spiner pulled at his collar and stared at the floor when asked what 'other things' could be found on its shelves.

Eventually he mumbled, "Clothes…if you want to call 'em that. Not enough cloth to make a cat a pair of pants. Gag stuff—you know, for bachelor parties. Masks. Handcuffs, stuff like for bondage. Sweets. Like that."

Moving on, the prosecutor wanted to nail down through Spiner what kind of items would cause HPD to send a Vice cop into a store like that. "Did someone make a complaint?"

"I saw the defendant in violation of the criminal code while making my regular rounds."

"What part of the code?"

Spiner managed to spit out the law. "Section 43.21 of the Texas Penal Code states that no one may sell or promote an obscene device, meaning one designed or marketed as useful primarily for the stimulation of human genital organs."

Lucky Sal, who had been studying racing forms on the bench, became more attentive.

"And did you observe someone selling such a device?"

"No… I went in to look around, you know, and the clerk wasn't there. The place was empty. So we looked in the back, you know, to be sure nobody wasn't being robbed or tied up or something…"

"You mean, against their will," the judge quipped, staring at Jessie and chuckling at his own joke. Jessie laughed too, and winked at him. She happened to know that Sal enjoyed an occasional sexual scenario with handcuffs involved, not from personal experience but from overhearing a reliable cop during a kidnapping case.

"Right." Spiner stopped, uncertain whether to enjoy the court's humor.

"Go on, go on." The judge waved his hand. "This is gonna get better."

"So we go into the stock room, and this lady's there, sitting on a box." Spiner pointed across the room. "That box." Two young assistant D.A.'s were wheeling the box that Jessie had inspected into the area below the judge's bench. "She was eating a sandwich or something. Said the clerk had run across the street to get some change."

"What else did you observe?"

"Well, I saw that this box she was sitting on, leaning on, kinda, had already been opened. And I saw what was inside. So I arrested her, and here we are."

"Would you point to the person you saw and arrested that day? Is she in the courtroom?"

Spiner obediently held up his hand and pointed directly at Laurie, who shrank inside her bolero dress in shame.

"Prosecution rests, your Honor," the prosecutor said. He sat down.

Hudson rattled a stack of papers on his table, killing time. His face was downcast, his brow wrinkled with stress.

From the second row, a folded piece of paper made its way down the line of courtroom observers and landed near Hudson's arm. The lawyer's eyebrows rose in surprise and puzzlement. He picked up, unfolded it, and read it.

He read it again, a tiny smile puckering his lips. Then, with a new spring in his step, he stepped to the middle of the courtroom to begin his cross.

"Officer Spiner, you've advised the court that my client did not work at Total Satisfaction, is that right?"

"She said she didn't. The clerk came back, and he said she didn't."

"Why didn't you arrest the clerk?"

"He came in the front of the store. He never went near the box."

"Was Laurie trying to sell what was in the box?"

"No, but she was close enough to it to be in possession of it. Possession of more than six devices raises a presumption that she's got them to sell. And, as I understand it, she *was* going to buy some of them, to sell at a party. That's what she came in for."

"Did you know my client before you arrested her?"

"No. Well, maybe I seen her around."

"So you came in and went into the back room. Did you go straight there?"

"No, I looked around a little. There was nobody working the register."

"Ah. And Laurie Voyaczic was, in fact, sitting on the box and eating her lunch when you first saw her that day, right?"

"Eating something."

"You don't know what she had for lunch, or what course she was on?"

"No."

"Okay, let's talk about the contents of the box. Have you ever looked at what's in it?"

"Sure. I flipped open the top before I arrested her and gave her the Miranda warning."

"And did you dig into the box?"

"Well, I kinda stirred 'em around. They're all just about the same. 'Cept for color."

Spiner wrinkled his nose with disgust, apparently at the idea that non-pinky-white individuals might have sex lives, too.

Hudson pushed up his sleeves like a hack magician. He approached the cardboard box and reached into it. "With the court's permission, your Honor, I'd like Officer Spiner to take a closer look at the item in question." Hudson pulled out one of the retail packages.

The item in question was pink cardboard. By now, Jessie had figured out why the seller had used cellophane on one side. You'd want to be sure you got the right color and didn't forget any necessary accessories, and you'd need batteries of the size your item required. Laurie had demonstrated an earlier version of Mr. Squiggledy for Jessie. It was operated via remote control, and if you put it down on a table and turned it on, it would 'walk.' Jessie thought it looked rather like an elongated Pillsbury doughboy marching into the oven.

Hudson, noting the court's nod of permission, marched up to Officer Spiner and thrust the contraband into his hands.

"Open it, please."

Spiner complied.

"Would you remove the merchandise. After your examination, I'd like to pass it to his Honor for inspection."

At this, Spiner's face snapped into "disgust" mode, his nose wrinkling, his upper lip pulled back. "Are you kiddin' me?" He looked up at Lucky Sal, who stared back at him, giving no quarter.

Jessie recognized the judge's eager curiosity to see the forbidden object by his raised eyebrows and the smile that threatened to widen his lips. Sal was no stranger to this class of merchandise, she surmised.

Spiner gave in. He pulled the Mr. Squiggledy out and held it up by its base.

Several observers in the gallery gasped—whether with shock, surprise or glee, Jessie wasn't sure.

It was indeed a prime specimen: pinkish-off white and eight inches long, with a base resembling two Haas avocados set in a tea cup. Jessie could see a square on the side where, one might suppose, the dildo would open to accept the requisite AA batteries.

Hudson continued. "Now, Officer Spiner, would you please bring the merchandise up to your nose and tell us what it smells like?"

This was too much. Spiner exploded. "Smell it? Are you fucking crazy?"

Hudson argued, "Look, it's never been used."

Spiner glared at Hudson, too angry to notice Judge Fortunato striving mightily to stifle a laugh, or to hear him bang his gavel. The gallery observers roared, some laughing, some demanding to know what he'd just said. The bailiff waved his hands for quiet and shushed the crowd.

"I don't want that thing anywhere near my nose! I don't even want to touch it!"

"Judge?"

Hudson had good reason to wonder how far he could push it. But Lucky Sal was enjoying the questioning now. "Don't see any reason for why you can't oblige Defense Counsel," he said.

Slowly, slowly, Spiner raised the dildo to his nose. When it got within half an inch of the tip, he stopped moving it and drew in a cautious breath. His nostrils flared, his eyebrows knotted, and a look of complete bewilderment crossed his face.

"What does it smell like, Officer?"

"Smells like… candy! Like…almonds. And chocolate."

"And you've spend a fair amount of time at the Chocolate Bar, haven't you, Officer? You recognize that smell."

Spiner nodded, unhappy.

"So do you still contend that this object, and all the others just like it, are 'useful *primarily* for the stimulation of human genital organs'?"

Stumped, Spiner stalled for time. He used his thumb to dig under the battery cover, which only resulted in crumbs of white chocolate falling onto his lap and being wedged under his thumbnail.

Without thinking, Spiner whisked the particles from his lap, then popped his thumb into his mouth to collect the candy residue.

Watching him suck his thumb in open court, Jessie knew he was done for. His eyes flitted back and forth as he searched for some way to make the case work. He wouldn't find one. The guys at the Chocolate Bar had done a superb sculpting job.

Still, Jessie enjoyed the sight of a row of defense attorneys— who, curiously enough, had been advised anonymously to keep their phone-cameras handy at a certain trial today— taking a picture of Spiner, thumb planted in his mouth, dildo in his hand.

The bailiff frowned at the sudden camera flashes, but Sal only banged his gavel one time and let the hub-bub die down on its own. The entire Houston bar would see those shots within the day, and they would be up on the Web inside of an hour.

"Shall I repeat the question, Officer? What's the primary use for candy?"

"To eat, I guess."

Hudson turned to the judge. "Your Honor, the defense moves to dismiss the charge against my client with prejudice."

"Officer Spiner, you're excused. Mr. Hudson—motion granted. Miss Voyaczic, you're free to go."

Spiner's face, ears and thick neck were the color of a fire hydrant, and he was spitting and muttering incoherent oaths against his new reality. He clambered out of the witness box, stubbed his toe on a counsel table, and windmilled his way up the center aisle.

As if to prove how thoroughly ridiculous he looked, two senior police detectives who had dropped by while waiting on another case, bent over with laughter, tears streaming down their faces, as he stumbled out of the room and into a flurry of clicking and flashing photographers and reporters. Jessie was satisfied.

Judge Fortunato shook his head and whispered to his clerk, "Stupido! Where do they get them? Four 'Spiner Specials' in one month." He left the bench, irritation showing in his forehead, and amusement pressed between his lips.

At counsel table, Hudson and his client beamed and happily exchanged high-fives. They turned to look for Jessie among the observers, but she had found a spot in the hall to make a cell phone call.

"Beau? Work's done here. Wanna go ride?"

Hudson and Laurie came out in time to see Jessie turn her shoulder away from them, to have some privacy. Laurie cringed at the shouts from the reporters but tried to smile like a winner.

Jessie snapped her cell phone shut and gave Laurie a thumbs-up. They were both headed home, and Beau had a new project lined up—a writing project, not the other kind.

Hudson pushed the reporters back and gave Laurie his arm to lead her to the elevator. As they passed, he leaned over to Jessie and whispered into her ear. "Evidence tampering is a felony, you know."

Jessie turned to wink at him. "So's murder. And since it was Spiner, it was one or the other. Think I let him off too light?"

Note: On Thursday, Valentine's Day 2008, the Texas "Dildo Statute," including the 1993 amendments, was struck down as unconstitutional by the U.S. Fifth Circuit Court of Appeals.

About The Authors

Cash Anthony brings back Jessie Carr, the avenging angel in her short stories *The Best Man* and *The Stand-In*, published in A DEATH IN TEXAS and DEAD AND BREAKFAST. Cash is an award-winning Houston screenwriter and author. Her life experiences as an attorney as well as her adventures on cross-country motorcycle trips inspire her stories. She is married to Timothy Hogan, and they live in Houston with Cora and Sam, their two cats, and Gypsy the Siberian Husky.

Laura Elvebak is the author of "Dying For Chocolate." Her debut mystery, Less Dead, came out in 2008 and features Niki Alexander, a counselor in a teen shelter. The second in the Niki Alexander series, Lost Witness, is due out in September 2009. Laura also appeared in The Final Twist anthology, A Death In Texas, with her short story, "Searching For Rachel." Laura is a member of The Final Twist, Sisters-In-Crime, and Mystery Writers of America. Find out more about Laura Elvebak at www.lldreamspell.com/LauraElvebak.htm and www.lauraelvebak.com

Diana L. Driver is the founder of The Final Twist. She was born in Cheyenne Wyoming and raised in Texas. Valentine's Day is her third piece of short fiction. Diana is the author of the novel, Ninth Lord of the Night and the nonfiction guidebook, The Maya, People of the Maize.

Cherri Galbiati attended college in Natchitoches, La. Afterwards she traveled throughout Great Britain and Europe. Her love for canines and their antics is what fuels her writing. She currently resides in Houston with her husband, their dogs, and lots of coffee. Cherri says it is a dog's heaven in her home...and it is. The short story, Conner Creek Fog inspired her to write a series using cadaver search dogs and the first in her series is now out, The Scent of Money. Future works will also include the second book titled, The Scent of Silence, and a mainstream darker novel, Tracking Thantos. Cherri is a member of The Final Twist, Houston mystery writers group—she served as its Vice President in 2004-2005. Read more about Cherri, her work and her dogs at www.cherrigalbiati.com.

Betty Gordon draws inspiration for her writing from years of experience in the legal arena as a law student, legal assistant and paralegal. This native Texan also has extensive backgrounds in dance instruction and sculpting. Betty holds a B.S. Degree in Professional Writing from the University of Houston-Downtown and graduate degrees in Literature (creative writing) and Visual Arts from the University of Houston-Clear Lake. Publishing credentials: "The Journal of Graduate Liberal Studies," poetry, two novels, "Murder in the Third Person" and "Deceptive Clarity" as well as numerous short stories in The Final Twist anthologies. Betty is a past president of The Final Twist Writers, a member of Mystery Writers of America, Sisters in Crime, Writers League of Texas, Ft. Bend Writers Guild, and Bay Area Writers League. Visit Betty at www.bettygordon.com.

Linda Houle is co-owner of the publishing company L&L Dreamspell. Her favorite part of the job is creating unique book covers. She's also written novels and short stories in several genres including mystery and romantic suspense.
Visit Linda Houle at www.lldreamspell.com/LindaHoule.htm.

Pauline Baird Jones is the award-winning author of eight novels of action-adventure, suspense, romantic suspense and comedy-mystery. She's also written two non-fiction books, Adapting Your Novel for Film and Made-up Mayhem and co-wrote Managing Your Book Writing Business with Jamie Engle. Her eighth novel, The Key, released in 2007 from LL Dreamspell and won an Independent Book Award Bronze Medal (IPPY) and is a Dream Realm Awards Winner. Her lastest novel, Girl Gone Nova will release winter 2009. Visit Pauline's website at www.perilouspauline.com.

Sally Love grew up in Austin and spent more than twenty-five years as a financial writer and a public relations/media relations specialist for financial and high-tech companies. She holds bachelor degrees in English and Journalism from The University of Texas and an MBA in Marketing from the University of Houston. Her short stories have won the Mystery Writers of America-Southwest Chapter's Murder by the Book Contest and the Houston Writers Guild Contest. They can be found in several upcoming LL Dreamspell anthologies. She is working on a series of mystery novels involving financial crimes. Sally and retired optometrist husband, Lou, live in Houston. Her hobbies include gardening and collecting antique glass.

Iona McAvoy is a native Floridian but has long considered Texas her true home. She even married a native Houstonian, Monty McAvoy, to prove it! Having lived in Houston and then being transferred to Minnesota, Georgia, and New York, it was to Houston she finally returned. Iona is an employment attorney, with a prior career as an environmental lawyer, corporate counsel and litigator. Her short story in this analogy, JADEAD, hails to Iona's love of mythology, rocks and crystals, and the Italian part of her heritage. Iona was living in New York, just outside Manhattan during 9/11. She has written a children's book which talks about 9/11, featuring two very talented German Shepherds, and hopes to have it published by the tenth anniversary, in 2011. She lives in the Heights area of Houston, Texas, with her husband, and her furbabies. You can read more about her at www.ionamcavoy.com. Howls.

Charlotte Phillips grew up in Allentown, Pennsylvania, where the Liberty Bell was hidden during the war of 1812. In addition to Pennsylvania, she lived in Florida and California before settling in Texas. Her degrees are from Florida Tech (BS-Marine Biology) and Houston Baptist University (MS-Management, Computing, and Systems). Charlotte lives in Houston with her husband Mark and their cat, Psychokitty.

Mark H. Phillips grew up in central Illinois reading the classics—especially Greek mythology, James Bond novels, and Batman comics. He is a graduate of both the University of Illinois (BA—Philosophy) and Northwestern University (MA—Philosophy). Mark currently lives in Houston with his wife, Charlotte, and teaches pre-calculus and political philosophy at Bellaire High School.

CeCe Smith helped to gain historic registration for her district, worked to build two city dog parks, and was involved in raising money for a new animal shelter. Animals, art and reading have been a part of CeCe's life since she was a young child. Having horses in Pennsylvania, raising a lion cub in Philly, owning a tea room and art gallery in Texas have all been dreams come true. She is an avid gardener and received several awards for gardens she created in St. Louis. While in St. Louis, she was the campaign manager for a state representative, president of a neighborhood association and authored the newsletter. She loves painting and sculpting, but writing has always been a passion. Now, back in Texas and living in Galveston—another dream has been realized.

Autumn Storm was born in Orange, Texas, raised in Florida and lived for a short time in both Cuba and Spain. She now lives in the La Porte area and is the 2009 secretary for The Final Twist. Interested in history, she served as a docent for the Historical Society in Lake Charles Louisiana and a few of her hobbies include touring lighthouses, plantation homes and old cemeteries.